A hundred years ago, in the introduction to his *Fairy and Folk Tales of the Irish Peasantry* (1888), the poet W. B. Yeats pointed to the key difference between English and Irish fairy tales: 'The personages of English fairy literature are merely mortals beautifully masquerading. Nobody ever laid new milk on their doorstep for them.' Irish fairy literature, on the other hand, is written for a people who *believed* absolutely in fairies and their power. The belief lingers on in rural Ireland even today, as anyone coming across a fairy thorn-tree will realize. There it stands, in some lonely country spot, a little tree mysteriously tricked out in handkerchiefs, tied to its branches by people with some hope – or belief – in the worth of such an exercise. It is not unlike those shrines in Mediterranean countries where Catholic worshippers have placed garments or belongings of a loved one – a sailor perhaps – to be guarded by their prayers to the Virgin from the perils of the deep sea.

Irish fairy-lore is often linked to a feature of the landscape such as a thorn-tree or a ruined hillfort (or rath), or a fairy well. Readers of 'Guleesh' or 'The Fairies' Revenge' will observe this.

Following Yeats, I have grouped the stories in the first six parts of this book according to whether they are about the good people or *sidhe* (fairy people); the red man or *fear dearg* (sometimes just called Far Darrig) and his gruesome pranks; the merrow or *murrughach* (mermaids and mermen); the leprehaun or *leith bhrogan* (fairy shoemaker); witches or giants. The stories in this part of the book are mostly from the school of collectors of the folk literature of Ireland, inspired by the work of Perrault in France, the Brothers Grimm in Germany and Sir Walter Scott in Scotland.

In Part Seven of the book, the stories are from even older sources. They include nine bardic stories from the Celtic sagas, first written down as long ago as the twelfth century. Some of these stories may in fact date from as long ago as the time of Christ, and they were handed down orally by the hereditary bards and singers and harpers employed at the Courts of the Irish Kings. Eleanor Hull's legend of Don-bo throws light on this period.

The great folklore scholar, Joseph Jacobs, in his *Celtic Fairy Tales* (1882 and still in print), commented on the delightful problem of selection in a folk literature as rich and varied as Ireland's. I can only echo this observation. This anthology represents the tip of a massive, marvellous and enduring iceberg. I hope readers will enjoy exploring it.

Gordon Jarvie

Other selections from Gordon Jarvie

SCOTTISH FOLK AND FAIRY TALES
THE GENIUS AND OTHER IRISH STORIES

Irish folk and fairy tales

Chosen and edited by
GORDON JARVIE

Illustrated by
BARBARA BROWN

THE
BLACKSTAFF
PRESS
BELFAST

ACKNOWLEDGEMENTS

Grateful acknowledgement is made to Douglas Sealey
and the Estate of Douglas Hyde for permission to include
in this collection the story entitled 'Guleesh',
from *Beside the Fire* (1891), by Dr Douglas Hyde.

'The Stolen Child' (W.B Yeats) appears by kind permission
of A.P. Watt Ltd on behalf of Michael B Yeats.

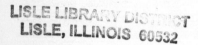
First published in 1992 by Puffin Books

This edition first published in 2002 by
Blackstaff Press Limited
Wildflower Way, Apollo Road
Belfast BT12 6TA, Northern Ireland

This selection, adaptations and Introduction
copyright © Gordon Jarvie, 1992
Illustrations copyright © Barbara Childs, 1992
All rights reserved

Printed and bound in Great Britain by Cox & Wyman

A CIP catalogue record for this book
is available from the British Library
ISBN 0-85640-731-3

www.blackstaffpress.com

CONTENTS

Contents

Part One

THE SIDHE

THE FAIRIES
William Allingham

Up the airy mountain,
  Down the rushy glen,
We daren't go a-hunting
  For fear of little men;
Wee folk, good folk,
  Trooping all together;
Green jacket, red cap,
  And white owl's feather!

Down along the rocky shore
  Some make their home,
They live on crispy pancakes
  Of yellow tide-foam;
Some in the reeds
  Of the black mountain lake,
With frogs for their watch-dogs,
  All night awake.

High on the hill-top
   The old King sits;
He is now so old and grey
   He's nigh lost his wits.
With a bridge of white mist
   Columbkill he crosses,
On his stately journeys
   From Slieveleague to Rosses;
Or going up with music
   On cold starry nights,
To sup with the Queen
   Of the gay Northern Lights.

They stole little Bridget
For seven years long;
   When she came down again
   Her friends were all gone.
They took her lightly back,
   Between the night and morrow,
They thought that she was fast asleep,
   But she was dead with sorrow.
They have kept her ever since
   Deep within the lake,
On a bed of flag-leaves,
   Watching till she wake.

By the craggy hill-side,
   Through the mosses bare,
They have planted thorn-trees
   For pleasure here and there.
Is any man so daring
   As dig them up in spite,
He shall find their sharpest thorns
   In his bed at night.

The Fairies

Up the airy mountain,
   Down the rushy glen,
We daren't go a-hunting
   For fear of little men;
Wee folk, good folk,
   Trooping all together;
Green jacket, red cap,
   And white owl's feather!

JAMIE FREEL AND THE
YOUNG LADY

Letitia Maclintock

Down in Fannet, in times gone by, lived Jamie Freel and his
mother. Jamie was the widow's sole support; his strong arm
worked for her untiringly, and as each Saturday night came
around, he poured his wages into her lap, thanking her
dutifully for the halfpence which she returned him for tobacco.

He was extolled by his neighbours as the best son ever
known or heard of. But he had neighbours of whose opinion
he was ignorant – neighbours who lived pretty close to him,
whom he had never seen, who are, indeed, rarely seen by
mortals, except on May eves and Hallowe'ens.

An old ruined castle, about a quarter of a mile from his
cabin, was said to be the abode of the 'wee folk'. Every
Hallowe'en were the ancient windows lighted up, and
passers-by saw little figures flitting to and fro inside the
building, while they heard the music of pipes and flutes.

6

It was well known that fairy revels took place; but nobody had the courage to intrude on them.

Jamie had often watched the little figures from a distance, and listened to the charming music, wondering what the inside of the castle was like; but one Hallowe'en he got up and took his cap, saying to his mother, 'I'm awa' to the castle to seek my fortune.'

'What!' cried she, 'would you venture there? You that's the poor widow's one son! Dinna be sae venturesome an' foolitch, Jamie! They'll kill you, an' then what'll come o' me?'

'Never fear, mother; nae harm 'ill happen me, but I maun gae.'

He set out, and as he crossed the potato-field, came in sight of the castle, whose windows were ablaze with light, that seemed to turn the russet leaves, still clinging to the crabtree branches, into gold.

Halting in the grove at one side of the ruin, he listened to the elfin revelry, and the laughter and singing made him all the more determined to proceed.

Numbers of little people, the largest about the size of a child of five years old, were dancing to the music of flutes and fiddles, while others drank and feasted.

'Welcome, Jamie Freel! Welcome, Jamie!' cried the company, perceiving their visitor. The word 'welcome' was caught up and repeated by every voice in the castle.

Time flew, and Jamie was enjoying himself very much, when his hosts said, 'We're going to ride to Dublin tonight to steal a young lady. Will you come too, Jamie Freel?'

'Ay, that I will!' cried the rash youth, thirsting for adventure.

A troop of horses stood at the door. Jamie mounted, and his steed rose with him into the air. He was presently flying over his mother's cottage, surrounded by the elfin troop, and on and on they went, over bold mountains, over little hills, over the deep Lough Swilley, over towns and cottages, where people were burning nuts, and eating apples, and keeping merry Hallowe'en. It seemed to Jamie that they flew all round Ireland before they got to Dublin.

'This is Derry,' said the fairies, flying over the cathedral spire; and what was said by one voice was repeated by all the rest, till fifty little voices were crying out, 'Derry! Derry! Derry!'

In like manner was Jamie informed as they passed over each town on the route, and at length he heard the silvery voices cry, 'Dublin! Dublin!'

It was no mean dwelling that was to be honoured by the fairy visit, but one of the finest houses in Stephen's Green.

The troop dismounted near a window, and Jamie saw a beautiful face, on a pillow in a splendid bed. He saw the young lady lifted and carried away, while the stick which was dropped in her place on the bed took her exact form.

The lady was placed before one rider and carried a short way, then given to another, and the names of the towns were cried out as before.

8

They were approaching home. Jamie heard 'Rathmullan', 'Milford', 'Tamney', and then he knew they were near his own house.

'You've all had your turn at carrying the young lady,' said he. 'Why wouldn't I get her for a wee piece?'

'Ay, Jamie,' replied they, pleasantly, 'you may take your turn at carrying her, to be sure.'

Holding his prize very tightly, he dropped down near his mother's door.

'Jamie Freel, Jamie Freel! Is that the way you treat us?' cried they, and they too dropped down near the door.

Jamie held fast, though he knew not what he was holding, for the little folk turned the lady into all sorts of strange shapes. At one moment she was a black dog, barking and trying to bite; at another, a glowing bar of iron, yet without heat; then, again, a sack of wool.

But still Jamie held her, and the baffled elves were turning away, when a tiny woman, the smallest of the party, exclaimed, 'Jamie Freel has her awa' frae us, but he sall hae nae gude o' her, for I'll mak' her deaf and dumb,' and she threw something over the young girl.

While they rode off disappointed, Jamie lifted the latch and went in.

'Jamie, man!' cried his mother, 'you've been awa' all night; what have they done on you?'

'Naething bad, mother; I ha' the very best of gude luck. Here's a beautiful young lady I ha' brought you for company.'

'Bless us an' save us!' exclaimed the mother, and for some minutes she was so astonished that she could not think of anything else to say.

Jamie told his story of the night's adventure, ending by saying, 'Surely you wouldna have allowed me to let her gang with them to be lost for ever?'

'But a *lady*, Jamie! How can a lady eat we'er poor diet, and live in we'er poor way? I ax you that, you foolitch fellow?'

'Weel, mother, sure it's better for her to be here nor over yonder,' and he pointed in the direction of the castle.

Meanwhile, the deaf and dumb girl shivered in her light clothing, stepping close to the humble turf fire.

'Poor crathur, she's quare and handsome! Nae wonder they set their hearts on her,' said the old woman, gazing at her guest with pity and admiration. 'We maun dress her first; but what, in the name o' fortune, hae I fit for the likes o' her to wear?'

She went to the press in 'the room', and took out her Sunday gown of brown drugget; she then opened a drawer, and drew forth a pair of white stockings, a long snowy garment of fine linen, and a cap, her 'dead dress', as she called it.

These articles of attire had long been ready for a certain sad ceremony, in which she would some day fill the chief part, and only saw the light occasionally, when they were hung out to air, but she was willing to give even these to the fair trembling visitor, who was turning in dumb sorrow and wonder from her to Jamie and from Jamie back to her.

The poor girl suffered herself to be dressed, and then sat down on a 'creepie' in the chimney corner, and buried her face in her hands.

'What'll we do to keep up a lady like yon?' cried the old woman.

'I'll work for you both, Mother,' replied her son.

'An' how could a lady live on we'er poor diet?' she repeated.

'I'll work for her,' was all Jamie's answer.

He kept his word. The young lady was very sad for a long time, and tears stole down her cheeks many an evening while the old woman spun by the fire, and Jamie made salmon nets, an accomplishment lately acquired by him, in hopes of adding to the comfort of his guest.

But she was always gentle, and tried to smile when she perceived them looking at her; and by degrees she adapted herself to their ways and mode of life. It was not very long before she began to feed the pig, mash potatoes and meal for the fowls, and knit blue worsted socks.

So a year passed, and Hallowe'en came round again.

'Mother,' said Jamie, taking down his cap, 'I'm off to the ould castle to seek my fortune.'

'Are you mad, Jamie?' cried his mother, in terror; 'sure they'll kill you this time for what you done on them last year.'

Jamie made light of her fears and went his way.

As he reached the crabtree grove, he saw bright lights in the castle windows as before, and heard loud talking. Creeping under the window, he heard the wee folk say, 'That was a poor trick Jamie Freel played us this night last year, when he stole the nice young lady from us.'

'Ay,' said the tiny woman, 'an' I punished him for it, for there she sits, a dumb image by his hearth; but he does na' know that three drops o' this glass I hold in my hand wad gie her her hearing and her speeches back again.'

Jamie's heart beat fast as he entered the hall. Again he was greeted by a chorus of welcomes from the company – 'Here comes Jamie Freel! Welcome, welcome, Jamie!'

As soon as the tumult subsided, the little woman said, 'You be to drink our health, Jamie, out o' this glass in my hand.'

Jamie snatched the glass from her hand and darted to the door. He never knew how he reached his cabin, but he arrived there breathless, and sank on a stone by the fire.

'You're kilt surely this time, my poor boy,' said his mother.

'No, indeed, better luck than ever this time!' and he gave the lady three drops of the liquid that still remained at the bottom of the glass, notwithstanding his mad race over the potato-field.

The lady began to speak, and her first words were words of thanks to Jamie.

The three inmates of the cabin had so much to say to one another, that long after cock-crow, when the fairy music had quite ceased, they were still talking round the fire.

'Jamie,' said the lady, 'be pleased to get me paper and pen and ink, that I may write to my father, and tell him what has become of me.'

She wrote, but weeks passed, and she received no answer. Again and again she wrote, and still no answer.

At length she said, 'You must come with me to Dublin, Jamie, to find my father.'

'I ha' no money to hire a car for you,' he replied, 'an' how can you travel to Dublin on your foot?'

But she implored him so much that he consented to set out with her, and walk all the way from Fannet to Dublin. It was not as easy as the fairy journey; but at last they rang the bell at the door of the fine house in Stephen's Green.

'Tell my father that his daughter is here,' said she to the servant who opened the door.

'The gentleman that lives here has no daughter, my girl. He had one, but she died better nor a year ago.'

'Do you not know me, Sullivan?'

'No, poor girl, I do not.'

'Let me see the gentleman. I only ask to see him.'

'Well, that's not much to ax; we'll see what can be done.'

In a few moments the lady's father came to the door.

'Dear father,' said she, 'don't you know me?'

'How dare you call me your father?' cried the old gentleman, angrily. 'You are an impostor. I have no daughter.'

'Look in my face, father, and surely you'll remember me.'

'My daughter is dead and buried. She died a long, long time ago.' The old gentleman's voice changed from anger to sorrow. 'You can go,' he concluded.

'Stop, dear father, till you look at this ring on my finger. Look at your name and mine engraved on it.'

'It certainly is my daughter's ring; but I do not know how you came by it. I fear in no honest way.'

'Call my mother, *she* will be sure to know me,' said the poor girl, who, by this time, was crying bitterly.

'My poor wife is beginning to forget her sorrow. She seldom speaks of her daughter now. Why should I renew her grief by reminding her of her loss?'

But the young lady persevered, till at last the mother was sent for.

'Mother,' she began, when the old lady came to the door, 'Don't you know your daughter?'

'I have no daughter; my daughter died and was buried a long, long time ago.'

'Only look in my face, and surely you'll know me.'

The old lady shook her head.

'You have all forgotten me; but look at this mole on my neck. Surely, Mother, you know me now?'

'Yes, yes,' said the mother, 'my Gracie had a mole on her neck like that; but then I saw her in her coffin, and saw the lid shut down upon her.'

It became Jamie's turn to speak, and he gave the history of the fairy journey, of the theft of the young lady, of the figure he had seen laid in the bed in its place, of her life with his mother in Fannet, of last Hallowe'en, and of the three drops that had released Gracie from her enchantment.

Gracie took up the story when he paused, and told how kind the mother and son had been to her.

The parents could not make enough of Jamie. They treated him with every distinction, and when he expressed his wish to return to Fannet, said they did not know what to do to show their gratitude.

But an awkward complication arose. The daughter would not let him go without her. 'If Jamie goes, I'll go too,' she said. 'He saved me from the fairies, and has worked for me ever since. If it had not been for him, dear Father and Mother, you would never have seen me again. If he goes, I'll go too.'

This being her resolution, the old gentleman said that

13

Jamie should become his son-in-law. The mother was brought from Fannet in a coach and four, and there was a splendid wedding.

They all lived together in the grand Dublin house, and Jamie was heir to untold wealth at his father-in-law's death.

THE LEGEND OF KNOCKGRAFTON
Thomas Crofton Croker

There was once a poor man who lived in the fertile glen of Aherlow, at the foot of the gloomy Galtee mountains, and he had a great hump on his back: he looked just as if his body had been rolled up and placed upon his shoulders; and his head was pressed down with the weight so much that his chin, when he was sitting, used to rest upon his knees for support. The country people were rather shy of meeting him in any lonesome place, for though, poor creature, he was as harmless and as inoffensive as a new-born infant, yet his deformity was so great that he scarcely appeared to be a human creature, and some ill-minded persons had started strange rumours about him. He was said to have a great knowledge of herbs and charms; but certain it was that he had a mighty skilful hand in plaiting straws and rushes into hats and baskets, which was the way he made his livelihood.

15

Lusmore, for that was the nickname put upon him by reason of his always wearing a sprig of the fairy cap, or lusmore (the foxglove), in his little straw hat, would always get more money for his plaited work than anyone else and perhaps that was the reason why someone, out of envy, had circulated the strange stories about him. Be that as it may, it happened that he was returning one evening from the pretty town of Cahir towards Cappagh, and as little Lusmore walked very slowly, on account of the great hump upon his back, it was quite dark when he came to the old moat of Knockgrafton, which stood on the right-hand side of his road. Tired and weary was he, and downcast at thinking how much farther he had to travel, and that he should be walking all the night; so he sat down under the moat to rest himself, and began looking mournfully enough upon the moon.

Presently there rose a wild strain of unearthly melody upon the ear of little Lusmore; he listened, and he thought that he had never heard such ravishing music before. It was like the sound of many voices, each mingling and blending with the other so strangely that they seemed to be one, though all singing different strains, and the words of the song were these –

Da Luan, Da Mort, Da Luan, Da Mort, Da Luan, Da Mort;[1]

when there would be a moment's pause, and then the round of melody went on again.

Lusmore listened attentively, scarcely drawing his breath lest he might lose the slightest note. He now plainly perceived that the singing was within the moat; and though at first it had charmed him so much, he began to get tired of hearing the same sound sung over and over so often without any change; so using the pause when *Da Luan, Da Mort*, had been sung three times, he took up the tune, and raised it

[1] Monday, Tuesday, Monday, Tuesday, Monday, Tuesday

with the words *augus Da Dardeen*[2] and then went on singing with the voices inside of the moat, *Da Luan, Da Mort*, finishing the melody, when the pause again came, with *augus Da Dardeen*.

The fairies within Knockgrafton, for the song was a fairy melody, when they heard this addition to the tune, were so much delighted that, with instant resolve, it was determined to bring the mortal among them, whose musical skill so far exceeded theirs, and little Lusmore was conveyed into their company with the eddying speed of a whirlwind.

Glorious to behold was the sight that burst upon him as he came down through the moat, twirling round and round, with the lightness of a straw, to the sweetest music that kept time to his motion. The greatest honour was then paid him, for he was put above all the musicians, and he had servants tending upon him, and everything to his heart's content, and a hearty welcome to all; and, in short, he was made as much of as if he had been the first man in the land.

Presently Lusmore saw a great consultation going forward among the fairies, and, notwithstanding all their civility, he felt very much frightened, until one stepping out from the rest came up to him and said –

> 'Lusmore! Lusmore!
> Doubt not, nor deplore,
> For the hump which you bore
> On your back is no more;
> Look down on the floor,
> And view it, Lusmore!'

When these words were said, poor little Lusmore felt himself so light, and so happy, that he thought he could have bounded at one jump over the moon, like the cow in the history of the cat and the fiddle; and he saw, with inexpressible pleasure, his hump tumble down upon the ground from

[2]And Wednesday too

17

his shoulders. He then tried to lift up his head, and he did so with becoming caution, fearing that he might knock it against the ceiling of the grand hall, where he was; he looked round and round again with the greatest wonder and delight upon everything, which appeared more and more beautiful; and, overpowered at beholding such a resplendent scene, his head grew dizzy, and his eyesight became dim. At last he fell into a sound sleep, and when he awoke he found it was broad daylight, the sun shining brightly, and the birds singing sweetly; and that he was lying just at the foot of the moat of Knockgrafton, with the cows and sheep grazing peaceably round about him. The first thing Lusmore did, after saying his prayers, was to put his hand behind to feel for his hump, but no sign of one was there on his back, and he looked at himself with great pride, for he had now become a well-shaped dapper little fellow, and more than that, found himself in a full suit of new clothes, which he concluded the fairies had made for him.

Towards Cappagh he went, stepping out as lightly, and springing up at every step as if he had been all his life a dancing-master. Not a creature who met Lusmore knew him without his hump, and he had a great work to persuade everyone that he was the same man – in truth he was not, so far as the outward appearance went.

Of course it was not long before the story of Lusmore's hump got about, and a great wonder was made of it. Through the country, for miles round, it was the talk of every one high and low.

One morning, as Lusmore was sitting contented enough at his cabin door, up came an old woman to him, and asked him if he could direct her to Cappagh.

'I need give you no directions, my good woman,' said Lusmore, 'for this is Cappagh; and whom may you want here?'

'I have come,' said the woman, 'out of Decie's country, in the county of Waterford, looking after one Lusmore, who, I have heard tell, had his hump taken off by the fairies; for there is a son of a friend of mine who has got a hump on him that will be his death; and maybe, if he could use the same charm as Lusmore, the hump may be taken off him. And now I have told you the reason of my coming so far: 'tis to find out about this charm, if I can.'

Lusmore, who was ever a good-natured little fellow, told the woman all the particulars, how he had raised the tune for the fairies at Knockgrafton, how his hump had been removed from his shoulders, and how he had got a new suit of clothes into the bargain.

The woman thanked him very much, and then went away quite happy and easy in her mind. When she came back to her friend's house, in the county of Waterford, she told her everything that Lusmore had said, and they put the little hump-backed man, who was a peevish and cunning creature from his birth, upon a cart, and took him all the way across the country. It was a long journey, but they did not care for that, as long as the hump was taken from off him; and they brought him, just at nightfall, and left him under the old moat of Knockgrafton.

Jack Madden, for that was the humpy man's name, had not been sitting there long when he heard the tune going on within the moat much sweeter than before; for the fairies were singing it the way Lusmore had settled their music for them, and the song was going on: *Da Luan, Da Mort, Da Luan, Da Mort, Da Luan, Da Mort, augus Da Dardeen*, without ever stopping. Jack Madden, who was in a great hurry to get quit of his hump, never thought of waiting until the fairies had done, or watching for a fit opportunity to raise the tune higher again than Lusmore had; so having heard them sing it over seven times without stopping, out he bawls, never minding the time or the humour of the tune, or how he could bring his words in properly, *augus Da Dardeen, augus Da Hena*[3] thinking that if one day was good,

[3] *Da Hena*: Thursday

two were better; and that if Lusmore had one new suit of clothes given him, he should have two.

No sooner had the words passed his lips than he was taken up and whisked into the moat with prodigious force; and the fairies came crowding round him with great anger, screeching and screaming, and roaring out, 'Who spoiled our tune? Who spoiled our tune?' and one stepped up to him above all the rest, and said –

> 'Jack Madden! Jack Madden!
> Your words came so bad in
> The tune we felt glad in; –
> This castle you're had in,
> That your life we may sadden;
> Here's two humps for Jack Madden!'

And twenty of the strongest fairies brought Lusmore's hump, and put it down upon poor Jack's back, over his own, where it became fixed as firmly as if it was nailed on with twelve-penny nails, by the best carpenter that ever drove one. Out of their castle they then kicked him; and in the morning, when Jack Madden's mother and her friend came to look after their little man, they found him half dead, lying at the foot of the moat, with the other hump upon his back. Well to be sure, how they did look at each other! But they were afraid to say anything, lest a hump might be put upon their own shoulders. Home they brought the unlucky Jack Madden with them, as downcast in their hearts and their looks as ever two friends were; and what through the weight of his other hump, and the long journey, he died soon after, leaving, they say, his heavy curse to anyone who would go to listen to fairy tunes again.

FRANK MARTIN AND THE
FAIRIES

William Carleton

Martin was a thin, pale man, when I saw him, of a sickly
look, and a constitution naturally feeble. His hair was a
light auburn, his beard mostly unshaven, and his hands of a
singular delicacy and whiteness, owing, I dare say, as much
to the soft and easy nature of his employment as to his
infirm health. In everything else he was as sensible, sober
and rational as any other man; but on the topic of fairies,
the man's mania was peculiarly strong and immovable.
Indeed, I remember that the expression of his eyes was
singularly wild and hollow, and his long narrow temples
sallow and emaciated.

Now, this man did not lead an unhappy life, nor did the
malady he laboured under seem to be productive of either
pain or terror to him, although one might be apt to imagine
otherwise. On the contrary, he and the fairies maintained
the most friendly intimacy, and their dialogues – which I

fear were woefully one-sided ones – must have been a source of great pleasure to him, for they were conducted with much mirth and laughter, on his part at least.

'Well, Frank, when did you see the fairies?'

'Whist! There's two dozen of them in the shop (the weaving-shop) this minute. There's a little ould fellow sittin' on the top of the weaving-machine, an' all to be rocked while I'm weavin'. The sorrow's in them, but they're the greatest little rogues alive, so they are. See, there's another of them at my cloth. Go out o' that, you blackguard; or, bad luck on me, if you don't, but I'll fetch you a smack! Ha! Cut, you thief you!'

'Frank, arn't you afeard o' them?'

'Is it me! Arra, what ud' I be afeard o' them for? Sure they have no power over me.'

'And why haven't they, Frank?'

'Because I was baptised against them.'

'What do you mean by that?'

'Why, the priest that christened me was tould by my father, to put in the proper prayer against the fairies – an' a priest can't refuse it when he's asked – an' he did so. Begorra, it's well for me that he did – (let the tallow alone, you little glutton – see, there's a weeny thief o' them aitin' my tallow) – becaise, you see, it was their intention to make me king o' the fairies.'

'Is it possible?'

'Devil a lie in it. Sure you may ax them, an' they'll tell you.'

'What size are they, Frank?'

'Oh, little wee fellows, with green coats, an' the purtiest little shoes ever you seen. There's two of them – both ould acquaintances o' mine – runnin' along the yarn-beam. That ould fellow with the bob-wig is called Jim Jam, an' the other chap, with the three-cocked hat, is called Nickey Nick. Nickey plays the pipes. Nickey, give us a tune, or I'll malivogue you – come now, "Lough Erne Shore". Whist, now – listen!'

The poor fellow, though weaving as fast as he could all the time, yet bestowed every possible mark of attention to the music, and seemed to enjoy it as much as if it had been real.

Many a time, when a mere child, not more than six or seven years of age, have I gone as far as Frank's weaving-shop, in order, with a heart divided between curiosity and fear, to listen to his conversation with the good people. From morning till night his tongue was going almost as incessantly as his shuttle; and it was well known that at night, whenever he awoke out of his sleep, the first thing he did was to put out his hand, and push them, as it were, off his bed.

'Go out o' this, you thieves, you – go out o' this now, an' let me alone. Nickey, is this any time to be playing the pipes, and me wants to sleep? Go off, now – troth if yez do, you'll see what I'll give yez tomorrow. Sure I'll be makin' new cloth; and if yez behave decently, maybe I'll lave yez the scrapin' o' the pot. There now. Och! Poor things, they're dacent crathurs. Sure they're all gone, barrin poor Red-cap, that doesn't like to lave me.' And then his one-track mind would fall back into what we trust was an innocent slumber.

About this time there was said to have occurred a very remarkable circumstance, which gave poor Frank a vast deal of importance among the neighbours. A man named Frank Thomas had a child sick, but of what complaint I cannot now remember, nor is it of any importance. One of the gables of Thomas's house was built against, or rather into, a Fort or Rath, called Towny, or properly Tonagh Fort. It was said to be haunted by the fairies, and what gave it a character peculiarly wild in my eyes was that there were on the southern side of it two or three little green mounds, which were said to be the graves of unchristened children, over which it was considered dangerous and unlucky to pass. At all events, the season was mid-summer; and one

evening about dusk, during the illness of the child, the noise
of a hand-saw was heard upon the Fort. This was considered
rather strange, and, after a little time, a few of those who
were assembled at Frank Thomas's went to see who it could
be that was sawing in such a place, or what they could be
sawing at so late an hour, for everyone knew that nobody in
the whole country about them would dare to cut down the
few white-thorns that grew upon the Fort. On going to
examine, however, judge of their surprise, when, after sur-
rounding and searching the whole place, they could discover
no trace of either saw or sawyer. In fact, with the exception
of themselves, there was no one, either natural or supernatural, visible. They then returned to the house, and had
scarcely sat down, when it was heard again within ten yards
of them. Another examination of the premises took place,
but with equal success. Now, however, while standing on
the Fort, they heard the sawing in a little hollow, about a
hundred and fifty yards below them, which was completely
exposed to their view, but they could see nobody. A party of
them immediately went down to ascertain, if possible, what
this singular noise and invisible labour could mean; but on
arriving at the spot, they heard the sawing, to which were
now added hammering, and the driving of nails upon the
Fort above, whilst those who stood on the Fort continued to
hear it in the hollow. On comparing notes, they resolved to
send down to Billy Nelson's for Frank Martin, a distance of
only about eighty or ninety yards. He was soon on the spot,
and without a moment's hesitation solved the enigma.

''Tis the fairies,' said he. 'I see them, and busy crathurs
they are.'

'But what are they sawing, Frank?'

'They are makin' a child's coffin,' he replied; 'they have
the body already made, an' they're now nailin' the lid together.'

That night the child died, and the story goes that on the
second evening afterwards, the carpenter who was called

upon to make the coffin brought a table out from Thomas's house to the Fort, as a temporary bench; and, it is said, that the sawing and hammering necessary for the completion of his task were precisely the same which had been heard the evening but one before – neither more nor less. I remember the death of the child myself, and the making of its coffin, but I think the story of the supernatural carpenter was not heard in the village for some months after its interment.

Frank had every appearance of a hypochondriac about him. At the time I saw him, he might be about thirty-four years of age, but I do not think, from the weakness of his frame and infirm health, that he has been alive for several years. He was an object of considerable interest and curiosity, and often have I been present when he was pointed out to strangers as 'the man that could see the good people'.

A DONEGAL FAIRY

after Letitia Maclintock

Ay, it's a bad thing to displeasure the wee folk, sure enoug
– they can be unfriendly if they're angered, an' they can b
the very best o' gude neighbours if they're treated kindly.

My mother's sister was all her lone in the house one day
wi' a big pot o' water boiling on the fire, and ane o' the we
folk fell down the chimney, and slipped wi' his leg in the hc
water. He let a terrible squeal out o' him, an' in a minut
the house was full o' wee crathurs pulling him out o' th
pot, an' carrying him across the floor.

'Did she scald you?' my aunt heard them ask him.

'Na, na, it was mysel' scalded my ain sel',' said the we
fellow.

'Ach weel, ach weel,' says they. 'If it was your ain fau
an' your ain sel' scalded yoursel', we'll say no more about i
but if she had scalded you, we'd ha' made her pay for it.'

THE HILL-MAN AND THE
HOUSE-WIFE

Juliana Horatia Ewing

It is well known that the good people cannot stand mean ways. Now, there once lived a house-wife who had a sharp eye to her own good in this world, and gave alms of what she had no use, for the good of her soul.

One day a hill-man knocked at her door. 'Can you lend us a saucepan, good mother?' said he. 'There's a wedding in the hill, and all the pots are in use.' 'Is he to have one?' asked the servant girl who opened the door. 'Ay, to be sure,' said the house-wife.

But when the maid was taking a saucepan from the shelf, the house-wife pinched her arm and whispered sharply, 'Not that good one, you stupid; get the old one out of the cupboard. It leaks, and the hill-men are so neat and such nimble workers that they are sure to mend it before they send it home. So we can do a good turn to the good people and save sixpence from the tinker.'

The maid fetched the saucepan, which had been laid by till the tinker's next visit, and gave it to the dwarf, who thanked her and went away.

The saucepan was soon returned neatly mended and ready for use. At supper-time the maid filled the pan with milk and set it on the fire for the children's supper, but in a few minutes the milk was so burnt and smoked that no one could touch it, and even the pigs would not drink the wash into which it was thrown.

'Ah, you good-for-nothing slut!' cried the house-wife, as she this time filled the pan herself. 'You would ruin the richest, with your careless ways; there's a whole quart of good milk spoilt at once.' '*And that's twopence,*' cried a voice from the chimney, a queer whining voice like some old body who was always grumbling over something.

The house-wife had not left the saucepan for two minutes when the milk boiled over, and it was all burnt and smoked as before. 'The pan must be dirty,' cried the house-wife in a rage; 'and there are two full quarts of milk as good as thrown to the dogs.' '*And that's fourpence*,' said the voice in the chimney.

After a long scrubbing the saucepan was once more filled and set on the fire, but it was not the least use, the milk was burnt and smoked again, and the house-wife burst into tears at the waste, crying out, 'Never before did such a thing happen to me since I kept house! Three quarts of milk burnt for one meal!' '*And that's sixpence*,' cried the voice from the chimney. 'You didn't save the tinker after all,' with which the hill-man himself came tumbling down the chimney, and went off laughing through the door. But from that time the saucepan was as good as any other.

THE FAIRIES' REVENGE
Lady Wilde

The fairies have a great objection to the fairy raths, where they meet at night, being built upon by mortal man. A farmer called Johnstone, having plenty of money, bought some land, and chose a beautiful green spot to build a house on, the very spot the fairies loved best.

The neighbours warned him that it was a fairy rath; but he laughed and never minded (for he was from the north), and looked on such things as mere old-wives' tales. So he built the house and made it beautiful to live in; and no people in the country were so well off as the Johnstones, so that the people said the farmer must have found a pot of gold in the fairy rath.

But the fairies were all the time plotting how they could punish the farmer for taking away their dancing ground, and for cutting down the hawthorn bush where they held their revels when the moon was full. And one day when the cows were milking, a little old woman in a blue cloak came to Mrs Johnstone and asked her for a porringer of milk.

30

'Go away,' said the mistress of the house, 'you shall have no milk from me. I'll have no tramps coming about my place.' And she told the farm servants to chase her away.

Some time after, the best and finest of the cows sickened and gave no milk, and lost her horns and teeth and finally died.

Then one day as Mrs Johnstone was sitting spinning flax in the parlour, the same little old woman in the blue cloak suddenly stood before her.

'Your maids are baking cakes in the kitchen,' she said; 'give me some off the griddle to carry away with me.'

'Go out of this,' cried the farmer's wife, angrily; 'you are a wicked old wretch, and have poisoned my best cow.' And she bade the farm servants drive her off with sticks.

Now the Johnstones had one only child; a beautiful bright boy, as strong as a young colt, and as full of life and merriment. But soon after this he began to grow queer and strange, and was disturbed in his sleep; for he said the

31

fairies came round him at night and pinched and beat him, and some sat on his chest and he could neither breathe nor move. And they told him they would never leave him in peace unless he promised to give them a supper every night of a griddle cake and a porringer of milk. So to soothe the child the mother had these things laid every night on a table beside his bed, and in the morning they were gone.

But still the child pined away, and his eyes got a strange, wild look, as if he saw nothing near or around him, only something far, far away that troubled his spirit. And when they asked him what ailed him, he said the fairies carried him away to the hills every night, where he danced and danced with them till morning, when they brought him back and laid him again in his bed.

At last the farmer and his wife were at their wits' end from grief and despair, for the child was pining away before their eyes and they could do nothing for him to help him. And one night he cried out in great agony –

'Mother! Mother! Send for the priest to take away the fairies, for they are killing me; they are here on my chest, crushing me to death,' and his eyes were wild with terror.

Now the farmer and his wife believed in no fairies, and in no priest; but to soothe the child they did as he asked and sent for the priest, who prayed over him and sprinkled him with holy water. The poor little fellow seemed calmer as the priest prayed, and he said the fairies were leaving him and going away, and then he sank into a quiet sleep. But when he woke in the morning, he told his parents that he had a beautiful dream and was walking in a lovely garden with the angels; and he knew it was heaven, and that he would be there before night, for the angels told him they would come for him.

Then they watched by the sick child all through the night, for they saw the fever was still on him, but hoped a change would come before morning; for he now slept quite calmly with a smile on his lips.

But just as the clock struck midnight he awoke and sat up, and when his mother put her arms round him weeping, he whispered to her – 'The angels are here, Mother,' and then he sank back, and so died.

Now after this calamity the farmer never held up his head. He ceased to mind his farm, and the crops went to ruin and the cattle died, and finally before a year and a day were over he was laid in the grave by the side of his little son; and the land passed into other hands, and as no one would live in the house it was pulled down. No one, either, would plant on the rath; so the grass grew again all over it, green and beautiful, and the fairies danced there once more in the moonlight as they used to do in the old time, free and happy; and thus the evil spell was broken for evermore.

But the people would have nothing to do with the childless mother, so she went away back to her own people, a broken-hearted, miserable woman – a warning to all who would arouse the vengeance of the fairies by interfering with their ancient rights and possessions and privileges.

THE STOLEN CHILD
W. B. Yeats

Where dips the rocky highland
  Of Sleuth Wood in the lake,
There lies a leafy island
  Where flapping herons wake
The drowsy water-rats.
There we've hid our fairy vats
Full of berries,
And of reddest stolen cherries.
Come away, O, human child!
To the woods and waters wild
With a fairy hand in hand,
For the world's more full of weeping than
         you can understand.

Where the wave of moonlight glosses
  The dim grey sands with light,
Far off by farthest Rosses
  We foot it all the night,

Weaving olden dances,
Mingling hands, and mingling glances,
   Till the moon has taken flight;
To and fro we leap,
   And chase the frothy bubbles,
   While the world is full of troubles.
And is anxious in its sleep.
Come away! O, human child!
To the woods and waters wild,
With a fairy hand in hand,
For the world's more full of weeping than
            you can understand.

Where the wandering water gushes
   From the hills above Glen-Car,
In pools among the rushes,
   That scarce could bathe a star,
We seek for slumbering trout,
   And whispering in their ears
      Give them unquiet dreams,
Leaning softly out
   From ferns that drop their tears
      Of dew on the young streams.
Come away, O, human child!
To the woods and waters wild,
With a fairy hand in hand,
For the world's more full of weeping than
            you can understand.

Away with us, he's going,
   The solemn-eyed;
He'll hear no more the lowing
   Of the calves on the warm hill-side.
Or the kettle on the hob
   Sing peace into his breast;
Or see the brown mice bob

W. B. Yeats

Round and round the oatmeal chest.
For he comes, the human child,
To the woods and waters wild,
With a fairy hand in hand,
From a world more full of weeping than
       he can understand.

GULEESH

after Douglas Hyde

There was once a boy in the county Mayo; Guleesh was his name. There was a ruined fort just by the gable of his house, and he often sat on the grassy bank that surrounded it. One night he stood, half leaning against the gable of the house, and looked up into the sky, watching the beautiful bright moon. After standing that way for some time, he said to himself: 'I wish I could get away from this place once in a while. I'd sooner be anywhere than here. Och, it's all right for you, old moon,' says he, 'that can turn around and move through the sky, and no man to say boo to you. I wish I was as free as you.'

Hardly was the word out of his mouth when he heard a great commotion like the sound of many people running together, and talking, and laughing, and joking, and the noise went past him like a whirl of wind, and he listened to it dying away into the ruined fort. 'Dear gracious, by my soul,' says he, 'that's a merry noise to follow.'

Inside the whirlwind was nothing less than the fairy host,

though of course Guleesh did not realize it, and he followed them into the ruins of the fort. There he caught up with their hullabaloo, every man of them crying out as loud as he could: 'My horse, my bridle, and saddle! My horse, my bridle, and saddle!'

'Dear gracious!' said Guleesh, 'I can shout like that too,' and he cried out as loud as they: 'My horse, my bridle, and saddle! My horse, my bridle, and saddle!' And immediately a fine horse with a bridle of gold, and saddle of silver, was standing before him. Guleesh leapt up on it, and the moment he was mounted, he saw that the whole ruin was full of horses, and of little people mounted on them.

Said one of the little people to him: 'Are you coming with us tonight, Guleesh?'

'I am surely,' said Guleesh.

'Well, come along then,' said the little man, and out they all trooped together, riding like the wind, faster than the fastest horse you ever saw a-hunting, and faster than the fox with the hounds at his tail. Faster than the cold winter's wind they went, and rushed along until they came to the brink of the sea.

Then every one of them cried: 'Up we go! Up we go!' and then they were far up in the air, and before Guleesh had time to think about it, they were down on dry land again, still going like the wind. At last they halted, and one of them said to Guleesh: 'Guleesh, do you know where you are?'

'No idea at all,' says Guleesh.

'You're in France, Guleesh,' said he. 'The daughter of the king of France is to be married tonight, the loveliest woman in the kingdom, and we are going to try and bring her away with us, if we can; and you must come with us, so that we can put her up behind you on your horse, for we cannot put her astride a fairy horse. But you're flesh and blood, and she can get a good grip of you, and she won't fall off your horse. Will you do that for us, Guleesh?'

'Happy to oblige a lady, I'm sure,' said Guleesh.

So then they got off their horses, and one of the fairy men said a word that Guleesh did not understand, and all at once Guleesh found himself and his little companions transported into the royal palace. There was a great feast going on there, and all the nobility and gentlefolk of the kingdom were there, dressed in their finest, and the night was as bright as the day with all the lamps and candles that were lit, and Guleesh had to shut his eyes at the brightness. When he opened them again and looked around him, he had never seen such an amazing sight. There were a hundred tables spread out, each one of them groaning with flesh-meat, and cakes and sweetmeats, and wine and ale, and every drink that ever a man saw. The musicians were at both ends of the great hall, playing the sweetest music that ever a person heard, and there were young men and women in the middle of the hall, dancing and turning and going round so quickly and lightly, that Guleesh got quite light-headed watching them. It was the biggest feast seen in France for twenty years, because the old king had no other children, and his daughter's wedding to the son of a neighbouring king was to take place that very night. Three days the feasting had been going on, but this was the night of the wedding, and the night that Guleesh and the little folk came, hoping, if they could, to carry off with them the king's young daughter.

Guleesh and his companions were standing together at the head of the hall, where a fine altar had been set up, with two bishops behind it waiting to marry the girl when the right moment came. Now none of the court could see the little people, for they had said a word as they came in, and that word made them all invisible, as if they had never been there.

'Tell me, which of them is the king's daughter?' asked Guleesh when he had got used to the noise and the bright lights.

'Don't you see her, over there?' asked the little man that he was talking to.

Guleesh looked over to where the little man was pointing, and there he saw the loveliest woman that ever moved on the ridge of the world. Her face was rose-bright and lily-smooth, her mouth as red as a strawberry, her foot as small as a person's hand, her hair like buckles of gold, and her form was slim and slender. Her garments and dress were woven with silver and gold, and the bright stone of the ring on her hand shone like the sun.

Guleesh was nearly blinded by the beauty of her; but when he looked again, he saw that she was crying and there were tears in her eyes. 'It can't be right,' said Guleesh to himself. 'Why is she so sad when all the folk around her are full of merriment and sport?'

'Dear gracious, she's sorely grieved,' said the little man; 'for it's against her will she is being married, and she has no love for the husband she is to marry. The king was going to marry her off three years ago, when she was only fifteen, but she begged him for a year's grace. Now she's had three years' grace, and the king will give her no longer – she must marry tonight, according to him. But I'll tell you this, Guleesh,' said the little man, 'it's no king's son she'll marry, if I can help it.'

Guleesh pitied the lovely lady when he heard all this, and he was heart-broken to think she would have to marry a man she didn't like, or take a nasty land-fairy for a husband. And though he said nothing aloud, he could not help cursing his bad luck, to be helping the fairies capture her and snatch her away from her family.

He was watching her when the king's son came up and asked her for a kiss, but she turned her head away from him. Guleesh was doubly sorry for her then, watching the lad take her by the soft white hand, and drawing her out to the dance. He watched them go through the motions of the dance, and he could plainly see the tears in her eyes.

When the dancing was over, the old king, her father, and her mother the queen, came up and said that now was the time for the marriage ceremony, that the bishops were ready, and it was time to put the wedding-ring on her finger and give her to her husband.

The king took the youth by the hand, and the queen took her daughter, and they went up together to the altar, with the lords and great people following them.

When they approached within about four yards of the altar, the little maneen stretched out his foot to trip the princess, and she fell. Before she had got up again, he threw something over her, said a couple of words, and in an instant the girl was gone from amongst them. Nobody could see her, for those words had made her invisible. The little maneen seized her and out with them all post-haste from the door of the great hall went the princess of France.

Well – the crying, and the hunting, and the searching, when the princess disappeared before the eyes of the whole court, and without any of them seeing what did it. Out of the front door of the palace rushed the fairy host, without let or hindrance, for nobody saw them go, and 'My horse, my bridle, and saddle!' cries every maneen of them. 'My horse, my bridle, and saddle!' cries Guleesh; and there was his horse standing ready before him.

'Now, jump up, Guleesh,' said the little man, 'and put the young lady behind you, and we will be going out of here, for morning is not far off now.'

Guleesh raised her up behind him on the horse's back, and, 'Giddy-up, horse,' said he; and his horse, and all the fairy horses with him, went at a great gallop until they came to the sea.

'Up we go!' cried every man of them.

'Up we go!' cried Guleesh; and all at once the horse rose under him, and cut a leap in the clouds, and came down in Erin.

They did not stop there, but raced on to Guleesh's house

beside the ruined fort in the county Mayo. And when they got there, Guleesh turned and caught the young girl in his two arms, and leapt off the horse with her.

'I call and cross you to myself, in the name of God!' said he. And on the spot, before another word was out of his mouth, his horse fell to earth, and there was nothing left on the ground but a plough handle; and so it was with the fairy horses too. Some of the little people had been riding old broomsticks, and others were hanging on to hemlock stems or thistle stalks.

The little people called out together when they heard what Guleesh had said: 'Oh Guleesh, you clown, you thief, may you come to grief for playing that trick on us!'

But they had lost their power over the girl, after Guleesh had consecrated her to himself.

'Oh Guleesh! That's a nice turn you did us, and we so kind to you! What good have we now out of our trip to France? Never mind, you clown, you'll pay us for this yet! Believe us, you'll repent this.'

'He'll get no good out of that young girl,' said the little man that had been talking to him in the palace earlier, and as he spoke he moved towards her and struck her a slap on the side of the head. 'Now,' said he, 'she'll be without speech; now, Guleesh, what use is a dumb woman to you? Think about that – and remember us, Guleesh!'

With that, he stretched out his two arms, and before Guleesh could answer, he and the rest of the fairies were away into the ruins of the fort, and Guleesh saw them no more.

Then Guleesh turned to the young woman and said to her: 'Thanks be to God, they're gone. You're a lot safer with me than with them.' The girl made no answer. 'There's shock and grief on her yet,' thought Guleesh, and he addressed her again: 'I'm afraid you must spend this night in my father's house, but if there's anything you need, you have only to ask, and I'll be your servant.'

The beautiful girl remained silent, but there were tears in her eyes, and her expression was distressed.

'Lady,' said Guleesh, 'tell me what you would like me to do now. I did not belong to that troop of fairies who carried you off with them. I am the son of an honest farmer, and I went with them without knowing what they were up to. If I can work out how to send you back to your father, I'll do it, and I hope you will tell me what you want.'

He looked into her face, and he saw the mouth moving as if she were trying to speak, but no words came.

'It cannot be,' said Guleesh, 'that you are dumb. Did I not hear you speak to the king's son in the palace tonight? Or has that fairy-devil really made you dumb, with that nasty blow to your jaw?'

The girl raised her smooth white hand, and laid her finger on her tongue, to show him that she had indeed lost her speech, and the tears ran out of her eyes like two streams, and Guleesh's own eyes were not dry, for he had a soft heart and hated to see the girl so unhappy.

He began wondering what he ought to do, whether to bring her home to his father's house, knowing that they would not believe him when he told them that he had been to France and brought back with him the king of France's daughter, and he was afraid they might mock the young lady or insult her.

While he was wondering what to do, he remembered the priest. 'Glory to God,' he thought, 'I know what I'll do; I'll bring her to the priest's house, and he'll look after her for me.' He explained his plan to the lady, and she bent her head to show that she was ready to follow him. So they went together to the priest's house, just as the sun was rising in the sky. Guleesh beat hard on the door, and although it was early, the priest was up and about, and soon opened up the house. He wondered when he saw Guleesh and the girl, and reckoned they wanted him to marry them.

'Guleesh, surely you don't want me to be marrying you and your sweetheart at this ungodly hour of the morning. And who is she anyway?' said he, suddenly, looking again at the young girl, 'where did you come from?'

'Father,' said Guleesh, 'all we want of you is a lodging for this young lady.'

The priest looked at him as if he had ten heads on him; but asking no further questions, he showed the pair of them in, sat them down, shut the door behind them, and waited.

'Now, Guleesh,' said he, 'I'm a busy man, and I want the facts of the matter, and I've no time for jokes.'

'I'm not telling you a word of a lie, nor joking,' said Guleesh seriously, 'but it was from the palace of the king of France I brought this lady, and she is the daughter of the king of France.'

And so Guleesh told the whole story to the priest, who was so surprised that he couldn't help exclaiming aloud from time to time, and clapping his hands in amazement.

When Guleesh said it was obvious the girl was unhappy about being married off, there came a red blush into the

44

girl's cheek, and he was more certain than ever that she had rather be stranded with him in Ireland than married off to a man she disliked. When Guleesh said he would be grateful to the priest for looking after her, the kind man said he'd be happy to give her a roof as long as she needed one, but that he would have to think about what to do with her in the longer term, because they had no means of sending her back to her father again.

Guleesh answered that he was worried about the same thing, and that he saw nothing for it but to keep the matter quiet until they had worked something out. They then decided between themselves that the priest should let on that it was his niece who was visiting him from the north, and that he should tell his neighbours she was dumb, and keep her out of the way of nosy folk. The girl showed with her eyes that she was grateful to them.

Guleesh went home then, and told his people that he had slept the night in a neighbour's barn.

There was much comment among the priest's neighbours at the girl who came so suddenly to his house without anyone knowing for sure where she was from, or what business she had there. Some of the people said that everything was not as it should be, and others commented that Guleesh was never out of the priest's house all of a sudden, which was not a bit like him.

And it was true that seldom a day went by but Guleesh would go to the priest's house, and talk to him, and hope to hear news of the young lady's recovery; but, alas! she remained dumb and silent, without relief or cure. Since she had no other means of talking, she carried on a sort of conversation with Guleesh by moving her hands and fingers, winking her eyes, nodding and shaking her head, laughing or smiling, and a thousand other signs, so that it was not long before they understood each other very well. Sometimes Guleesh still wondered how to send her back safely to her father; but there was no one to take her, and he himself didn't know the road, for he had never been out of the county Mayo before the night he rode out with the little people. Nor had the priest any better knowledge than he; but when Guleesh asked him, he wrote three or four letters to the king of France, and gave them to merchants who were travelling over the seas; but never a word came back to Ireland.

So things went on for many months, and Guleesh fell deeper and deeper in love with the girl, and it was plain to himself and the priest that she too liked him. At last the boy became fearful lest the king should indeed find where his daughter was, and take her away from him, so he asked the priest to write no more, but to leave the matter to God.

After a year of this, there came a day when Guleesh was lying by himself on the grassy bank, thinking over in his mind of all that had happened to him since the night when he rode out with the fairy folk across the sea. Then suddenly he remembered that it was on Hallowe'en night that he had been standing at the gable of the house, when the whirlwind came, and the fairy folk in it, and he said to himself: 'Hallowe'en night comes round again tonight. I must stand in the same place as I stood last year, and see if the good people come again. Perhaps I might learn something that would be useful to me, and help me bring back her speech to Mary' – which was the name himself and the priest now called the king's daughter, for neither of them knew her right name. Guleesh explained his intentions to the priest, and the priest gave him his blessing.

That night after dark, Guleesh went to the old ruined fort, and stood leaning on an old grey flagstone, waiting for the witching hour. The moon rose slowly in the sky, and it was like a knob of fire at his back; and a white fog lay over the flat fields of grass and all the damp places, through the coolness of the night after a hot day. The night was calm as a lake without a breath of wind to ruffle its surface, and there was no sound to be heard but the cricking of insects

going by from time to time, or the sudden hoarse scream of
the wild geese as they passed from lake to lake, half a mile
up in the air over his head; or the sharp whistle of the
golden and green plover, rising and lying, lying and rising,
as they do on a calm night. A thousand bright stars shone
over his head, and a light frost left the grass white and crisp
under his foot.

An hour he stood there, two hours, three hours, and the
frost increasing all the time, so that he heard the crispness
under his foot as often as he moved. At last, he decided the
fairy folk were not going to appear that night, when he
heard a far-off sound coming towards him, and he recognized what it was at once. The sound increased, and at first
it was like the beating of waves on a pebbly shore, and then
it was like the falling of a great waterfall, and at last it was
like a loud storm in the tops of the trees, and then the
whirlwind burst into the ruins, and the little folk were in it.

Scarcely had they all gathered into the ruins till they all
began shouting, and screaming, and talking amongst themselves; and then each one of them cried out: 'My horse, my
bridle, and saddle! My horse, my bridle, and saddle!' So
Guleesh took his courage in his hands, and called out as
loudly as any of them: 'My horse, my bridle, and saddle! My
horse, my bridle, and saddle!' But before the words were
well out of his mouth, another little man cried out: 'Oh ho!
Guleesh, my boy, are you among us again? How are you
getting on with your woman? Don't you be calling for your
horse tonight! You'll not play that trick on us a second time!
It was a good trick the first time, no doubt!'

'Not bad at all,' said another little man, 'but he won't do
that again.'

'Isn't he a fine lad, the same boy! to take a woman with
him that can't say as much as "How do you do?" since this
time last year!' said a third little man.

'Perhaps he likes to be looking at her,' said another voice.

'And if the fool only knew there's a herb growing beside

his own door, and if he were to boil it up and give it to her, she'd be well,' said another voice.

'That's true enough.'

'He is a fool.'

'Don't bother your head with him; let's go.'

'Leave the goblin standing there.'

And with that they rose up into the air, and away with them with one hullabaloo just as they'd come; and they left poor Guleesh standing where they'd found him, his two eyes almost jumping out of his head, looking after them and wondering . . .

He didn't stand long till he returned home, thinking over all he had seen and heard, wondering whether there really was a herb at his door which could give Mary back her speech. 'It can't be,' says he to himself, 'that they wanted me to overhear all that; perhaps it just slipped out by mistake. But I'll search for that plant as soon as the sun rises.'

Guleesh got up as soon as the sun was up, and went out and searched through the grass round about the house, trying to find the strange herb. And indeed, he was not long searching till he noticed a large funny-looking herb growing up beside the gable of the house.

He went over to it and examined it carefully, and saw that there were seven little branches coming from the stalk, and seven leaves growing on every brancheen of them, and that there was a white sap in the leaves. 'Isn't that amazing,' said he to himself, 'I never noticed this plant before. If herbs have any powers at all, surely this strange plant will do something for us.'

He drew out his knife, cut the plant, and carried it into his house; stripped the leaves off it and cut up the stalk; and there came a thick white juice out of it, as comes out of the sow thistle when it is bruised, except that this juice was more like oil.

He put it in a little pot of water, and boiled it over the fire, and then he took a cup half-filled with the juice and put it to his own mouth. It occurred to him that it might be poisonous, and that the good people were trying to do away with him, or make him put the girl to death by accident. He put the cup down again, dipped the tip of his finger in the liquid, and put it to his mouth. It was not bitter, and indeed it had a sweet, agreeable taste. Guleesh grew bolder then, and drank a thimbleful of the liquid, and then as much again, and soon he had half the cup drunk. He fell asleep after that, and did not wake till it was night, and there was great hunger and thirst on him.

He had to wait then till daybreak; but he determined, as soon as possible, to go to the king's daughter and give her a drink of the juice of the herb.

Next morning, he went straight to the priest's house with the drink in his hand, and he never felt himself so bold and valiant and light-hearted as that day, and he was quite certain that it was the herbal drink which made him feel so good.

When he came to the house, he found the priest and the young lady within, and they were wondering greatly why he had not visited them for two days.

He told them all his news, and said that he was certain there was great power in the herb, and that it would do the lady no harm, for he himself had tested it and got good from it, and then he let her taste it, assuring her that there was no danger in it.

Guleesh handed her the cup, and she drank half of it, and then she fell back on her bed and a heavy sleep came on her, and she never woke out of that sleep till the following afternoon.

Guleesh and the priest sat up with her the entire time, waiting till she should wake, half hoping and half fearing what might become of her.

She awoke at last after the sun had gone half its way through the heavens. She rubbed her eyes and looked like a person who did not know where she was. She was like one astonished when she saw Guleesh and the priest beside her, and she sat up doing her best to collect her thoughts.

The two men were in great anxiety waiting to see would she speak, or not speak, and after a couple of minutes of silence, the priest said gently to her: 'Did you sleep well, Mary?'

And she answered him: 'I slept, thank you.'

No sooner did Guleesh hear her talking than he let out a shout of joy, and ran over to her, and fell on his knees, and said: 'A thousand thanks to God, who has given you back your speech; lady of my heart, speak again to me.'

The lady answered that she understood that it was he who had got her that drink; that she was obliged to him from her heart for all the kindness he had shown her since the day she first came to Ireland, and that he might be certain that she would never forget it. Guleesh was ready to die with satisfaction and delight. Then they brought her food, and she ate with a good appetite, and was merry and joyous, and never left off talking with them while she was eating.

After that, Guleesh went home to his house, and stretched himself on his bed and fell asleep again, for the power of the herb was not all spent, and he passed another day and a night sleeping. When he woke up he went back to the priest's house, and found that the young lady had also been asleep almost since the time he had left her.

He went into her room with the priest, and they watched her till she woke again and spoke as well as ever, and Guleesh was greatly delighted. And so their friendship increased.

In due course, they married one another, and that was one fine wedding. And I heard from a little bird that there was neither want nor woe, sickness nor sorrow, mishap nor misfortune on them till the hour of their death, and may the same be with me, and with us all!

Part Two

THE PHOUKA AND THE RED MAN

THE PHOUKA
Lady Wilde

The Phouka is a friendly being, and often helps the farmer at his work if he is treated well and kindly. One day a farmer's son was minding cattle in the field, when something rushed past him like the wind; but he was not frightened, for he knew it was the Phouka on his way to the old mill by the moat where the fairies met every night. So he called out, 'Phouka, Phouka! show me what you are like, and I'll give you my big coat to keep you warm.' Then a young bull came to him lashing his tail like mad; but Phadrig threw the coat over him, and in a moment he was quiet as a lamb, and told the boy to come to the mill that night when the moon was up, and he would have good luck.

So Phadrig went, but saw nothing except sacks of corn all lying about on the ground, for the men had fallen asleep, and no work was done. Then he lay down also and slept, for he was very tired; and when he woke up early in the morning there was all the meal ground, though certainly the men had not done it, for they still slept. And this happened

53

for three nights, after which Phadrig determined to keep awake and watch.

Now there was an old chest in the mill, and he crept into this to hide, and just looked through the keyhole to see what would happen. And exactly at midnight six little fellows came in, each carrying a sack of corn on his back; and after them came an old man in tattered rags of clothes, and he bade them turn the mill, and they turned and turned it till all was ground.

Then Phadrig ran to tell his father, and the miller determined to watch the next night with his son, and both together saw the same thing happen.

'Now,' said the farmer, 'I see it is the Phouka's work, and let him work if it pleases him, for the men are idle and lazy and only sleep. So I'll pack the whole set off tomorrow, and leave the grinding of the corn to this excellent old Phouka.'

After this the farmer grew so rich that there was no end to his money, for he had no men to pay, and all his corn was ground without his spending a penny. Of course the people wondered much over his riches, but he never told them about the Phouka, or their curiosity would have spoiled the luck.

Now Phadrig went often to the mill and hid in the chest that he might watch the fairies at work; but he had great pity for the poor old Phouka in his tattered clothes, who yet directed everything and had hard work of it sometimes, keeping the little Phoukas in order. So Phadrig, out of love and gratitude, bought a fine suit of cloth and silk and laid it one night on the floor of the mill just where the old Phouka always stood to give his orders to the little men, and then he crept into the chest to watch.

'How is this?' said the Phouka when he saw the clothes. 'Are these for me? I shall be turned into a fine gentleman.'

And he put them on, and then began to walk up and down admiring himself. But suddenly he remembered the corn, and went to grind as usual, then stopped and cried out –

'No, no. No more work for me. Fine gentlemen don't grind corn. I'll go out and see a little of the world and show my fine clothes.' And he kicked away the old rags into a corner, and went out.

No corn was ground that night, nor the next, nor the next; all the little Phoukas ran away, and not a sound was heard in the mill. Then Phadrig grew very sorry for the loss of his old friend, and used to go out into the fields and call out, 'Phouka, Phouka! come back to me. Let me see your face.' But the old Phouka never came back, and all his life long Phadrig never looked on the face of his friend again. However, the farmer had made so much money that he wanted no more help; and he sold the mill and reared up Phadrig to be a great scholar and a gentleman, who had his own house and land and servants. And in time he married a beautiful lady, so beautiful that the people said she must be daughter to the king of the fairies.

A strange thing happened at the wedding, for when they all stood up to drink the bride's health, Phadrig saw beside him a golden cup filled with wine. And no one knew how the golden cup had come to his hand; but Phadrig guessed it was the Phouka's gift, and he drank the wine without fear and made his bride drink also. And ever after their lives were happy and prosperous, and the golden cup was kept as a treasure in the family, and the descendants of Phadrig have it in their possession to this day.

THE RED MAN IN DONEGAL
Letitia Maclintock

Pat Diver, the tinker, was a man well accustomed to a wandering life, and to strange shelters; he had shared the beggar's blanket in smoky cabins; he had crouched beside the still in many a nook and corner where poteen was made on the wild Inishowen mountains; he had even slept on the bare heather, or on the ditch, with no roof over him but the vault of heaven; yet all his nights of adventure were tame and commonplace when compared with one especial night.

During the day preceding that night, he had mended all the kettles and saucepans in Moville and Greencastle, and was on his way to Culdaff, when night overtook him on a lonely mountain road.

He knocked at one door after another asking for a night's lodging, while he jingled the halfpence in his pocket, but was everywhere refused.

Where was the boasted hospitality of Inishowen, which he had never before known to fail? It was of no use to be able to pay when the people seemed so churlish. Thus thinking, he made his way towards a light a little farther on, and knocked at another cabin door.

An old man and woman were seated one at each side of the fire.

'Will you be pleased to give me a night's lodging, sir?' asked Pat respectfully.

'Can you tell a story?' returned the old man.

'No, then, sir, I canna say I'm good at story-telling,' replied the puzzled tinker.

'Then you maun just gang farther, for none but them that can tell a story will get in here.'

This reply was made in so decided a tone that Pat did not attempt to repeat his appeal, but turned away reluctantly to resume his weary journey.

'A story, indeed,' muttered he. 'Auld wives' fables to please the weans!'

As he took up his bundle of tinkering implements, he observed a barn standing rather behind the dwelling-house, and, aided by the rising moon, he made his way towards it.

It was a clean, roomy barn, with a piled-up heap of straw in one corner. Here was a shelter not to be despised; so Pat crept under the straw and was soon asleep.

He could not have slept very long when he was awakened by the tramp of feet, and, peeping cautiously through a crevice in his straw covering, he saw four immensely tall men enter the barn, dragging a body which they threw roughly upon the floor.

They next lighted a fire in the middle of the barn, and fastened the corpse by the feet with a great rope to a beam in the roof. One of them began to turn it slowly before the fire. 'Come on,' said he, addressing a gigantic fellow, the tallest of the four – 'I'm tired; you be to tak' your turn.'

'Faix an' troth, I'll no' turn him,' replied the big man. 'There's Pat Diver in under the straw, why wouldn't he tak' his turn?'

With hideous clamour the four men called the wretched

Pat, who, seeing there was no escape, thought it was his wisest plan to come forth as he was bidden.

'Now, Pat,' said they, 'you'll turn the corpse, but if you let him burn you'll be tied up there and roasted in his place.'

Pat's hair stood on end, and the cold perspiration poured from his forehead, but there was nothing for it but to perform his dreadful task.

Seeing him fairly embarked in it, the tall men went away.

Soon, however, the flames rose so high as to singe the rope, and the corpse fell with a great thud upon the fire, scattering the ashes and embers, and extracting a howl of anguish from the miserable cook, who rushed to the door, and ran for his life.

He ran on until he was ready to drop with fatigue, when, seeing a drain overgrown with tall, rank grass, he thought he would creep in there and lie hidden till morning.

But he was not many minutes in the drain before he heard the heavy tramping again, and the four men came up with their burden, which they laid down on the edge of the drain.

'I'm tired,' said one, to the giant; 'it's your turn to carry him a piece now.'

'Faix and troth, I'll no' carry him,' replied he, 'but there's Pat Diver in the drain, why wouldn't he come out and tak' his turn?'

'Come out, Pat, come out,' roared all the men, and Pat, almost dead with fright, crept out.

He staggered on under weight of the corpse until he reached Kiltown Abbey, a ruin festooned with ivy, where the brown owl hooted all night long, and the forgotten dead slept around the walls, under dense, matted tangles of brambles and ben-weed.

No one ever buried there now, but Pat's tall companions turned into the wild graveyard, and began digging a grave.

Pat, seeing them thus engaged, thought he might once more try to escape, and climbed up into a hawthorn tree in the fence, hoping to be hidden in the boughs.

'I'm tired,' said the man who was digging the grave; 'here, take the spade,' addressing the big man, 'it's your turn.'

'Faix an' troth, it's no' my turn,' replied he, as before. 'There's Pat Diver in the tree, why wouldn't he come down and tak' his turn?'

Pat came down to take the spade, but just then the cocks in the little farmyards and cabins round the abbey began to crow, and the men looked at one another.

'We must go,' said they, 'and well is it for you, Pat Diver, that the cocks crowed, for if they had not, you'd just ha' been bundled into that grave with the corpse.'

Two months passed, and Pat had wandered far and wide over the county Donegal, when he chanced to arrive at Raphoe during a fair.

Among the crowd that filled the Diamond he came suddenly on the big man.

'How are you, Pat Diver?' said the big man, bending down to look into the tinker's face.

'You've the advantage of me, sir, for I havna' the pleasure of knowing you,' faltered Pat.

'Do you not know me, Pat?' Whisper – 'When you go back to Inishowen, you'll have a story to tell!'

DANIEL O'ROURKE
Thomas Crofton Croker

People may have heard of the renowned adventures of
Daniel O'Rourke, but how few are there who know that the
cause of all his perils, above and below, was neither more
nor less than having slept under the walls of the Phouka's
tower. I knew the man well. He lived at the bottom of
Hungry Hill, just at the right-hand side of the road as you
go towards Bantry. He was an old man at the time he told
me the story, with grey hair and a red nose; and it was on
the 25th of June 1813 that I heard it from his own lips, as he
sat smoking his pipe under the old poplar tree, on as fine an
evening as ever shone from the sky. I was going to visit the
caves in Dursey Island, having spent the morning at Glen-
gariff.

'I am often axed to tell it, sir,' said he, 'so that this is not
the first time. The master's son, you see, had come from
beyond foreign parts in France and Spain, as young gentlemen used to go before Bonaparte or any such was heard of;
and sure enough there was a dinner given to all the people

60

on the ground, gentle and simple, high and low, rich and poor. The *ould* gentlemen were the gentlemen after all, saving your honour's presence. They'd swear at a body a little, to be sure, and, maybe, give one a cut of a whip now and then, but we were no losers by it in the end; and they were so easy and civil, and kept such rattling houses, and thousands of welcomes; and there was no grinding for rent, and there was hardly a tenant on the estate that did not taste of his landlord's bounty often and often in a year; but now it's another thing. No matter for that, sir, for I'd better be telling you my story.

'Well, we had everything of the best, and plenty of it; and we ate, and we drank, and we danced, and the young master by the same token danced with Peggy Barry, from the Bohereen – a lovely young couple they were, though they are both low enough now. To make a long story short, I got, as a body may say, the same thing as tipsy almost, for I can't remember ever at all, no ways, how it was I left the place; only I did leave it, that's certain. Well, I thought, for all that, in myself, I'd just step to Molly Cronohan's, the fairy woman, to speak a word about the bracket heifer that was bewitched; and so as I was crossing the stepping-stones of the ford of Ballyasheenogh, and was looking up at the stars and blessing myself – for why? it was Lady-day – I missed my foot, and souse I fell into the water. "Death alive!" thought I, "I'll be drowned now!" However, I began swimming, swimming away for the dear life, till at last I got ashore, somehow or other, but never the one of me can tell how, upon a *dissolute* island.

'I wandered and wandered about there, without knowing where I wandered, until at last I got into a big bog. The moon was shining as bright as day, or your fair lady's eyes, sir (with your pardon for mentioning her), and I looked east and west, and north and south, and every way, and nothing did I see but bog, bog, bog – I could never find out how I got into it; and my heart grew cold with fear, for sure and certain I was that it would be my *berrin* place. So I sat down upon a stone which, as good luck would have it, was close by me, and I began to scratch my head, and sing the *Ullagone* – when all of a sudden the moon grew black, and I looked up, and saw something for all the world as if it was moving down between me and it, and I could not tell what it was. Down it came with a pounce, and looked at me full in the face; and what was it but an eagle? as fine a one as ever flew from the kingdom of Kerry. So he looked at me in the face, and says he to me, "Daniel O'Rourke," says he, "how do you do?" "Very well, I thank you, sir," says I; "I hope you're well;" wondering out of my senses all the time how an eagle came to speak like a Christian. "What brings you here, Dan?" says he. "Nothing at all, sir," says I; "only I wish I was safe home again." "Is it out of the island you want to go, Dan?" says he. "'Tis, sir," says I: so I up and told him how I had taken a drop too much, and fell into the water; how I swam to the island; and how I got into the bog and did not know my way out of it. "Dan," says he, after a minute's thought, "though it is very improper for you to get drunk on Lady-day, yet as you are a decent sober man, who 'tends Mass well, and never flings stones at me or mine, nor cries out after us in the fields – my life for yours," says he; "so get up on my back, and grip me well for fear you'd fall off, and I'll fly you out of the bog." "I am afraid," says I, "your honour's making game of me; for whoever heard of riding a horseback on an eagle before?" "'Pon the honour of a gentleman," says he, putting his right foot on his breast, "I am quite in earnest: and so now either take my offer or starve in the bog – besides, I see that your weight is sinking the stone."

'It was true enough as he said, for I found the stone every minute sinking under me. I had no choice; so thinks I to myself, faint heart never won fair lady, and this is a fair chance. "I thank your honour," says I, "for the loan of your civility; and I'll take your kind offer." I therefore

mounted upon the back of the eagle, and held him tight
enough by the throat, and up he flew in the air like a lark.
Little I knew the trick he was going to serve me. Up – up –
up, God knows how far up he flew. "Why then," said I to
him – thinking he did not know the right road home – very
civilly, because why? I was in his power entirely; "Sir," says
I, "please your honour's glory, and with humble submission
to your better judgment, if you'd fly down a bit, you're now
just over my cabin, and I could be put down there, and
many thanks to your worship."

"'Arrah, Dan," said he, "do you think me a fool? Look
down in the next field, and don't you see two men and a
gun? By my word it would be no joke to be shot this way, to
oblige a drunken blackguard that I picked up off of a cold
stone in a bog." "Bother you," said I to myself, but I did
not speak out, for where was the use? Well, sir, up he kept,
flying, flying, and I asking him every minute to fly down,
and all to no use. "Where in the world are you going, sir?"

says I to him. "Hold your tongue, Dan," says he: "mind your own business, and don't be interfering with the business of other people." "Faith, this is my business I think," says I. "Be quiet, Dan," says he: so I said no more.

'At last where should we come to, but to the moon itself. Now you can't see it from this, but there is, or there was in my time, a reaping-hook sticking out of the side of the moon.

'"Dan," said the eagle, "I'm tired with this long fly; I had no notion 'twas so far." "And my lord, sir," said I, "who in the world *axed* you to fly so far – was it I? did not I beg and pray and beseech you to stop half an hour ago?" "There's no use talking, Dan," said he; "I'm tired bad enough, so you must get off, and sit down on the moon until I rest myself." "Is it sit down on the moon?" said I; "is it upon that little round thing, then? why, then, sure I'd fall off in a minute, and be kilt and spilt, and smashed all to bits; you are a vile deceiver – so you are." "Not at all, Dan," said he; "you can catch fast hold of the reaping-hook that's sticking out of the side of the moon, and 'twill keep you up." "I won't then," said I. "Maybe not," said he, quite quiet. "If you don't, my man, I shall just give you a shake, and one slap of my wing, and send you down to the ground, where every bone in your body will be smashed as small as a drop of dew on a cabbage in the morning." "Why, then, I'm in a fine way," said I to myself, "ever to have come along with the likes of you;" and so giving him a hearty curse in Irish, for fear he'd know what I said, I got off his back with a heavy heart, took hold of the reaping-hook, and sat down upon the moon, and a mighty cold seat it was, I can tell you that.

'When he had me there fairly landed, he turned about on me, and said, "Good morning to you, Daniel O'Rourke," said he; "I think I've nicked you fairly now. You robbed my nest last year" ('twas true enough for him, but how he found out is hard to say), "and in return you are freely welcome to cool your heels dangling upon the moon like an idiot."

'"Is that all, and is this the way you leave me, you brute, you," says I. "You ugly unnatural baste, and is this the way you serve me at last? Bad luck to yourself; with your hook'd nose, and to all your breed, you blackguard." 'Twas all to no manner of use; he spread out his great big wings, burst out a-laughing, and flew away like lightning. I bawled after him to stop; but I might have called and bawled forever, without his minding me. Away he went, and I never saw him from that day to this – sorrow fly away with him! You may be sure I was in a disconsolate condition, and kept roaring out for the bare grief, when all at once a door opened right in the middle of the moon, creaking on its hinges as if it had not been opened for a month before, I suppose they never thought of greasing 'em, and out there walks – who do you think but the man in the moon himself? I knew him by his bush.

'"Good morrow to you, Daniel O'Rourke," said he; "how do you do?" "Very well, thank your honour," said I. "I hope your honour's well." "What brought you here, Dan?" said he. So I told him how I was a little overtaken in liquor at the master's, and how I was cast on a *dissolute* island, and how I lost my way in the bog, and how the thief of an eagle promised to fly me out of it, and how, instead of that, he had fled me up to the moon.

'"Dan," said the man in the moon, taking a pinch of snuff when I was done, "you must not stay here." "Indeed, sir," says I, "'tis much against my will I'm here at all; but how am I to go back?" "That's your business," said he; "Dan, mine is to tell you that here you must not stay; so be off in less than no time." "I'm doing no harm," says I, "only holding on hard by the reaping-hook, lest I fall off." "That's what you must not do, Dan," says he. "Pray, sir," says I, "may I ask how many you are in family, that you would not give a poor traveller lodging: I'm sure 'tis not often you're troubled with strangers coming to see you, for 'tis a long way." "I'm by myself, Dan," says he; "but you'd better let go the reaping-hook that was keeping you up." "No way," says I, "and the more you bids me, the more I won't let go; – so I will." "You had better, Dan," says he again. "Why, then, my little fellow," says I, taking the whole weight of him with my eye from head to foot, "there are two words to that bargain; and I'll not budge, but you may if you like." "We'll see how that is to be," says he; and back he went, giving the door such a great bang after him (for it was plain he was huffed) that I thought the moon and all would fall down with it.

'Well, I was preparing myself to try strength with him, when back again he comes, with the kitchen cleaver in his hand, and, without saying a word, he gives two bangs to the handle of the reaping-hook that was keeping me up, and *whap*! it came in two. "Good morning to you, Dan," says the spiteful little old blackguard, when he saw me cleanly falling down with a bit of the handle in my hand; "I thank you for your visit, and fair weather after you, Daniel." I had not time to make any answer to him, for I was tumbling over and over, and rolling and rolling, at the rate of a fox-hunt. "God help me!" says I, "but this is a pretty pickle for a decent man to be seen in at this time of night: I am now sold fairly." The word was not out of my mouth when whiz! what should fly by close to my ear but a flock of wild geese, all the way from my own bog of Ballyasheenogh, else how should they know me? The ould gander, who was their general, turning about his head, cried out to me, "Is that you, Dan?" "The same," said I, not a bit daunted now at what he said, for I was by this time used to all kinds of bedevilment, and, besides, I knew him of ould. "Good morrow to you," says he, "Daniel O'Rourke; how are you in health this morning?" "Very well, sir," says I, "I thank you kindly," drawing my breath, for I was mightily in want of some. "I hope your honour's the same." "I think 'tis falling you are, Daniel," says he. "You may say that, sir," says I. "And where are you going all the way so fast?" said the gander. So I told him how I had taken the drop, and how I came on the island, and how I lost my way in the bog, and how the thief of an eagle flew me up to the moon, and how the man in the moon turned me out. "Dan," said he, "I'll save you: put out your hand and catch me by the leg, and I'll fly you home." "Sweet is your hand in a pitcher of honey, my jewel," says I, though all the time I thought within myself that I don't much trust you; but there was no help, so I caught the gander by the leg, and away I and the other geese flew after him as fast as hops.

'We flew, and we flew, and we flew, until we came right over the wide ocean. I knew it well, for I saw Cape Clear to my right hand, sticking up out of the water. "Ah, my lord," said I to the goose, for I thought it best to keep a civil tongue in my head any way, "fly to land if you please." "It is impossible, you see, Dan," said he, "for a while, because you see we are going to Arabia." "To Arabia!" said I; "that's surely some place in foreign parts, far away. Oh! Mr Goose: why then, to be sure, I'm a man to be pitied among you." "Whist, whist, you fool," said he, "hold your tongue; I tell you Arabia is a very decent sort of place, as like West Carbery as one egg is like another, only there is a little more sand there."

'Just as we were talking, a ship hove in sight, scudding so beautiful before the wind. "Ah! then, sir," said I, "will you drop me on the ship, if you please?" "We are not fair over it," said he; "if I dropped you now you would go splash into the sea." "I would not," says I; "I know better than that, for it is just clean under us, so let me drop now at once."

'"If you must, you must," said he; "there, take your own way;" and he opened his claw, and faith he was right – sure enough I came down plump into the very bottom of the salt sea! Down to the very bottom I went, and I gave myself up then forever, when a whale walked up to me, scratching himself after his night's sleep, and he looked me full in the face, and never the word did he say, but lifting up his tail, he splashed me all over again with the cold salt water till there wasn't a dry stitch upon my whole carcass! and I heard somebody saying – 'twas a voice I knew, too – "Get up you drunken brute, off o' that"; and with that I woke up, and there was Judy with a tub full of water, which she was splashing all over me – for, rest her soul! though she was a good wife, she never could bear to see me in drink, and had a bitter hand of her own.

'"Get up," said she again: "and of all places in the parish would no place sarve your turn to lie down upon but under the ould walls of Carrigapooka? an uneasy resting I am sure you had of it." And sure enough I had: for I was fairly bothered out of my senses with eagles, and men of the moons, and flying ganders, and whales, driving me through bogs, and up to the moon, and down to the bottom of the green ocean. If I was in drink ten times over, long would it be before I'd lie down in the same spot again, I know that.'

Part Three

THE MERROW AND THE
WATER SPIRITS

THE LADY OF GOLLERUS
Thomas Crofton Croker

On the shore of Smerwick harbour, one fine summer's morning, just at day-break, stood Dick Fitzgerald 'shoghing the dudeen', which may be translated, smoking his pipe. The sun was gradually rising behind the lofty Brandon, the dark sea was getting green in the light, and the mists, clearing away out of the valleys, went rolling and curling like the smoke from the corner of Dick's mouth.

''Tis just the pattern of a pretty morning,' said Dick, taking the pipe from between his lips, and looking towards the distant ocean, which lay as still and tranquil as a tomb of polished marble.

'Well, to be sure,' continued he, after a pause, ''tis mighty lonesome to be talking to one's self by way of company, and not to have another soul to answer one – nothing but the child of one's own voice, the echo! I know this, that if I had the luck, or maybe the misfortune,' said Dick with a melancholy smile, 'to have a wife, it would not be this way with me! – and what in the wide world is a man without a wife?

He's no more surely than a bottle without a drop of drink in it, or dancing without music, or the left leg of a scissors, or a fishing-line without a hook, or any other matter that is no ways complete. – Is it not so?' said Dick Fitzgerald, casting his eyes towards a rock upon the strand, which, though it could not speak, stood up as firm and looked as bold as ever Kerry witness did.

But what was his astonishment at beholding, just at the foot of that rock a beautiful young creature combing her hair, which was of a sea-green colour, and now the salt water shining on it, appeared, in the morning light, like melted butter upon cabbage.

Dick guessed at once that she was a Merrow, although he had never seen one before, for he spied the cohuleen driuth, or little enchanted cap, which the sea people use for diving down into the ocean, lying upon the strand, near her; and he had heard, that if once he could possess himself of the cap, she would lose the power of going away into the water. So he seized it with all speed, and she, hearing the noise, turned her head about as quickly as any Christian.

When the Merrow saw that her little diving-cap was gone, the salt tears – doubly salt, no doubt, from her – came trickling down her cheeks, and she began a low mournful cry with just the tender voice of a new-born infant. Dick, although he knew well enough what she was crying for, determined to keep the cohuleen driuth, let her cry never so much, to see what luck would come out of it. Yet he could not help pitying her, and when the dumb thing looked up in his face, and her cheeks all moist with tears, 'twas enough to make any one feel for her, let alone Dick, who had ever and always, like most of his countrymen, a mighty tender heart of his own.

'Don't cry, my darling,' said Dick Fitzgerald; but the Merrow, like any bold child, only cried the more for that.

Dick sat himself down by her side, and took hold of her hand, by way of comforting her. 'Twas in no particular an ugly hand, only there was a small web between the fingers, as there is in a duck's foot, but 'twas as thin and as white as the skin between egg and shell.

'What's your name, my darling?' says Dick, thinking to make her conversant with him, but he got no answer, and he was certain sure now, either that she could not speak, or did not understand him. He therefore squeezed her hand in his, as the only way he had of talking to her. It's the universal language; and there's not a woman in the world, be she fish or lady, that does not understand it.

The Merrow did not seem much displeased at this mode of conversation and, making an end of her whining all at once, 'Man,' says she, looking up in Dick Fitzgerald's face, 'Man, will you eat me?'

'By all the red petticoats and check aprons between Dingle and Tralee,' cried Dick, jumping up in amazement, 'I'd as soon eat myself, my jewel! Is it I eat you, my pet? – Now 'twas some ugly ill-looking thief of a fish put that notion into your own pretty head, with the nice green hair down upon it, that is so cleanly combed out this morning!'

'Man,' said the Merrow, 'what will you do with me, if you won't eat me?'

Dick's thoughts were running on a wife. He saw, at the first glimpse, that she was handsome; but since she spoke, and spoke too like any real woman, he was fairly in love with her. 'Twas the neat way she called him 'man', that settled the matter entirely.

'Fish,' says Dick, trying to speak to her after her own short fashion; 'fish,' says he, 'here's my word, fresh and fasting, for you this blessed morning, that I'll make you Mistress Fitzgerald before all the world, and that's what I'll do.'

'Never say the word twice,' says she; 'I'm ready and willing to be yours, Mister Fitzgerald; but stop, if you please, 'till I twist up my hair.'

It was some time before she had settled it entirely to her

liking, for she guessed, I suppose, that she was going among strangers, where she would be looked at. When that was done, the Merrow put the comb in her pocket, and then bent down her head and whispered some words to the water that was close to the foot of the rock.

Dick saw the murmur of the words upon the top of the sea, going out towards the wide ocean, just like a breath of wind rippling along, and says he in the greatest wonder, 'Is it speaking you are, my darling, to the salt water?'

'It's nothing else,' says she, quite carelessly, 'I'm just sending word home to my father, not to be waiting breakfast for me; just to keep him from being uneasy in his mind.'

'And who's your father, my duck?' says Dick.

'What!' said the Merrow, 'did you never hear of my father? He's the king of the waves, to be sure!'

'And yourself, then, is a real king's daughter?' said Dick, opening his two eyes to take a full and true survey of his wife that was to be. 'Oh, I'm nothing else but a made man with you, and a king your father – to be sure he has all the money that's down in the bottom of the sea!'

'Money,' repeated the Merrow, 'what's money?'

''Tis no bad thing to have when one wants it,' replied Dick, 'and maybe now the fishes have the understanding to bring up whatever you bid them?'

'Oh! yes,' said the Merrow, 'they bring me what I want.'

'To speak the truth, then,' said Dick, ''tis a straw bed I have at home before you, and that I'm thinking, is no ways fitting for a king's daughter. So, if 'twould not be displeasing to you, just to mention a nice feather-bed, with a pair of new blankets – but what am I talking about? Maybe you have not such things as beds down under the water?'

'By all means,' said she, 'Mr Fitzgerald – plenty of beds at your service. I've fourteen oyster-beds of my own, not to mention one just planting for the rearing of young ones.'

'You have?' says Dick, scratching his head and looking a little puzzled. ''Tis a feather-bed I was speaking of – but

74

clearly, yours is the very cut of a decent plan, to have bed and supper so handy to each other, that a person when they'd have the one, need never ask for the other.'

However, bed or no bed, money or no money, Dick Fitzgerald determined to marry the Merrow, and the Merrow had given her consent. Away they went, therefore, across the strand, from Gollerus to Ballinrunnig, where Father Fitzgibbon happened to be that morning.

'There are two words to this bargain, Dick Fitzgerald,' said his Reverence, looking mighty glum. 'And is it a fishy woman you'd marry? – the Lord preserve us! – send the scaly creature home to her own people, that's my advice to you, wherever she came from.'

Dick had the cohuleen driuth in his hand, and was about to give it back to the Merrow, who looked covetously at it, but he thought for a moment, and then, says he, 'Please your Reverence, she's a king's daughter.'

'If she was the daughter of fifty kings,' said Father Fitzgibbon, 'I tell you, you can't marry her, she being a fish.'

'Please your Reverence,' said Dick again in an undertone, 'she is as mild and as beautiful as the moon.'

'If she was as mild and as beautiful as the sun, moon and stars, all put together, I tell you, Dick Fitzgerald,' said the Priest, stamping his right foot, 'you can't marry her, she being a fish!'

'But she has all the gold that's down in the sea only for the asking, and I'm a made man if I marry her; and,' said Dick, looking up slyly, 'I can make it worth anyone's while to do the job.'

'Oh! that alters the case entirely,' replied the Priest. 'Why there's some reason now in what you say: why didn't you tell me this before? Marry her by all means if she was ten times a fish. Money, you know, is not to be refused in these bad times, and I may as well have the use of it as another, that maybe would not take half the pains in counselling you as I have done.'

So Father Fitzgibbon married Dick Fitzgerald to the Merrow, and like any loving couple, they returned to Gollerus well pleased with each other. Everything prospered with Dick – he was at the sunny side of the world. The Merrow made the best of wives, and they lived together in the greatest contentment.

It was wonderful to see, considering where she had been brought up, how she would busy herself about the house, and how well she nursed the children; for at the end of three years there were as many young Fitzgeralds – two boys and a girl.

In short, Dick was a happy man, and so he might have continued to the end of his days, if he had only the sense to take proper care of what he had got; many another man, however, besides Dick, has not had wit enough to do that.

One day when Dick was obliged to go to Tralee, he left his wife minding the children at home after him and thinking she had plenty to do without disturbing his fishing tackle.

Dick was no sooner gone than Mrs Fitzgerald set about cleaning up the house and, chancing to pull down a fishing-net, what should she find behind it in a hole in the wall but her own cohuleen driuth.

She took it out and looked at it, and then she thought of her father the king, and her mother the queen, and her brothers and sisters, and she felt a longing to go back to them. She sat down on a little stool and thought over the happy days she had spent under the sea; then she looked at her children, and thought on the love and affection of poor Dick, and how it would break his heart to lose her. 'But,' says she, 'he won't lose me entirely, for I'll come back to him again; and who can blame me for going to see my father and my mother, after being so long away from them.'

She got up and went towards the door, but came back again to look once more at the child that was sleeping in the cradle. She kissed it gently, and as she kissed it, a tear trembled for an instant in her eye and then fell on its rosy cheek. She wiped away the tear, and turning to the eldest little girl, told her to take good care of her brothers, and to be a good child herself, until she came back. The Merrow then went down to the strand.

The sea was lying calm and smooth, just heaving and glittering in the sun, and she thought she heard a faint sweet singing, inviting her to come down. All her old ideas and feelings came flooding over her mind, Dick and her children were at the instant forgotten, and placing the cohuleen driuth on her head, she plunged in.

Dick came home in the evening and, missing his wife, he asked Kathleen, his little girl, what had become of her mother, but she could not tell him. He then inquired of the neighbours, and he learned that she was seen going towards the strand with a strange-looking thing liked a cocked hat in her hand. He returned to his cabin to search for the cohuleen driuth. It was gone, and the truth now flashed upon him.

Year after year did Dick Fitzgerald wait, expecting the return of his wife, but he never saw her more. Dick never married again, always thinking that the Merrow would sooner or later return to him, and nothing could ever persuade him but that her father the king kept her below the sea by main force. 'For,' said Dick, 'she surely would not of herself give up her husband and her children.'

While she was with him, she was so good a wife in every respect, that to this day she is spoken of in the tradition of the country as the pattern for one, under the name of 'The Lady of Gollerus'.

EONÍN

Mary Patton

Eonín was a little boy who lived in Aran on the Big Island. His home was a little out of Kilronan on the shore facing the Galway coast, and was quite a comfortable one, for Eonín's father owned a boat and was well known and well thought of in the three islands. Eonín was not old enough to go to the fishing with his father as yet, for he had only just begun to go to school, but he loved the sea and was never so happy as when it was fine and his father would take him out in the boat if he was only going out for a short time.

Sorcha, his mother, did not love the sea, and would never set foot in the boat, but stayed at home minding Una, the baby, and keeping the house ready for Seán, her husband, when he came in tired and wet after a night's fishing. She dreaded the storms that blew in from the Atlantic so suddenly, and would sit up half the night if Seán was out on the water.

''Tis no use to be taking on so, woman dear,' said the old grandmother, who sat in the warm corner by the fire. 'We all must get death some time, and we may be taken on land as well as on sea. We are all just in God's hands.'

'It is as God wills it indeed,' said Sorcha, only in her heart she cried, 'Let him be spared to me this long while, Mother of God!' And she looked at Eonín and wondered how she would bring up the boy without the man to help her.

They were talking like this one evening, waiting for Seán to come home, while Eonín was learning his lesson for the morrow by the fireside, and he began to wonder if he would hear his father coming up the road and giving a shout to let them know he was there, or would they carry him up in a sail like Seamus Rua. He was so relieved when he heard the usual call that he threw down his book and ran out of the house to meet him. It was bright moonlight and there was very little wind to make a noise at sea, but when Eonín was lifted up to his father's shoulder above the level of the loose stone wall he was sure he heard something besides the rattle of the pebbles as they were drawn back by the receding waves. It sounded like someone singing far out in the bay, and as Eonín was very fond of singing, he sat quite still and listened till he was carried into the house and set down.

'There is music out on the sea,' he called out to his mother. 'Will you not come out and listen to it? It is lovely.'

'God stand between us and harm!' cried his mother, and she ran to the door and shut it tight to keep out the sound, for every Aran woman knows that if her son hears the mermaids singing he will be drowned in the end.

'The boats are coming in, and it is some of the men singing that he hears,' said Seán, laughing at her. 'You think too much of those sayings, Sorcha. We are learning better than that nowadays.' And he took Una out of her cradle to have a look at her, and danced her up and down till she screamed with delight.

'It is what I am always telling her,' said the grandmother from her corner; 'but indeed you are a good head to the house, Seán, and have never grudged me the best of tea and sugar or the bit of tobacco.' And she lit her pipe and smoked by the fire while Sorcha set the food out on the table.

It was early in the autumn when Sorcha came back from Kilronan saying that the old Protestant clergyman living in the Rectory there was ill, and not likely to recover. He lived all alone, for his wife was dead and his daughter married abroad, and though he had very few of his own congregation he was well known and well liked by all the islanders, for he never interfered with anybody and gave a good price for the fish. So Sorcha was really sorry when she heard the news.

'And the housekeeper tells me,' she said, 'that she doesn't know what she will do at all. The steamer will not be back for more than a week, and she has no way of sending to Galway to let them know. If the poor gentleman dies there will be no one to bury him.'

'There is a clergyman at Inverin on the mainland,' said Seán. 'I will go over and fetch him back,' and he glanced up at the sky as he spoke. Sorcha glanced too, for she knew the weather signs as well as he did, if not better. There was not much wind, but the clouds were very high and spread in narrow streamers, and there was a noise in the air that meant the sea was coming in a heavy swell through the sound.

'There will be no boats from Aran putting out for the fishing tonight,' she said.

'Think if it was myself lying there with no one of my own near me,' said Seán. 'It is but nine miles to Cashla; I will be back before the storm breaks.'

So he went down to the quay and hoisted sail for the mainland, while Sorcha went back into the house after she watched the boat out of sight on the first long tack eastward.

The gale sprang up sooner than she expected, a real Aran squall, short in duration perhaps but violent enough while it lasted. Eonín coming back from school was nearly blown off his legs as he met the wind coming over the hill. He was astonished not to see his father when he got home.

'Is he gone out in the boat?' he asked his mother.

'He is so!' she said. 'God send him home safe to us!'

She would say no more, but got Eonín his dinner and then sat down with some sewing for Una, to keep herself from thinking. It was too wild to go out, and Eonín tried to start a game of his own in a corner, but it was the longest evening he had ever known. His mother sewed silently, his granny sat talking to herself by the fire, and Una asleep in her cradle was the only comfortable one of the lot. He was not one bit sorry when his mother put down her work and said it was time for him to go to bed.

His bed was in a little room just off the living-room, and he could not tell how long he might have slept when he was wakened by a sound in the kitchen, and sitting up in bed he saw there was a light still there. He slipped from out the bed-clothes noiselessly, and creeping to the door opened it cautiously and peeped through. The turf fire was burning brightly and beside it his grandmother was still sitting. On the table was spread his father's usual supper, and in the window was a lighted candle and his mother sitting beside it with a look on her face he had never seen before.

'A great many of the Costellos got their death on the sea,' said the grandmother. 'My own man always said to me, "And isn't it better than lying on a bed ailing for weeks and all the money going out of the house to the doctor?"' But his mother made no answer except to burst into a fit of weeping. Then Eonín crept back and sat on the edge of his bed thinking a moment, for he knew that now as the only man in the house it was for him to be up and doing something.

Presently he reached for his clothes in the dark and pulled them on.

Seán's house was better built and more comfortable than most of the fishermen's houses in Aran, and the window in

Eonín's bedroom could really open and shut. The wind was not on that side of the house, and moving carefully he slid up the lower sash and climbed out without the women hearing him. He closed the window behind him and stood in the little cabbage-plot.

The wind had commenced to slacken somewhat, and stars shone out here and there through the racing clouds. It was light enough to see his way to the stone wall which bounded the garden, and once over that he stood in the lane which reached to the shore. His skin shoes made no noise on the stones and no one knew that he had left the house or made any attempt to stop him as he ran towards a line of rocks which stretched out black among the surging waves.

Every Aran boy knows about mermaids, and some of them will tell you they have seen them. Eonín had never seen a mermaid, but he was a very little boy and his idea now was to scramble out to the farthest point of the rocks and see if he could find one. If he caught hold of her and held her tight she would have to tell him where his father was and promise to bring him home safe. So he slid and groped his way over the wet stones and slippery seaweed till he reached the farthest rock.

There was no mermaid to be seen looking up out of the water as he had half expected, and he did not know if they would hear him if he called out to them. He knelt down on the rock and tried to look through the heavy mass of weed. As he did so a huge wave swept over the rock entirely submerging it, and carrying Eonín fighting and struggling for breath back with it into the very depths of the sea.

How far he was falling he could not tell, but after the first horrible choking sensation was over he seemed to be sinking quite easily through the water till he came with a bump on something that heaved and writhed and twisted around him with a queer hissing sound. Eonín rolled off it and found himself lying on a broad ledge of rock with a huge conger eel coiled on it staring at him.

'Now who have I here?' said the conger, when he had recovered a little from the shock.

'God and Mary save you,' said Eonín, 'and it's little manners you have not to give me the greeting.'

'Where would I get manners,' said the conger, 'living in this backward place? The People of the Sea do not care much for my society, and if it were not for the Fox Sharks and the Sword-fish I would have no one to associate with. But who are you, and where do you come from?'

'I am Eonín, the son of big Seán Costello,' said Eonín, 'and I live on the Strand road a little way from Kilronan.'

'I know big Seán the fisherman,' said the conger. 'Indeed he is well known in all the seas of Aran. When I was a little fellow only a foot and a half long he caught me in his net and threw me back into the water. "Grow a bit more," he said, "before I catch you again." A meaner man would have used me for bait. I have always had a great wish for Seán ever since then and I am pleased to see his son, and you may tell him that I am ten feet long, and can bite through a man's hand. I am not like the little yellow congers of the sand. I think he would be a proud man if he could catch me now.'

'I may never tell my father anything about you,' Eonín sobbed. 'He has never reached home tonight, and it was trying to find where he is that I came to be here.'

'Tell me all about it,' said the conger, coiling himself up again to listen.

So Eonín told him how he had gone out to find a mermaid, and how a big wave had swept the rock and sucked him under.

'I have no great opinion of the mermaids,' said the conger when Eonín had told him the whole story. 'They are too interfering and too fond of coming between an honest fish and his food. Telling the hake where I am lying indeed! A conger has to get on in the world as well as another. I would be living on jellyfish if they had their own way.

'I can show you where the mermaids live, but more than that I cannot promise, for the truth is we are not friends at all. They think too much of themselves with their songs and their golden combs for their hair. It's very little cause they have for pride to my mind,' he went on. 'Have they tails like mine or teeth like mine? Is there one of them could crunch a lobster as I can? However, since you want to see them I will take you down, for they live lower down than I do, and I would be glad to do a service to the son of big Seán the fisherman.'

So he flattened the great fin that ran from his head to his tail and told Eonín to put his arms around his neck and stretch himself along his back, and when he was settled firmly the conger shot head first off the rock and dived downwards with a beautiful swift motion.

They landed at last on a bed of the most beautiful white sand Eonín had ever seen. There were beautiful seaweeds of various colours growing here and there, and all kinds of shining shells. Around the sands great rocks towered up, and in the rocks were caves from one of which came a sound of very sweet singing.

'If you go straight in there,' said the conger, pointing with his side fin at this cave, 'you will find them at their antics. And put a bold face on you, and ask for what you want, and do not give in to them, or let them put upon you. I am sorry I cannot go in with you, but I would not give them the satisfaction of finding me here. So now goodbye, and I wish you luck.'

He shot off up through the water, and Eonín was left alone. He felt a little scared, especially after what the conger had said about the mermaids, but the singing inside the cave was so sweet it drew him towards it, and at last he took courage to enter.

He found himself in a great hall formed out of the rock. It was not dark as he had thought a cave would be, but lit with the pale green light that seemed to represent daylight under the water. The floor was of shining sand and the roof seemed made of masses of floating seaweed through which the fish came darting.

But Eonín could look at nothing but the mermaids. There were a great many of them, and some of them were floating and swimming about pretending to chase the fish, while the rest were gathered in a group singing the song that had attracted him in. They stopped as he stood at the entrance, and turned and looked at him, and he thought they could not be as unkind as the conger had made out, for they had very sweet faces though their long hair was of a strange greenish golden colour and they had long tails like a fish, covered with silver scales. They gathered round Eonín, smiling and holding out their hands, and then he saw that there was one who seemed taller than the others seated on a rock at the end of the hall. She was leaning her head on her hand as if thinking, and when she raised it he saw she was more beautiful and that she wore a band of shining stones around

her head. She looked up and beckoned with her hand.

'You are very welcome, Eonín, son of big Seán the fisherman,' said the mermaid of the rock. 'Now, what have you come seeking?'

'The big conger said that my father might be with you,' said Eonín, when he had recovered from his astonishment at finding they knew who he was. 'But I do not think you would harm him,' he added.

'I will take you to see him,' said the mermaid, 'but you must tell me first, are you a brave boy?'

'I am a very brave boy,' said Eonín. 'I go down through the Fairies' Gap to the well in the dusk of the evening if my mother wants water for the house, and there are bigger boys than I am in Aran who will not do that.'

'That is well,' said the mermaid; 'and now you may come with me.'

She took him in her arms and swam swiftly with him across the cave and out into the space beyond till they came to another ridge of rocks thickly covered with brown weed. She set Eonín on the top of this and told him to look over. There was another stretch of sand at the foot of the ridge, and there Eonín saw his father lying as if asleep. His head was resting on one arm and his body rocked slightly with the motion of the water.

'Can I not go and wake him?' asked Eonín. 'He would be terribly vexed to be lying there asleep and my mother wanting him at home.'

'No,' said the mermaid, 'you may not wake him.'

'Will you not let him go back, and we all of us wanting him so bad? My mother will lose her life if you will not let him go.'

'There is a rule of life under the sea as well as on the land,' said the mermaid, 'and I may not let him go for the asking. But if you will stay with us and take his place, we may let him go back.'

A terrible dread came over Eonín at the thought of

staying down at the bottom of the sea and never going home
to his mother and Una again, and all he could say for the
moment was, 'Is that the way it is?' 'That is the way, and no
other way,' said the mermaid.

'Then I will stay,' said Eonín with a great sob, 'for I am
not big enough to take out the boat, and there will be no
head to the house if my father does not go home. But I will
be terribly lonesome away from them all.' The tears came
into his eyes and he would have burst out crying only he
remembered he had said he was brave.

'See,' said the mermaid, 'your father is no longer there.'
And when he looked there was nothing but the sand to be
seen. Then she placed her hand over his heart and it was so
cold that he felt the chill right through his body, and she
kissed him on the forehead till his life on land faded out
of his mind, and he forgot his home and his people and
was as gay and happy as if he had never thought of missing them.

The days passed by, though you could only tell night
from day by the green light becoming darker and lighter.
There was no sun or moon or stars to be seen, and indeed
Eonín had forgotten all about them. Soon he could swim
and float quite well, but if the mermaids wished to take him
any distance they put him astride a huge codfish so that he
might keep up with them easily. He soon found that they
were not always playing or singing but had quite a lot to do,
tidying up the rock-pools after a storm, looking after the
fishes and seeing that the smaller ones were not oppressed
by the bigger.

When the mermaids went to tidy the rock-pools they
always took Eonín with them, and he would help them to
clear away the torn seaweed and see that the anemones and
sea-urchins were fast on their rocks, and play with the little
red rock-fish. But sometimes they had something to do of
which they never spoke to him.

He was never left quite alone until the day after a great

87

storm had been raging overhead for many hours. He thought they would have had a great expedition round the pools seeing what damage had been done, but instead they told him he must play by himself for a while, as they must all go away and could not take him where they were going.

He did as he was told and tried to amuse himself playing with the shells that lay about the sand, but it was dull work all alone, and presently he strayed out of the cave on to the stretch of sand outside. Something dark shot through the water overhead, and presently the big conger landed beside him. Eonín had no recollection of anything that had happened before the mermaid kissed him, so he only looked at the conger wondering who he was and what had brought him.

'Well, and how do you get on with them?' said the conger, who as we know had no manners.

Eonín only looked at him in a puzzled way. 'Do you mean the mermaids?' he said. 'They are all away somewhere.'

'There is a big wreck off the Hag's Head,' said the conger, 'and they have all gone off to look after the drowned sailors. I have not often a good word for them, but I like to be just, and I will say this, they show every respect and care for the drowned. It is only when you are alive that they torment you. But are you content to be here, and do you never think of going back to your home?'

'What is home?' asked Eonín. 'I live here, and I play with the fishes and the shells and I help the mermaids to settle the pools after a storm. I do not know of any other kind of life.'

'I see they have been playing their tricks with you,' said the conger, 'but I know a cure for that, and I will fetch it straight away, for indeed I have come to talk to you on a matter of some importance. Now do not stir from this till I come back.'

And he shot up through the water, leaving the boy staring

after him. He was gone some little time, and Eonín wondered if he was really coming back.

By and by he saw the conger shooting swiftly downwards. He carried something in his mouth.

'Take this bit of seaweed out of my mouth and eat it,' he told Eonín.

It was reddish-brown with notched edges and had a salt taste. As Eonín chewed it he suddenly knew it was 'Dulsk' or dry seaweed he was eating, and the memory of the life he used to lead on land came back to him. He could see his home standing back a little from the road, and the fields covered with grey slabs of stone, and the little white cabins of Kilronan in the distance. He remembered his mother and father and little sister, and his granny who sat always in her corner near the fire, the boat lying beside the quay and the sunlight shining on the water. An immense grief and a longing to be back again came over him.

'Do you remember where you came from?' asked the conger, eyeing him curiously. But Eonín could not speak, his heart was so full.

'It is what I came to talk to you about,' said the conger, 'for there is no peace or rest for the dwellers among the rocks of Aran. Day and night men are searching with poles and grappling-irons till the congers are driven from their homes and dare not return. And so it came into my mind that it is you they are seeking, and you must go back if we are to have any life at all.'

'How will I go back?' said Eonín. 'Now that I remember, I have a terrible wish to go home.'

'I will carry you on my back,' said the conger, 'and leave you on the very rock you fell in off, if you will put your arms round my neck and hold on tight.'

But a sudden fear came over Eonín. 'I said I would stay here instead of my father,' he cried, 'and so I cannot go. He would come back himself if he knew I had gone back on my word, and my mother could not do without him. So I must stay with the mermaids.'

He cried bitterly, for the more he remembered, the harder it was not to go.

'You have very inconvenient notions,' said the conger. 'And if this is your decision, the congers may leave Aran, for there will be no end to this searching. When they call out to your father that it is useless to go on, and to give up, he cries out he will search all his life. There is but one thing now that I can think of doing, and I do not think it can be any harm. We must go out to Skerdmore and consult the Great Grey Seal who lives there. He says he is a cousin of the mermaids and is sometimes taken for them. He may be able to tell us some way of getting over the difficulty.'

Then the conger flattened the fin on his back and Eonín lay along it and put his arms round the conger's neck and away they shot through the water. They went very fast, but it was a long way to Skerdmore, and Eonín's arms began to ache from holding on so tightly, when they rose suddenly to the surface of the sea. Then he saw they had reached a tiny island with a great many rocks showing on one side of it, and on one of these was lying a great grey seal.

The conger hooked his tail round a point of the rock, and Eonín scrambled up on to it.

'We have come to consult your Honour on a difficult point,' said the conger very politely, for he knew the Grey Seal could have bitten him in two, 'and we hope that you will give us the benefit of your great wisdom and learning. Here is a little boy who has been living with the mermaids in order to release his father, and now he would like to go home himself if he could do so without breaking his promise.'

'The mermaids are distant relations of mine,' said the Grey Seal, raising himself on his two front flippers. 'We are both musical and you may have heard me singing. I should not care to annoy them at the request of a mere conger. Why should this little boy want to go home?'

'It is because I have remembered my home and my mother and my father,' said Eonín, 'and all the things I used to do on land. My mother will have no one to get in the water for the house, or to be running in when my father is away at the fishing. But I would not vex the mermaids or go unless they would let me.'

'We all know,' said the conger, 'that there are a great deal too many boys in this world, and that they are good for very little except to throw stones at the seals and disturb them by splashing round the rocks, but there is more at stake in this matter than you might think. The fate of all the congers of Aran depends on his going home. We have no rest or peace while they are searching for him, and if we are driven away we shall no longer be able to listen to the lovely music which you make on the summer nights.'

'I see, I see,' said the Grey Seal, greatly pleased. 'Since you like my voice I should be sorry if you had no opportunity of hearing it. But it will not be easy for him to win his release. There is a rule of life under the sea as well as on land, and they may not let him go for the asking.'

'What am I to do?' asked Eonín.

'You will have to find out what they want most in the world,' said the Grey Seal, 'and then you will have to give it to them.'

Eonín's heart sank, for he could not think how he could accomplish such a task, but the conger thanked the seal profusely and asked Eonín to get on his back again.

'I am always pleased to help anyone who appreciates music,' said the Grey Seal.

They left the seal on his rock bellowing most dismally and made all speed back to the mermaids' cave. The night had fallen and with all their haste the mermaids were there before them, so that when they reached the entrance they heard them singing softly inside.

'Now go in,' said the conger, 'and keep your wits about you and do not fail me, for it would break my heart to live

91

even as far off as Inishbofin. I will wait behind the rocks here to see what happens.'

Eonín slowly went in, wondering what he should say and how he would get them what they wanted most in the world even if he could find it out. They were all seated round the cave and none of them playing, but singing so sad an air that it brought the tears to his eyes. The mermaid who always sat at the end on the rock beckoned to him, and when he reached her she lifted him up on to her lap.

'Now, Eonín,' she said, 'tell me all that is in your heart.'

Eonín laid his head against her breast and told her all that had happened since they left him alone.

'I have a sore longing to get home,' he said, when he had finished his story, 'and so will you please tell me what you want most in the world, and I will try and get it for you.'

The mermaid looked very thoughtful and then she signed to the others, who all stopped singing and gathered round her.

'Now I will tell you, Eonín,' she said, 'when there is a wreck on the coast we go to look after those that may be drowned, and we sing to them that they may rest peacefully until they are called from our care. We know a great many songs, both gay and sad, but tonight we need one that we have never heard or learned. Can you sing us a song that we do not know?'

Then Eonín thought of all the songs he had ever heard and he sang them the songs the fishermen sing when the boats are coming in, or when they are raising the nets or hauling at the ropes, but the mermaids shook their heads and looked sorrowful and said they knew all those.

'It will be some English song you are wanting,' he cried, 'and I have no English.'

'No, no,' they cried, 'it is not that we want at all.'

Then Eonín suddenly bethought him of a song they could never have heard, for when his mother sang it she shut the door tight to keep out the sound of the sea. She sang it always to put Una to sleep and he knew it well. He lifted up his voice and sang, 'Oh, little head of gold. Oh, candle of the house –' and they listened without a word till he came to the very end.

'That is the song we want!' they all cried when he had finished, 'and now we will show you why we want it.'

They swam with him to another part of the cave, and there, lying asleep on a bed made of the softest sea-moss, he saw a tiny child, not much bigger than Una and with golden curls shining against the dark green weed.

'We knew no song that she would have cared to hear,' they said; 'but now you have taught us one. You have earned your release, though we are sorry to lose you.'

The tallest mermaid lifted him on to her lap again and she placed her hand on his heart and kissed him on the lips, but this time her lips and her hands were so warm that he felt the warmth right through his body, and when she had done that she looked him in the eyes and smiling, said: 'Now all that has happened shall be as though it has never happened, and the conger shall take you to the very rock you fell in off.'

They called the conger in, and when he knew that he was to take Eonín home his delight knew no bounds, and he span round and round to show how pleased he was till they all felt quite giddy and told him he should not have as much as a sprat to eat if he did not stop. Then he calmed down, and they placed Eonín on his back when they had all said goodbye, and stood waving their hands and singing while he shot up out of sight with his burden.

'I too will say goodbye,' said the conger when Eonín had scrambled off his back on to the rock. 'I must now go and tell the other congers the great news that you are back and that there will be no more searching of the rocks. And mind you tell your father I am ten feet long and can bite through a man's hand. I think he will be proud to hear of me again.'

'We will go fishing for you together,' cried Eonín, and

the conger waved his side fin and sank down through the water.

Eonín found himself alone lying on the rock, and as he looked round and saw the familiar scene his life under the sea faded out of his mind and he could not quite tell why he was on the rock or what had brought him there. The sun had risen and the storm had passed over. The sky was quite clear and the sun shining, and except that the sea was still rather rough, there was no trace of a gale. He stood up and saw a boat running into the harbour and knew it for his father's boat. By running quickly he reached the quay as it came alongside, and in it was his father safe and sound and another man in the stern wrapped in a dark overcoat.

'What brings you out here at this hour, Eonín?' said his father, for it was still very early. 'But since you are here, run home with a message from me, for I must show this gentleman the way to the Rectory. Tell your mother we could not get out of Cashla the way the wind was, and that that was the delay, for I am sure she was uneasy.'

Eonín ran back hard and met his mother on the pathway, for she too had seen the boat.

'How did you get out without my seeing you?' she asked, bewildered, when he had given the message; but she was too happy to scold, and he ran on in, not quite sure of how it had happened himself.

Sometimes when he is making up a story for Una it all comes back to him, and he tells it to her, while she listens with great attention, sucking her thumb the while. But he can get no one else to believe him when he says he has talked with the Great Grey Seal at Skerdmore.

Part Four

THE LEPREHAUN

THE LEPREHAUN
Lady Wilde

The Leprehauns are merry, industrious, tricksy little sprites, who do all the shoemaker's work and the tailor's and the cobbler's for the fairy gentry, and are often seen at sunset under the hedge singing and stitching. They know all the secrets of hidden treasure, and if they take a fancy to a person will guide him to the spot in the fairy rath where the pot of gold lies buried. It is believed that a family now living near Castlerea came by their riches in a strange way, all through the good offices of a friendly Leprehaun. And the legend has been handed down through many generations as an established fact.

There was a poor boy once, one of their forefathers, who used to drive his cart of turf daily back and forward, and make what money he could by the sale; but he was a strange boy, very silent and moody, and the people said he was a fairy changeling, for he joined in no sports and scarcely ever spoke to any one, but spent the nights reading all the old bits of books he picked up in his rambles. The one thing he longed for above all others was to get rich, and to be able to give up the old weary turf cart, and live in peace and quietness all alone, with nothing but books round him, in a beautiful house and garden all by himself.

Now he had read in the old books how the Leprehauns knew all the secret places where gold lay hid, and day by day he watched for a sight of the little cobbler, and listened for the click, click of his hammer as he sat under the hedge mending the shoes.

At last, one evening just as the sun set, he saw a little fellow under a dock leaf, working away, dressed all in green, with a cocked hat on his head. So the boy jumped down from the cart and seized him by the neck.

'Now you don't stir from this,' he cried, 'till you tell me where to find the hidden gold.'

'Easy now,' said the Leprehaun, 'don't hurt me, and I will tell you all about it. But mind you, I could hurt you if I chose, for I have the power; but I won't do it, for we are cousins once removed. So as we are near relations I'll just be good, and show you the place of the secret gold that none can have or keep except those of fairy blood and race. Come along with me, then, to the old fort of Lipenshaw, for there it lies. But make haste, for when the last red glow of the sun vanishes the gold will disappear also, and you will never find it again.'

'Come away, then,' said the boy, and he carried the Leprehaun into the turf cart, and drove off. And in a second they were at the old fort, and went in through a door made in the stone wall.

'Now look round,' said the Leprehaun, and the boy saw the whole ground covered with gold pieces, and there were vessels of silver lying about in such plenty that all the riches of all the world seemed gathered there.

'Now take what you want,' said the Leprehaun; 'but hasten, for if that door shuts you will never leave this place as long as you live.'

So the boy gathered up his arms full of gold and silver, and flung them into the cart; and was on his way back for more when the door of the fort shut with a clap like thunder, and all the place became dark as night. And he saw no more of the Leprehaun, and had not time even to thank him.

So he thought it best to drive home at once with his treasure, and when he arrived and was all alone by himself he counted his riches, and all the bright yellow gold pieces, enough for a king's ransom.

And he was very wise and told no one; but went off next day to Dublin and put all his treasures into the bank, and found that he was now indeed as rich as a lord.

So he ordered a fine house to be built with spacious gardens, and he had servants and carriages and books to his heart's content. And he gathered all the wise men round him to give him the learning of a gentleman; and he became a great and powerful man in the country, where his memory is still held in high honour, and his descendants are living to this day rich and prosperous; for their wealth has never decreased though they have ever given largely to the poor, and are noted above all things for the friendly heart and the liberal hand.

But the Leprehauns can be bitterly malicious if they are offended, and one should be very cautious in dealing with them, and always treat them with great civility, or they will take revenge and never reveal the secret of the hidden gold.

One day a young lad was out in the fields at work when he saw a little fellow, not the height of his hand, mending shoes under a dock leaf. And he went over, never taking his eyes off him for fear he would vanish away; and when he got quite close he made a grab at the creature, and lifted him up and put him in his pocket.

Then he ran away home as fast as he could, and when he had the Leprehaun safe in the house, he tied him by an iron chain to the hob.

'Now tell me,' he said, 'where am I to find a pot of gold? Let me know the place or I'll punish you.'

'I know of no pot of gold,' said the Leprehaun; 'but let me go that I may finish mending the shoes.'

'Then I'll make you tell me,' said the lad.

And with that he made up a great fire, and put the little fellow on it and scorched him.

'Oh, take me off, take me off!' cried the Leprehaun, 'and I'll tell you. Just there, under the dock leaf where you found me there is a pot of gold. Go; dig and find.'

So the lad was delighted, and ran to the door; but it so happened that his mother was just then coming in with the pail of fresh milk, and in his haste he knocked the pail out of her hand, and all the milk was spilled on the floor.

Then when the mother saw the Leprehaun she grew very angry and beat him. 'Go away, you little wretch!' she cried. 'You have bewitched the mill with your evil eye, and brought ill-luck.' And she kicked him out of the house.

The lad ran off to find the dock leaf, though he came back very sorrowful in the evening, for he had dug and dug nearly down to the middle of the earth; but no pot of gold was to be seen.

That same night the husband was coming home from his work, and as he passed the old fort he heard voices and laughter, and one said –

'They are looking for a pot of gold; but they little know that a crock of gold is lying down in the bottom of the old quarry, hid under the stones close by the garden wall. But whoever gets it must go of a dark night at twelve o'clock, and beware of bringing his wife with him.'

So the man hurried home and told his wife he would go that very night, for it was black dark, and she must stay at home and watch for him, and not stir from the house till he came back. Then he went out into the dark night alone.

'Now,' thought the wife, when he was gone, 'if I could

only get to the quarry before him I would have the pot of gold all to myself; while if he gets it I shall have nothing.'

And with that she went out and ran like the wind until she reached the quarry, and then she began to creep down very quietly in the black dark. But a great stone was in her path, and she stumbled over it, and fell down and down till she reached the bottom, and there she lay groaning, for her leg was broken by the fall.

Just then her husband came to the edge of the quarry and began to descend. But when he heard the groans he was frightened.

'Cross of Christ about us!' he exclaimed; 'what is that down below? Is it evil, or is it good?'

'Oh, come down, come down and help me!' cried the woman. 'It's your wife is here, and my leg is broken, and I'll die if you don't help me.'

'And is this my pot of gold?' exclaimed the poor man. 'Only my wife with a broken leg lying at the bottom of the quarry.'

And he was at his wits' end to know what to do, for the night was so dark he could not see a hand before him. So he roused up a neighbour, and between them they dragged up the poor woman and carried her home, and laid her on her bed half dead from fright, and it was many a day before she was able to get about as usual; indeed she limped all her life long, so that the people said the curse of the Leprehaun was on her.

But as to the pot of gold, from that day to this not one of the family, father, or son, or any belonging to them, ever set eyes on it. However, the little Leprehaun still sits under the dock leaf of the hedge, and laughs at them as he mends the shoes with his little hammer – tick tack, tick tack – but they are afraid to touch him, for now they know he can take his revenge.

THE FIELD OF THISTLES
after Thomas Crofton Croker

One fine day at harvest-time, Tom Fitzpatrick was taking a walk down along the hedgerow. All of a sudden, he heard a sort of clacking noise from the other side of the hedge. 'What's that?' Tom wondered, thinking he could steal up quietly and get sight of what was making the noise. As he was tiptoeing along, the noise stopped suddenly. Quick as a flash, Tom looked sharply through the bushes. What should he see in a nook of the hedge but a big brown gallon jug; and by-and-by he noticed a little wee teeny tiny bit of an old man, with a *teenshy* cocked hat stuck on top of his head, and a *deeshy* little leather apron covering his front. The little fellow was in the process of standing on top of a wooden stool, and reaching up to the gallon jug, from which he drew a pitcher full of drink. Having quaffed his drink, he then sat down on the stool and began to work at putting a heel-piece on a tiny brogue just fit for his own dainty foot. 'Well, by the powers,' said Tom to himself, 'I never thought I'd live to see a Leprehaun – but here's one for sure. All I have to do is keep my eyes on him, and I'm made for life. For don't they all have a crock of gold hidden away? And don't they say that if you keep your eyes firmly fixed on them, they can't escape, and by all the laws of the fairy trade they have to take you right to their crock of gold?'

Tom now approached closer towards the little shoemaker, never taking his eyes off him – just like a cat with a mouse. 'God bless your work, neighbour,' said Tom suddenly.

The little man raised his head, and 'Thank you kindly, sir,' said he.

'I wonder why you would be working on a holiday?' said Tom.

'That's my business entirely,' was the reply.

'Well, at least you'll tell me what you've got in your pitcher there, won't you?' said Tom.

'That I will, with pleasure,' said the Leprehaun; 'it's good beer.'

'Beer!' said Tom, greatly surprised; 'where did you get beer?'

'Where do you think I got it – I made it,' said the Leprehaun.

'Of malt?' asked Tom.

'No, of heath,' said the little fellow.

'Ah, you're pulling my leg!' said Tom, bursting out laughing; 'you don't think I'd believe that, do you?'

'Suit yourself,' said the little fellow grumpily, 'but I'm telling you the truth. Did you never hear tell of the Danes?'

'What about *them*?' said Tom.

'Just that it was the Danes, in the old days long ago, taught us how to make beer out of heath, and the secret's been in my family ever since.'

'Well, well,' said Tom. 'Will you give me a taste of your beer?'

'Look here, young man,' said the Leprehaun. 'You'd be better employed looking after your father's cattle than bothering decent folk with your prattle and questions. Look over there, will you? While you've been idling your time with me, your cattle have broken into that cornfield, and they've got the crops all trampled about.'

Tom was so surprised by this news that he was on the point of turning round. Then, in the nick of time, he remembered: never take your eyes off a Leprehaun. So he made a grab at the little fellow, and caught him up in his hand – but in his hurry he knocked over the pitcher, and spilt all the beer, so that he could not now get a taste of it. Tom then swore he would kill the little fellow if he did not show him where his money was hidden – and he looked so fierce and wicked that the little man was quite terrified of him. 'Come along with me across a couple of fields,' said he to Tom, 'and I'll show you my crock of gold.'

So off they went, Tom keeping a tight hold of the Leprehaun, and never taking his eyes off him even though they had hedges and ditches and bogs to cross, and at last they came to a great field all full of thistles, and the Leprehaun pointed to a big thistle, and said, 'See that thistle? Dig down under that, and you'll get the crock of golden coins.'

In his hurry to get to the crock of gold, Tom had completely forgotten to bring a spade with him, so he made up his mind to run back home and fetch one; and in order to be sure he came back to the right thistle, he took off one of his red socks, and tied it tight round the thistle.

Then he turned to the Leprehaun and said, 'Swear you'll not take that sock from that thistle.' And the Leprehaun swore right away not to touch it.

'I suppose,' said the Leprehaun then, very politely, 'you have no further use for me?'

'No,' says Tom; 'you may go away now, if you wish, and good luck to you wherever you go.'

'Well, goodbye to you, Tom Fitzpatrick,' said the Leprehaun; 'and good luck to you too, and I must say!'

So Tom ran home for dear life, and got a good spade, and

then ran back to the thistle-field with it; but when he got there, lo and behold! every single thistle in that huge field had a red sock tied around it, each one the very model of Tom's own! And there was no way that Tom could dig up that whole huge field, for there were more than forty good Irish acres in it.

So Tom went home again with his spade on his shoulder, a little cooler than when he ran out to claim the crock of gold and make his fortune. And he never saw a Leprehaun again.

Part Five

WITCHES

THE HORNED WOMEN
Lady Wilde

A rich woman sat up late one night carding and preparing wool, while all the family and servants were asleep. Suddenly a knock was given at the door, and a voice called – 'Open! open!'

'Who is there?' said the woman of the house.

'I am the Witch of the one Horn,' was answered.

The mistress, supposing that one of her neighbours had called and required assistance, opened the door, and a woman entered, having in her hand a pair of wool carders, and bearing a horn on her forehead, as if growing there. She sat down by the fire in silence, and began to card the wool with violent haste. Suddenly she paused, and said aloud: 'Where are the women? they delay too long.'

Then a second knock came to the door, and a voice called as before, 'Open! open!'

The mistress felt herself constrained to rise and open to the call, and immediately a second witch entered, having two horns on her forehead, and in her hand a wheel for spinning wool.

109

'Give me place,' she said, 'I am the Witch of the two Horns,' and she began to spin as quick as lightning.

And so the knocks went on, and the call was heard, and the witches entered, until at last twelve women sat round the fire – the first with one horn, the last with twelve horns.

And they carded the thread, and turned their spinning wheels, and wound and wove.

All singing together an ancient rhyme, but no word did they speak to the mistress of the house. Strange to hear, and frightful to look upon, were these twelve women, with their horns and their wheels; and the mistress felt near to death, and she tried to rise that she might call for help, but she could not move, nor could she utter a word or a cry, for the spell of the witches was upon her.

Then one of them called to her in Irish, and said –'Rise, woman, and make us a cake.' Then the mistress searched for a vessel to bring water from the well that she might mix the meal and make the cake, but she could find none.

And they said to her, 'Take a sieve and bring water in it.'

And she took the sieve and went to the well; but the water poured from it, and she could fetch none for the cake, and she sat down by the well and wept.

Then a voice came by her and said, 'Take yellow clay and moss, and bind them together, and plaster the sieve so that it will hold.'

This she did, and the sieve held water for the cake; and the voice said again –

'Return, and when you come to the north angle of the house, cry aloud three times and say, "The mountain of the Fenian women and the sky over it is all on fire".'

And she did so.

When the witches inside heard the call, a great and terrible cry broke from their lips, and they rushed forth with wild lamentations and shrieks, and fled away to Slievenamon, where was their chief abode. But the Spirit of the Well bade the mistress of the house to enter and prepare her home against the enchantments of witches if they returned again.

And first, to break their spells, she sprinkled the water in which she had washed her child's feet (the feet-water) outside the door on the threshold; secondly, she took the cake which the witches had made in her absence of meal mixed with the blood drawn from the sleeping family, and she broke the cake in bits, and placed a bit in the mouth of each sleeper, and they were restored; and she took the cloth they had woven and placed it half in and half out of the chest with the padlock; and lastly, she secured the door with a great crossbeam fastened in the jambs, so that they could not enter, and having done these things she waited.

Not long were the witches in coming back, and they raged and called for vengeance.

'Open, open!' they screamed, 'open, feet-water!'

'I cannot,' said the feet-water, 'I am scattered on the ground, and my path is down to the Lough.'

'Open, open, wood and trees and beam!' they cried to the door.

'I cannot,' said the door, 'for the beam is fixed in the jambs and I have no power to move.'

'Open, open, cake that we have made and mingled with blood!' they cried again.

'I cannot,' said the cake, 'for I am broken and bruised, and my blood is on the lips of the sleeping children.'

Then the witches rushed through the air with great cries, and fled back to Slievenamon, uttering strange curses on the Spirit of the Well, who had wished their ruin; but the woman and the house were left in peace, and a mantle dropped by one of the witches in her flight was kept hung up by the mistress as a sign of the night's awful contest; and this mantle was in possession of the same family from generation to generation for five hundred years after.

BEWITCHED BUTTER

Letitia Maclintock

Not far from Rathmullan in Donegal lived, last spring, a family called Hanlon; and in a farmhouse, some fields distant, people named Dogherty. Both families had good cows, but the Hanlons were fortunate in possessing a Kerry cow that gave more milk and yellower butter than the others.

Grace Dogherty, a young girl, who was more admired than loved in the neighbourhood, took much interest in the Kerry cow, and appeared one night at Mrs Hanlon's door with the modest request –

'Will you let me milk your Moiley[1] cow?'

'An' why wad you wish to milk wee Moiley, Grace, dear?' inquired Mrs Hanlon.

'Oh, just becase you're sae throng at the present time.'

'Thank you kindly, Grace, but I'm no too throng to do

---

[1] In Connaught called a 'mweeal' cow – ie, a cow without horns. Irish *maol*, literally, blunt.

my ain work. I'll no trouble you to milk.'

The girl turned away with a discontented air; but the next evening, and the next, found her at the cow-house door with the same request.

At length Mrs Hanlon, not knowing well how to persist in her refusal, yielded, and permitted Grace to milk the Kerry cow.

She soon had reason to regret her want of firmness. Moiley gave no milk to her owner.

When this melancholy state of things lasted for three days, the Hanlons applied to a certain Mark McCarrion, who lived near Binion.

'That cow has been milked by someone with an evil eye,' said he. 'Will she give you a wee drop, do you think? The full of a pint measure wad do.'

'Oh, ay, Mark, dear; I'll get that much milk frae her, anyway.'

'Weel, Mrs Hanlon, lock the door, an' get nine new pins that was never used in clothes, an' put them into a saucepan wi' the pint o' milk. Set them on the fire, an' let them come to the boil.'

The nine pins soon began to simmer in Moiley's milk.

Rapid steps were heard approaching the door, agitated knocks followed, and Grace Dogherty's high-toned voice was raised in eager entreaty.

'Let me in, Mrs Hanlon!' she cried. 'Tak off that cruel pot! Tak out them pins, for they're pricking holes in my heart, an' I'll never offer to touch milk of yours again.'

Part Six

GIANTS

THE GIANT'S STAIRS
Thomas Crofton Croker

On the road between Passage and Cork there is an old mansion called Ronayne's Court. It may be easily known from the stack of chimneys and the gable-ends, which are to be seen, look at it which way you will. Here it was that Maurice Ronayne and his wife Margaret Gould kept house, as may be learned to this day from the great old chimney-piece, on which is carved their arms. They were a mighty worthy couple, and had but one son, who was called Philip, after no less a person than the King of Spain.

Immediately on his smelling the cold air of this world the child sneezed, which was naturally taken to be a good sign of his having a clear head; and the subsequent rapidity of his learning was truly amazing, for on the very first day a primer was put into his hands, he tore out the A, B, C page and destroyed it, as a thing quite beneath his notice. No wonder, then, that both father and mother were proud of their heir, who gave such indisputable proofs of genius, or, as they called it in that part of the world, '*genus*'.

117

One morning, however, Master Phil, who was then just seven years old, was missing, and no one could tell what had become of him: servants were sent in all directions to seek him, on horseback and on foot, but they returned without any tidings of the boy, whose disappearance altogether was most unaccountable. A large reward was offered, but it produced them no intelligence, and years rolled away without Mr and Mrs Ronayne having obtained any satisfactory account of the fate of their lost child.

There lived at this time, near Carrigaline, one Robin Kelly, a blacksmith by trade. He was what is termed a handy man, and his abilities were held in much estimation by the lads and the lasses of the neighbourhood; for independent of shoeing horses, which he did to great perfection, and making plough-irons, he interpreted dreams for the young women, sung 'Arthur O'Bradley' at their weddings, and was so good-natured a fellow at a christening, that he was gossip to half the country round.

Now it happened that Robin had a dream himself, and young Philip Ronayne appeared to him in it, at the dead hour of the night. Robin thought he saw the boy mounted upon a beautiful white horse, and that he told him how he was made a page to the giant Mahon MacMahon, who had carried him off, and who held his court in the hard heart of the rock. 'The seven years – my time of service – are clean out, Robin,' said he, 'and if you release me this night I will be the making of you forever after.'

'And how will I know,' said Robin – cunning enough, even in his sleep – 'but this is all a dream?'

'Take that,' said the boy, 'for a token' – and at the word the white horse struck out with one of his hind legs, and gave poor Robin such a kick in the forehead that, thinking he was a dead man, he roared as loud as he could after his brains, and woke up, calling a thousand murders. He found himself in bed, but he had the mark of the blow, the regular print of a horseshoe, upon his forehead as red as blood; and

118

Robin Kelly, who never before found himself puzzled at the dream of any other person, did not know what to think of his own.

Robin was well acquainted with the Giant's Stairs – as, indeed, who is not that knows the harbour? They consist of great masses of rock, which, piled one above another, rise like a flight of steps from very deep water, against the bold cliff of Carrigmahon. Nor are they badly suited for stairs to those who have legs of sufficient length to stride over a moderate-sized house, or to enable them to clear the space of a mile in a hop, step and jump. Both these feats the giant MacMahon was said to have performed in the days of Finnian glory; and the common tradition of the country placed his dwelling within the cliff up whose side the stairs led.

Such was the impression which the dream made on Robin, that he determined to put its truth to the test. It occurred to him, however, before setting out on his adventure, that a plough-iron may be no bad companion, as, from experience, he knew that it was an excellent knock-down argument, having on more occasions than one settled a little disagreement very quietly: so, putting one on his shoulder, off he marched, in the cool of the evening, through Glaun a Thowk (the Hawk's Glen) to Monkstown. Here an old friend of his (Tom Clancey by name) lived, who on hearing Robin's dream, promised him the use of his skiff, and moreover, offered to assist in rowing it to the Giant's Stairs.

After supper, which was of the best, they embarked. It was a beautiful still night, and the little boat glided swiftly along. The regular dip of the oars, the distant song of the sailor, and sometimes the voice of a belated traveller at the ferry of Carrigaloe, alone broke the quietness of the land and sea and sky. The tide was in their favour, and in a few minutes Robin and his friend rested on their oars under the dark shadow of the Giant's Stairs. Robin looked anxiously for the entrance to the Giant's palace, which, it was said, may be found by any one seeking it at midnight; but no such entrance could he see. His impatience had hurried him there too early, and after waiting a considerable time in a state of suspense not to be described, Robin, with pure vexation, could not help exclaiming to his companion, "Tis a pair of fools we are, Tom Clancey, for coming here at all on the strength of a dream.'

'And whose doing is it,' said Tom, 'but your own?'

At the moment he spoke they perceived a faint glimmering of light to proceed from the cliff, which gradually increased until a porch big enough for a king's palace unfolded itself almost on a level with the water. They pulled the skiff towards the opening, and Robin Kelly, seizing his plough-iron, boldly entered with a strong hand and a stout heart. Wild and strange was that entrance, the whole of which appeared formed of grim and grotesque faces, blending so strangely each with the other that it was impossible to define any: the chin of one formed the nose of another; what appeared to be a fixed and stern eye, if dwelt upon, changed to a gaping mouth; and the lines of the lofty forehead grew into a majestic and flowing beard. The more Robin allowed himself to contemplate the forms around him, the more terrific they became; and the stony expression of this crowd of faces assumed a savage ferocity as his imagination converted feature after feature into a different shape and character. Losing the twilight in which these indefinite forms were visible, he advanced through a dark and devious passage, whilst a deep and rumbling noise sounded as if the rock was about to close upon him, and swallow him up alive forever. Now, indeed, poor Robin felt afraid.

'Robin, Robin,' said he, 'if you were a fool for coming here, what in the name of fortune are you now?' But, as before, he had scarcely spoken, when he saw a small light twinkling through the darkness of the distance, like a star in the midnight sky. To retreat was out of the question; for so many turnings and windings were in the passage, that he considered he had but little chance of making his way back. He, therefore, proceeded towards the bit of light, and came at last into a spacious chamber, from the roof of which hung the solitary lamp that had guided him. Emerging from such profound gloom the single lamp afforded Robin abundant light to discover several gigantic figures seated round a massive stone table, as if in serious deliberation, but no word disturbed the breathless silence which prevailed. At the head of this table sat Mahon MacMahon himself, whose majestic beard had taken root, and in the course of ages grown into the stone slab. He was the first who perceived Robin; and instantly starting up, drew his long beard from out the huge piece of rock in such haste and with so sudden a jerk that it was shattered into a thousand pieces.

'What seek you?' he demanded in a voice of thunder.

'I come,' answered Robin, with as much boldness as he could put on, for his heart was almost fainting within him; 'I come,' said he, 'to claim Philip Ronayne, whose time of service is out this night.'

'And who sent you here?' said the giant.

''Twas of my own accord I came,' said Robin.

'Then you must single him out from among my pages,' said the giant; 'and if you fix on the wrong one, your life is forfeit. Follow me.' He led Robin into a hall of vast extent and filled with lights; along either side of which were rows of beautiful children, all apparently seven years old, and none beyond that age, dressed in green, and every one exactly dressed alike.

'Here,' said Mahon, 'you are free to take Philip Ronayne, if you will; but, remember, I give you but one choice.'

Robin was sadly perplexed; for there were hundreds upon hundreds of children; and he had no very clear recollection of the boy he sought. But he walked along the hall, by the side of Mahon, as if nothing was the matter, although his great iron dress clanked fearfully at every step, sounding louder than Robin's own sledge-hammer battering on his anvil.

They had nearly reached the end without speaking, when Robin, seeing that the only means he had was to make friends with the giant, determined to try what effect a few soft words might have.

"Tis a fine wholesome appearance the poor children carry,' remarked Robin, 'although they have been here so long shut out from the fresh air and the blessed light of heaven. 'Tis tenderly your honour must have reared them!'

'Ay,' said the giant, 'that is true enough; so give me your hand; for you are, I believe, a very honest fellow for a black-smith.'

Robin at the first look did not much like the huge size of the hand, and, therefore, presented his plough-iron, which the giant seizing, twisted in his grasp round and round again as if it had been a potato stalk. On seeing this all the children set up a shout of laughter. In the midst of their mirth Robin thought he heard his name called; and all ear and eye, he put his hand on the boy who he fancied had spoken, crying out at the same time, 'Let me live or die for it, but this is young Phil Ronayne.'

'It is Philip Ronayne – happy Philip Ronayne,' said his young companions; and in an instant the hall became dark. Crashing noises were heard, and all was in strange confusion; but Robin held fast his prize, and found himself lying in the grey dawn of the morning at the head of the Giant's Stairs with the boy clasped in his arms.

Robin had plenty of friends to spread the story of his wonderful adventure: Passage, Monkstown, Carrigaline – the whole barony of Kerricurrihy rung with it.

'Are you quite sure, Robin, it is young Phil Ronayne you have brought back with you?' was the regular question; for although the boy had been seven years away, his appearance now was just the same as on the day he was missed. He had neither grown taller nor older in look, and he spoke of things which had happened before he was carried off as one awakened from sleep, or as if they had occurred yesterday.

'Am I sure? Well, that's a queer question,' was Robin's reply; 'seeing the boy has the blue eye of the mother, with the foxy hair of the father; to say nothing of the *purty* wart on the right side of his little nose.'

However Robin Kelly may have been questioned, the worthy couple of Ronayne's Court doubted not that he was the deliverer of their child from the power of the giant MacMahon; and the reward they bestowed on him equalled their gratitude.

Philip Ronayne lived to be an old man; and he was remarkable to the day of his death for his skill in working brass and iron, which it was believed he had learned during his seven years' apprenticeship to the giant Mahon Mac-Mahon.

A LEGEND OF KNOCKMANY
William Carleton

What Irish man, woman or child has not heard of our renowned Hibernian Hercules, the great and glorious Finn M'Coul? Not one, from Cape Clear to the Giant's Causeway, nor from that back again to Cape Clear. And, by the way, speaking of the Giant's Causeway brings me at once to the beginning of my story. Well, it so happened that Finn and his men were all working at the Causeway, in order to make a bridge across to Scotland; when Finn, who was very fond of his wife Oonagh, took it into his head that he would go home and see how the poor woman got on in his absence. So, accordingly, he pulled up a fir-tree, and, after lopping off the roots and branches, made a walking-stick of it, and set out on his way to Oonagh.

Oonagh, or rather Finn, lived at this time on the very tip-top of Knockmany Hill, which faces a cousin of its own called Cullamore, that rises up, half-hill, half-mountain, on the opposite side.

There was at that time another giant, named Cucullin –

124

me say he was Irish, and some say he was Scotch – but hether Scotch or Irish, there was no question but he was a rror. No other giant of the day could stand before him; d such was his strength, that, when well vexed, he could ve a stamp that shook the country about him. The fame d name of him went far and near; and nothing in the ape of a man, it was said, had any chance with him in a ht. By one blow of his fists he flattened a thunderbolt and pt it in his pocket, in the shape of a pancake, to show to l his enemies, when they were about to fight him. Undoubt-ly he had given every giant in Ireland a considerable ating, barring Finn M'Coul himself; and he swore that he ould never rest, night or day, winter or summer, till he ould serve Finn with the same sauce, if he could catch him. owever, the short and long of it was, with reverence be it oken, that Finn heard Cucullin was coming to the Cause-ay to have a trial of strength with him; and he was seized ith a very warm and sudden fit of affection for his wife, or woman, leading a very lonely, uncomfortable life of it his absence. He accordingly pulled up the fir-tree, as I id before, and having snedded it into a walking-stick, set it on his travels to see his darling Oonagh on the top of ockmany, by the way.

In truth, the people wondered very much why it was that nn selected such a windy spot for his dwelling-house, and ey even went so far as to tell him as much.

'What can you mane, Mr M'Coul,' said they, 'by pitching ur tent upon the top of Knockmany, where you never are thout a breeze, day or night, winter or summer; where, sides this, there's the sorrow's own want of water?'

'Why,' said Finn, 'ever since I was the height of a round wer, I was known to be fond of having a good prospect of y own; and where the dickens, neighbours, could I find a tter spot for a good prospect than the top of Knockmany? for water, I am sinking a pump, and, plase goodness, as on as the Causeway's made, I intend to finish it.'

Now, this was more of Finn's philosophy; for the re[a]
state of the case was, that he pitched upon the top [o]
Knockmany in order that he might be able to see Cuculli[n]
coming towards the house. All we have to say is, that if h[e]
wanted a spot from which to keep a sharp look-out – an[d]
between ourselves, he did want it grievously – barring Sliev[e]
Croob, or Slieve Donard, or its own cousin, Cullamore, h[e]
could not find a neater or more convenient situation for it i[n]
the sweet and sagacious province of Ulster.

'God save all here!' said Finn, good-humouredly, o[n]
putting his honest face into his own door.

'Musha, Finn, avick, an' you're welcome home to you[r]
own Oonagh, you darlin' bully.' Here followed a smack tha[t]
is said to have made the waters of the lake at the bottom [of]
the hill curl, as it were, with kindness and sympathy.

Finn spent two or three happy days with Oonagh, and fe[lt]
himself very comfortable, considering the dread he had [of]
Cucullin. This, however, grew upon him so much that h[is]
wife could not but perceive something lay on his min[d]
which he kept altogether to himself. Let a woman alone, [in]
the meantime, for ferreting or wheedling a secret out of h[er]
good man, when she wishes. Finn was a proof of this.

'It's this Cucullin,' said he, 'that's troubling me. When t[he]
fellow gets angry, and begins to stamp, he'll shake you[r]
whole townland; and it's well known that he can stop [a]
thunderbolt, for he always carries one about him in t[he]
shape of a pancake, to show to anyone that might b[e]
planning to fight him.'

As he spoke, he clapped his thumb in his mouth, which h[e]
always did when he wanted to prophesy, or to know an[y]
thing that happened in his absence; and the wife asked hi[m]
what he did it for.

'He's coming,' said Finn; 'I see him below Dungannon.'

'Thank goodness, dear! an' who is it, avick? Glory be [to]
God!'

'That baste, Cucullin,' replied Finn; 'and how to manag[e]

don't know. If I run away, I am disgraced; and I know that sooner or later I must meet him, for my thumb tells me so.'

'When will he be here?' said she.

'Tomorrow, about two o'clock,' replied Finn with a groan.

'Well, my bully, don't be cast down,' said Oonagh; 'depend on me, and maybe I'll bring you better out of this scrape than ever you could bring yourself, by your rule o' thumb.'

She then made a high smoke fire on the top of the hill, after which she put her finger in her mouth, and gave three whistles, and by that Cucullin knew he was invited to Cullamore – for this was the way that the Irish long ago gave a sign to all strangers and travellers, to let them know they were welcome to come and take share of whatever was going.

In the meantime, Finn was very melancholy, and did not know what to do, or how to act at all. Cucullin was an ugly customer to meet with; and, the idea of the 'pancake' aforesaid flattened the very heart within him. What chance could he have, strong and brave though he was, with a man who could, when put in a passion, walk the country into earthquakes and knock thunderbolts into pancakes? Finn didn't know where to turn for help. Right or left – backward or forward – where to go he could form no guess whatsoever.

'Oonagh,' said he, 'can you do nothing for me? Where's all your invention? Am I to be skivered like a rabbit before your eyes, and to have my name disgraced forever in the sight of all my tribe, and me the best man among them? How am I to fight this man-mountain – this huge cross between an earthquake and a thunderbolt? – with a pancake in his pocket that was once –'

'Take it easy, Finn,' replied Oonagh; 'troth, I'm ashamed of you. Keep your head, will you? Talking of pancakes, maybe, we'll give him as good as any he brings with him –

thunderbolt or otherwise. If I don't treat him to as smart feeding as he's got this many a day, never trust Oonagh again. Leave him to me, and do just as I bid you.'

This relieved Finn very much; for, after all, he had great confidence in his wife, knowing, as he did, that she had got him out of many a quandary before. Oonagh then drew the nine woollen threads of different colours, which she always did to find out the best way of succeeding in anything of importance she went about. She then platted them into three plats with three colours in each, putting one on her right arm, one round her heart, and the third round her right ankle, for then she knew that nothing could fail with her that she undertook.

Having everything now prepared, she sent round to the neighbours and borrowed one-and-twenty iron griddles, which she took and kneaded into the hearts of one-and-twenty cakes of bread, and these she baked on the fire in the usual way, setting them aside in the cupboard according as they were done. She then put down a large pot of new milk, which she made into curds and whey. Having done all this, she sat down quite contented, waiting for Cucullin's arrival on the next day about two o'clock, that being the hour at which he was expected – for Finn knew as much by the sucking of his thumb. Now this was a curious property that Finn's thumb had. In this very thing, moreover, he was very much resembled by his great foe, Cucullin; for it was well known that the huge strength he possessed all lay in the middle finger of his right hand, and that, if he happened by any mischance to lose it, he was no more, for all his bulk, than a common man.

At length, the next day, Cucullin was seen coming across the valley, and Oonagh knew that it was time to commence operations. She immediately brought the cradle, and made Finn to lie down in it, and cover himself up with the clothes.

'You must pass for your own child,' said she; 'so just lie there snug, and say nothing, but be guided by me.'

About two o'clock, as he had been expected, Cucullin came in. 'God save all here!' said he; 'is this where the great Finn M'Coul lives?'

'Indeed it is, honest man,' replied Oonagh; 'God save you kindly – won't you be sitting?'

'Thank you, ma'am,' says he, sitting down; 'you're Mrs M'Coul, I suppose?'

'I am,' said she; 'and I have no reason, I hope, to be ashamed of my husband.'

'No,' said the other, 'he has the name of being the strongest and bravest man in Ireland; but for all that, there's a man not far from you that's very desirous of taking a shake with him. Is he at home?'

'Why, then, no,' she replied; 'and if ever a man left his house in a fury, he did. It appears that some one told him of a big basthoon of a giant called Cucullin being down at the Causeway to look for him, and so he set out there to try if he could catch him. Well, truthfully, I hope, for the poor giant's sake, he won't meet with him, for if he does, Finn will make paste of him at once.'

'Well,' said the other, 'I am Cucullin, and I have been seeking him these twelve months, but he always kept clear of me; and I will never rest night or day till I lay my hands on him.'

At this Oonagh set up a loud laugh, of great contempt, by the way, and looked at him as if he was only a mere handful of a man.

'Did you ever see Finn?' said she, changing her manner all at once.

'How could I?' said Cucullin; 'he always took care to keep his distance.'

'I thought so,' she replied; 'I judged as much; and if you take my advice, you poor-looking creature, you'll pray night and day that you may never see him, for I tell you it will be a black day for you when you do. But, in the meantime, you perceive that the wind's on the door, and as Finn himself is

129

away from home, maybe you'd be civil enough to turn the house, for it's always what Finn does when he's here.'

This was a startler even to Cucullin; but he got up, however, and after pulling the middle finger of his right hand until it cracked three times, he went outside, and getting his arms about the house, turned it as she had wished. When Finn saw this, he felt the sweat of fear oozing out through every pore of his skin; but Oonagh, depending upon her woman's wit, felt not a whit daunted.

'Arrah, then,' said she, 'as you are so civil, maybe you'd do another obliging turn for us, as Finn's not here to do it himself. You see, after this long stretch of dry weather we've had, we feel very badly off for want of water. Now, Finn says there's a fine spring-well somewhere under the rocks behind the hill here below, and it was his intention to pull them asunder; but having heard of you, he left the place in such a fury, that he forgot it. Now, if you try to find it, in truth I'd feel it a kindness.'

She then brought Cucullin down to see the place, which was then all one solid rock; and, after looking at it for some time, he cracked his right middle finger nine times, and, stooping down, tore a cleft about four hundred feet deep, and a quarter of a mile in length, which has since been christened by the name of Lumford's Glen.

'You'll now come in,' said she, 'and eat a bit of such humble fare as we can give you. Finn, even although he and you are enemies, would scorn not to treat you kindly in his own house; and, indeed, if I didn't do it even in his absence, he would not be pleased with me.'

She accordingly brought him in, and placing half a dozen of the cakes we spoke of before him, together with a can or two of butter, a side of boiled bacon, and a stack of cabbage, she desired him to help himself – for this, be it known, was long before the invention of potatoes. Cucullin put one of the cakes in his mouth to take a huge whack out of it, when he made a thundering noise, something between a growl and a yell. 'Blood and fury!' he shouted; 'how is this? Here are two of my teeth out! What kind of bread is this you gave me?'

'What's the matter?' said Oonagh coolly.

'Matter!' shouted the other again; 'why, here are the two best teeth in my head gone.'

'Why,' said she, 'that's Finn's bread – the only bread he ever eats when at home; but, indeed, I forgot to tell you that nobody can eat it but himself, and that child in the cradle there. I thought, however, that, as you were reported to be rather a stout little fellow for your size, you might be able to manage it, and I did not wish to affront a man that thinks himself able to fight Finn. Here's another cake – maybe it's not so hard as that.'

Cucullin at the moment was not only hungry, but ravenous, so he accordingly made a fresh set at the second cake, and immediately another yell was heard twice as loud as the first. 'Thunder and gibbets!' he roared 'take your bread out of this, or I will not have a tooth left in my head; there's another pair of them gone!'

'Well, honest man,' replied Oonagh, 'if you're not able to eat the bread, say so quietly, and don't be wakening the child in the cradle there. There, now, he's awake upon me.'

Finn now gave a skirl that startled the giant, as coming from such a youngster as he was supposed to be. 'Mother,' said he, 'I'm hungry – get me something to eat.'

Oonagh went over, and putting into his hand a cake that had no griddle in it, Finn, whose appetite in the meantime had been sharpened by seeing eating going forward, soon swallowed it. Cucullin was thunderstruck, and secretly thanked his stars that he had the good fortune to miss meeting Finn, for, as he said to himself, 'I'd have no chance with a man who could eat such bread as that, which even his son that's but in his cradle can munch before my eyes.'

'I'd like to take a glimpse at the lad in the cradle,' said he to Oonagh; 'for I can tell you that the infant who can

manage that nutriment is no joke to look at, or to feed of a scarce summer.'

'With all the veins of my heart,' replied Oonagh; 'get up, acushla, and show this decent little man something that won't be unworthy of your father, Finn M'Coul.'

Finn, who was dressed for the occasion as much like a baby boy as possible, got up, and asks Cucullin, 'Are you strong?' said he.

'Mercy on us!' exclaimed the other, 'what a voice in so small a chap!'

'Are you strong?' said Finn again; 'are you able to squeeze water out of that white stone?' he asked, putting one into Cucullin's hand. The latter squeezed and squeezed the stone, but in vain.

'Ah, you're a poor creature!' said Finn. 'You a giant! Give me the stone here, and when I'll show what Finn's little son can do, you may then judge of what my daddy himself is.'

Finn then took the stone, and exchanging it for the curds,

he squeezed the latter until the whey, as clear as water, oozed out in a little shower from his hand.

'I'll now go in,' said he, 'to my cradle; for I scorn to lose my time with anyone that's not able to eat my daddy's bread, or squeeze water out of a stone. Bedad, you had better be off out of this before he comes back; for if he catches you, it's in jelly he'd have you in two minutes.'

Cucullin, seeing what he had seen, was of the same opinion himself; his knees knocked together with the terror of Finn's return, and he accordingly hastened to bid Oonagh farewell, and to assure her, that from that day out, he never wished to hear of, much less to see, her husband. 'I admit fairly that I'm not a match for him,' said he, 'strong as I am; tell him I will avoid him as I would the plague, and that I will make myself scarce in this part of the country while I live.'

Finn, in the meantime, had gone into the cradle, where he lay very quietly, his heart at his mouth with delight that Cucullin was about to take his departure, without discovering the tricks that had been played on him.

'It's well for you,' said Oonagh, 'that he doesn't happen to be here, for it's nothing but hawk's meat he'd make of you.'

'I know that,' says Cucullin; 'divil a thing else he'd make of me; but before I go, will you let me feel what kind of teeth Finn's lad has got that can eat griddle-bread like that?'

'With all pleasure in life,' said she; 'only, as they're far back in his head, you must put your finger a good way in.'

Cucullin was surprised to find such a powerful set of grinders in one so young; but he was still much more so on finding, when he took his hand from Finn's mouth, that he had left the very finger upon which his whole strength depended, behind him. He gave one loud groan, and fell down at once with terror and weakness. This was all Finn wanted, who now knew that his most powerful and bitterest enemy was at his mercy. He started out of the cradle, and in a few minutes the great Cucullin, that was for such a length of time the terror of him and all his followers, lay a corpse before him. Thus did Finn, through the wit and invention of Oonagh, his wife, succeed in overcoming his enemy by cunning, which he never could have done by force.

Part Seven

TRADITIONAL STORIES AND CELTIC SAGA STORIES

COUNTRY-UNDER-WAVE
Alice Furlong

There was once a little child, and he could not learn. It was not his fault. Every summer eve, and every winter night, he stood by the knee of his mother, and she said for him the names of the days of the week, and the seasons of the year, and told him how to call the sun and the moon and the stars. She gave him to know that the wheat was sown in one time, and reaped in another; that the oxen drew the plough, and the swift, nimble steed the chariot; that there were seven degrees of folks in the land, and seven orders among the poets, and seven colours to be distributed among the folks and among the poets, according to rank and station. And many other things the mother taught him, standing by her knee. The child listened, and was of attentive mind.

But in the morning, she asked him what was shining in the heavens, and he made answer, 'The moon.' And she asked him when did men take sickles and go a-reaping, and he said, 'In the season of Beltaine' (which is the early summer season when birds are on the bough, and blossom on the thorn). And she bade him tell her what animal it was that drew the plough over red, loamy fields, and he answered, 'The swift, nimble horse.' And she questioned him of the seven folks, and the seven orders, and the seven colours, and he had no right understanding concerning any of these.

'Ill-luck is on me, that I am the mother of a fool!' said the poor woman many a time. Then the child used to steal away to the dim, green orchard, and hide among the mossy trees, and weep.

After a time, the mother gave up trying to teach him, and taught his younger brothers and his sister, instead. The boy then took the lowest place at table, and his fare was given him last, and he was, in that homestead, the person held in least respect by menservants and maids.

There was a wise woman tarrying in the place one day, putting herbs of healing about an ailing cow. She saw the boy, and his fair head hanging, and shame in his eyes. 'What is wrong with this fair-headed lad?' said she.

'The head is wrong with him,' answered the mother of the boy. 'He has no utterance nor understanding. A heavy trouble to me, that! For there was none among my kin and people but had the wisdom and the knowledge fitting for his station.'

The wise woman muttered and mumbled to herself.

'Get him the Nuts of Knowledge', said she, after that.

'I have heard tell of them,' said the mother, 'but hard is their getting.' The brothers and the sister of the child that could not learn stood round about, and listened to the talk between the mother and the wise woman, Dechtera.

'The Nuts of Knowledge, they grow upon the Hazels of Knowledge, over a Well of Enchantment in the Country-under-Wave,' said Dechtera. 'If it be that you desire wisdom for your boy, good woman, you must send there some person to bring the nuts to you.'

The second son, Kian, flung back his hair. He was a

proud youth, and full of courage as a ripe apple is full of sweetness.

'Let me be going, that the disgrace may be taken from my mother, and the sons of my mother,' said he.

The wise woman fingered her long lip.

'If you would go, 'tis soon you must be going,' she said. 'It is near the Eve of Beltaine, an eve of great witchery. Between the rising and the setting of the moon, that night, the loughs and the seas of Erin become gates of glass that will open to let through any person who seeks the Country-under-Wave. Is this to your mind, my son?'

'It is pleasing to my mind,' said the lad.

'It is well pleasing to my mind,' said the mother.

The wise woman went on telling them of the way to reach Country-under-Wave.

'He must bid farewell to kith and kin, and go in his loneness to the lough shore that night,' she said. 'And when the gates of glass are shut behind him, he must tarry in the Under-water Land from Beltaine until Samhain and harvest, when the nuts of the Magic Hazels will ripen to scarlet red. And on the eve of Samhain, he will draw near the Well of Enchantment and wait for the dropping of the nuts. He must be swift to stretch out the hand and snatch them as they drop. For the Salmon of Knowledge, he too is waiting in the Well, to eat the fruit as it falls. In that hour, a rosy surge rises upon the water, and the Salmon eats and swims away, swimming all the seas of the round, rolling world. And he has a knowledge of everything that passes, over-seas, and under-seas, and in hidden places and desert ways. But if this youth lets the nuts slip through his fingers, he shall be in the power of Them in the Country-under-Wave.'

'Good are my fingers to catch and hold,' said the boy, Kian.

The wise woman went away to the hills then, after curing the ailing cow.

Came the eve of Beltaine, the night of witchery. The lad

said farewell to his house and home, and embraced hi
brothers and his sister and his mother. He went out alon
under the moon, and there was fairy singing in the win
that night, and over the dewy fields the silver track of fair
feet. He came to the lough shore, and saw the water as gate
of glass. He went boldly through and travelled crystal road
ways and riverways until he came to the Country-under
Wave.

The grass was greener than emeralds there; the trees wer
bowers of blossom. A radiant mist was on the mountains
The level plain was more thick with flowers than the sk
with stars of a night when there is neither moon nor cloud
'A better country than my mother's country!' said the yout
to himself.

He was walking over a shining pebbly way until he cam
to a house. Every plank of the wall was of a different colou
to the one beside it; the doors and windows were frame
and pillared in wrought gold; the roof was fashioned c
plumage so finely spread that it seemed like one feather with
out parting or division.

People were passing to and fro about this fair hous
Noble of mien were they, with hair of the hue of primrose
with eyes sloe-black, the blush of the rosy foxglove on ever
cheek, the pure whiteness of milk on every brow. They cam
in a shining troop to meet Kian, the boy, and they said t
him, 'A hundred welcomes before you!'

The lad saluted them. They brought him within th
palace, and invited him to abide there for the night. He sai
he was willing. The time went pleasantly with mirth an
music. Soon the lad inquired where was the Well of Enchant
ment? 'More than a day's journey from this spot,' the lor
of the mansion made answer. On the red dawn of th
morrow, the lad took his leave of them. They gave him
fair-woven napkin spun of silk as fine as the web of
spider.

'When there comes upon you hunger or thirst, spread th

napkin on the grass and it shall be covered with the choicest of foods and drinks,' said the lord of the coloured house.

The lad gave them thanks.

'It is a great country you have of it down here,' he said. The noble people were pleased.

'You never were in its like before,' they said.

The boy, Kian, felt his high spirit rise up in him. He was a proud lad, and could not listen to a country being praised over his own. That was no fault. But he spoke a word, and the word was not true.

'I have seen as many wonders in my mother's country, and more,' said he. Then he followed the crystal waterways and roadways, seeking the Well of Enchantment.

The folks of that mansion were watching him along the way. 'A lie in his mouth in return for our hospitality!' said they one to another. 'Well, let it be so. He is not in our power now, but that may be mended another day.'

The boy followed his road. He was travelling till evening, and he came to the shore of the sea. The sand was in grains of gold, the waves fell with the sound of singing. He beheld white-maned seahorses race upon the strand, and wonderful people in chariots behind the horses. He sat down among the flowers, and he spread the fine-spun napkin, and it was covered with choice food and drinks. He ate his supper, and then looked about to find a place to rest for the night.

He saw a fair woman coming towards him, and gave her greeting.

'A hundred welcomes before you, Kian,' said she to him. He wondered how she knew his name. 'You are in want of a resting-place for the night?' said she.

'I want that, among other things,' said the lad.

The fair woman led him to a palace among the rocks. It was finer and better than the first house he had been in, if that were possible. Every person there had a star on the forehead and flowing pale-gold hair, like the ripple of the foam of the sea. And the clothing of every person was of the tint of waves, blue and green, shifting and changing with their stir and movement.

'This is the house of Manannan Mac Lir, who commands the winds and the storms and the tempests that wreck ships and drown fishers,' said the woman.

The boy remained there that night. Pleasant was the entertainment he got in the house of Manannan Mac Lir. On the morn of the morrow, he went forth again to find the Well of Enchantment. The folks of the house gave him a little bit of a cloak, no bigger than would go over the lad's shoulders.

'When you are in want of a shelter and sleeping booth for the night, hang this cloak from the first straight twig you pick up from the grass. The twig will be a pillar and the cloak a tent, therewith.'

He gave them thanks, and said, 'Wonders upon wonders! What more can you do down here?'

The sea-folks laughed out. They laughed more softly than the sigh of summer waves. They were pleased with the youth.

'You have not fallen in with such people before,' said they. The spirit of the lad rose up. He forgot himself again. He told another lie.

'The foot-boys of the King of Erin are better people,' he said, and followed his journey. The folks of that sea-mansion laughed again. But now their laughter was like the whistle of the wind that bids the storm begin.

'A boast he has instead of thanks for us,' said they. 'Let it be so. He is not in our power now. That will be mended another day.'

Kian, the boy, abode in the Country-under-Wave while the meadows ripened in his mother's country, and mowers went forth with scythes, and maids tossed the hay. The apple was green and the cherry was red. After that, it drew nigh the harvest, and the apple reddened, and the cherry tree began to change the hue of its leaves.

Down in the Country-under-Wave, the youth was walking to and fro, seeking the Well of Enchantment. The day before the eve of Samhain, he came upon it, in a deep forest, where the wind murmured always and always. He saw the magic hazels, and knew them by the crimson of their fruit. And the nut-cluster drooped over the water of the Well, and leaned to its own rosy shadow beneath. 'Now my journey is ended,' said Kian, the boy.

He hung his cloak from the first twig he met in the green, green grass, and it rose to be a pillar, and the cloak spread to be a tent. He threw his fine-spun napkin upon the flowers, and it was covered with food and drinks. He ate his supper, and he took his rest.

But the people of the first mansion had put a sleeping-potion in the drink, and it was long that Kian remained in slumber. All the morning he slept; and the noonday sun saw him sleeping, and the rising moon that night. But just before the midnight he awoke, for he seemed to hear his young sister calling upon him to haste, haste, haste. He ran out in the moonlight, and saw the Well shining, and the magic cluster swaying from the bough.

'It is my time now,' said he.

He stood beside the water, and there was the shimmering salmon, with upturned eye, below. But while he waited, all of a sudden, from the tent behind him came the most woeful crying he had ever heard. He thought it was the voice of his mother, and he turned his head. And then, he heard a splash in the water of the Well of Enchantment. The crying ceased as soon as it began. It was a high, wild cry of laughter he caught, like the wind at night when the tempest is out. And the waters of the Well began to rise in a rosy surge, and there was no cluster hanging to its own shadow, but a fruitless bough.

'Now, ill-luck is upon me!' said Kian, the boy.

The water sank, and the Salmon of Knowledge swam through the seas of the round, rolling world. The boy sat down by the brink, and covered his head with his mantle, lest any eye might discern his tears. And as he was thus, a deep sleep fell upon him, like to death itself. Then the people of the coloured mansion, and the sea-folks of the palace of Manannan came round him, and they put a grey flagstone over him, and left him by the Well.

November eve came and went, and the mother of Kian was looking for his return, but he never came. 'I had a bad dream concerning him,' said the little sister, Fedelm.

The mother sent for the wise woman on the hill.

'Some mishap has befallen,' said Dechtera. 'I do not know what you had best do now, except you send the third brother to help him. But you must wait for next May-eve.'

The woman of the house made lament and moan. 'All for a fool has this trouble fallen,' said she. She drove the eldest boy from her presence, and made him sit with the servants. But little Fedelm wept until, for peace sake, the mother had to let him back to his own place. The poor boy that could not learn was filled with shame.

In due season, came again the time of Beltaine, the eve of witchery. Lugaid, the third of the brothers, went forth, in his loneness. He heard the fairy talk in the wind, and saw, among the dew, the silver track of the feet of Queens from the Raths. He stepped upon the lough shore, and the gates of glass stood open, and 'he went through. Not gleefully he went, but against his will, for he cared for no person in the world but himself – neither for the shame of the fool, nor for the lost, bright boy, nor for the sorrow of his mother. But he said to himself, 'Bad is it that I must go upon this search. But worse it will be if I stay at home, for our house is full of weeping and misery, and there is no comfort to be had in it.'

He was walking crystal streets and roads until he came to the Country-under-Wave, in like manner to his brother. He beheld the bowers and the flowers, the mist of light upon the mountains. He saw the coloured house, and the noble people in their beauty.

They came to him. 'A hundred welcomes before you!' said they. He was too fond of his own comfort to doff his head-dress to them.

'In a strange country, no stranger goes without supper,' he said.

The people whispered among themselves. They said then, 'If you had not asked it, it would have been given to you.' They brought him within the palace, and gave him his supper, full and plenty of all kinds. They kept him there that night.

When morning was come, and the crowing of cocks, and a red sun rising, he said to them, 'Is it far to the Well of Enchantment?'

'It will take you nigh a season to find it,' said they to him. He sighed at that, and the lord of the mansion took pity upon him. He gave him a fine-spun napkin, and told him it would be spread with breakfast, dinner and supper for him, as long as he remained in that place. The lad bade them joy, and went off whistling. He did not doff his head-dress to the women, and he going.

The noble people were angry. 'A churl this is, no lie,' they said. 'Well, he is not in our power today, but that will be mended another day.'

Lugaid went up and down that country. He came to the shore, and the ribbed, yellow sands, and the waves that made music in their plash and fall. The steeds of Manannan Mac Lir raced upon the sea. His chariots glistened; his people were there, in glinting, sheeny garments, all changing from green to blue, and from blue to green again.

It was nightfall when the lad beheld them, and no light was abroad but the light from the star on the brow of every one of these strange sea-people. One of them came to him. 'You will be in want of shelter tonight?' she said. The boy had been sleeping in dry places under hedges and southern banks. He felt he would like better the comfort of a bed.

'Shelter is a good thing to a tired person, and the night to be at hand,' he answered. She brought him with her into the palace among the rocks. He sat on a couch made of the down of sea swans; he drank out of a cup that was speckled with great emeralds as the grass of a May morning with beads of dew.

There was reciting of hero-tales, and harping and piping, after the banquet. The lad, Lugaid, was heavy with sleep. He let his head fall down, and snored.

'O, 'tis a churl we have here!' cried the people of Manannan. 'Throw him out with the calves in the byre!'

The fair woman who had spoken first with the boy, took his part. 'Long travel he has put behind him,' said she, 'and in the shelter of a house he has not slept for nights upon nights.' They let him be, then, until it was morning.

When the morn of the morrow came, the sea-folks gave him the little cloak. 'A tent it will be for you when you need it,' said they.

It was a little grey thing, mean to look at. The lad did not believe in the power of the sea-people. He took the cloak and threw it upon his back, and went away, swaggering, and making faces at them over his shoulder. But as he went, he heard them all begin to talk together, and their voices were like the rising of the far tide. 'It is not in our power to harm him, now,' they were saying, 'but that will be amended another day.'

The young lad abode in that Country-under-Wave until Samhain. Everywhere he went, he kept his eyes open for a sight of his brother. But he asked no questions of anybody. In due time he found the deep forest, and the dark Well, the hazels and the ruddy fruit, leaning to its own shadow.

It was sunset on the eve of Samhain. The boy sat down on the ground, near an old grey flagstone. He spread the napkin out, and there was an abundance both of food and drink upon it, at that. He ate and drank.

But the people of the coloured house had put a sleeping-potion into the drink, for on this eve they had power to work spells and charms against mortals. The boy drank then, and a heavy slumber fell upon him, and he was there lying in the dew until midnight drew nigh.

He heard in his sleep the voice of his sister, Fedelm. 'O, haste, haste, haste!' said the voice. He rose and ran to the Well of Enchantment. The rosy cluster was loosening from the bough. Lugaid, the boy, stretched his hand, and his eye caught the silver gleam of the Salmon of Knowledge below in the water of the Well. But a gust of hollow wind sprang up, all at once, and blew the leaves of the magic hazels into his eyes. Then he heard the fall of the fruit upon the water, and the crimson surge swelled up with little dim noises, and the Salmon ate the nuts, and swam away through the seas of the round, rolling world.

The deep death-trance fell upon Lugaid. He dropped down beside the Well. The sea-folks, and the people of the coloured mansion came, and put a grey flagstone over him and left him by his brother.

The mother waited for her boy's return, but he did not return.

'I saw him in my dream,' said Fedelm, the girl. 'I saw him, and he was in a trance of sleep.'

The mother sent for Dechtera, the wise woman.

'Lugaid has gone the way of Kian,' said the poor mother. 'What will I be doing now, with no son left me but a fool?'

'Send the daughter after them,' said Dechtera.

'I will not send the daughter,' said the woman of the house. She kissed and embraced the child, and said that she would not part with her. The boy that could not learn said he would not part with her. The mother blessed him for that, and put him into his own proper place at the head of his father's table. There was peace and sorrow among them until it was May-eve again.

'I will go to my rest early tonight,' said Fedelm, the girl.

They did not know what she had in her mind to do. They let her away to her little bower, to her rest. But she wound a silken curtain about the bedpost, and let herself down through the window. She went over the bawn-wall in the light of the moon, and heard the fairy-women singing in the wind, and saw the glimmer of fairy feet dancing over the honey-dew.

She went in her loneness to the lough shore, and the gates of glass stood open. She took a quick breath, and leaped through, and travelled the crystal highways and glassy roads until she came to the Country-under-Wave.

She found the lovely meads, thick-set with blossoms and the embowering trees. She saw the mountain mist, like silver fleeces spread far and thin. She fared to the coloured mansion with its golden pillars, and met the wise people of that house.

'A hundred welcomes before you, fair maid!' said they to her.

'A hundred tears are falling after me,' said Fedelm.

They brought her within, and laid choice foods before her. She ate a little honey and bread, and no more. She asked them to tell her the road to the Well of Enchantment.

'It is more than a month's journey from here,' said they.

She rose up then, and said she must be on her way though the night was falling. But they begged her, and craved of her to remain in their company that night, since there was now nothing to be seen by the Well but hazels with rosy buds upon them. She waited, then, that night.

In the morning they said to her, 'Here is a napkin. Whenever you are hungry or thirsty spread it on the ground, and it shall hold itself full of food and drink.'

Fedelm took it, and made them a curtsy. 'Is there anything I may do for ye, in return for this gift,' said she.

'Teach a boy to speak truth,' said the lord of the mansion. 'You will not see us again.'

The girl went her way. She fared north and south. She fared east and west. She came to the green-billowed, foam-ridged, hollow sea. The waves were making a melodious, wandering music. The seahorses pawed the floor of the ocean, and tossed the surf of the high, towering tide.

Manannan and his people were in their chariots, racing and riding on the watery meads. Little Fedelm stood watching them, and the evening fell, and she was so entranced that she forgot to eat or drink.

Then a fair radiant woman came to her, over the seas. She was more lustrous than the evening star when it hangs over the new moon in a twilight blue sky.

'I saw a face like this before,' said she. 'And I saw such clear bright eyes. Who will this little mortal maiden be?' And she stood before Fedelm, and looked her up and down.

'A maiden on a sad quest,' said the girl. 'The dauther of a sad mother; the sister of a sad brother.' Her tears fell, and left her eyes more clear and bright again. The majestic women brought her into the sea palace. They made her remain with them for that night. There was music and singing, and they asked her if the same was pleasing. She answered, 'If one were in mournful mood that harping and those singing voices would be enough to make him forget his sadness, though it were the whole world's burden should be upon him.'

'A well-spoken maiden,' said the sea-folks among themselves.

On the morn of the morrow, they gave her the small grey cloak, and knowledge of the use of it.

'What shall I do to repay you for this gift?' said Fedelm, curtsying before them.

'Teach a churl fine manners,' said the sea-folks. 'This is our first and last meeting.'

The girl was in the Country-under-Wave until November eve. She found the dim ever-murmuring wood, and the dark deep Well of Enchantment, and the Magic Hazels. The cluster was scarlet-red, swaying above its shadow in the water. The two grey flagstones were beside. The girl looked at the first of them. It had a streak of moss down the middle of the top.

'That puts me in mind of the curl on the white forehead of Kian, my brother,' said the maid. 'But it was hair brighter than gold, and this is the old green moss on the old grey flagstone.'

She went wandering about the lone place, and stood by the second flagstone. There was a score down the middle of the top.

'That, moreover, puts me in mind of my brother, Lugaid, and the frown he used to have on his brow, a furrow of discontent,' said she, musing. 'But what is this but an old grey stone, and he had a brow fairer than snow.'

After that, the evening fell, and all the murmuring, whispering wind of the woods went into a strange silence. And soon the moon rose, round as an apple, and the stars came out, twinkling and beaming over the dew.

Fedelm ate her supper off the magic napkin, and rested a while beneath the enchanted cloak. She was weary. A sleep fell upon her. But in the slumber she seemed to hear faint voices crying and calling. It went to her heart to hear them, for she knew them as the voices of her two lost brothers. She came to herself at the sound. It was the people of the coloured house made her hear the voices. She walked out upon the brink of the Well of Enchantment.

'I discern a creaking in that bough,' she said. If it had not been that the forest was full of silence, she would not have heard it; but this was the work of the sea-folks, to lay a spell of silence on the leaves, that the girl might know the hour was at hand.

It drew near the midnight, and Fedelm stood upon the brink of the Well, and watched the swaying of the bough, and the magic cluster, crimson-red. She saw below her in the wave a great silver salmon, waiting, with upturned eye. And then, the bough creaked, the stalk snapped, and the nuts, shining like fiery rubies, came dropping down upon the water. But the magic cluster never reached the wave, for Fedelm's little fingers seized it as it fell.

The moment the nuts were in her hand she knew all things. She knew the flagstone with the streak of moss upon it was her dear brother, Kian, who had told a lie to the people of the coloured mansion. She knew the flagstone with the furrow was Lugaid, the churlish, selfish brother. And she knew how to break the spell upon the one and the other by shaking the water of the Well of Enchantment over them from her little kind hand.

She did that, and they came into their right shapes, and embraced her, and laughed and cried. She led them out by the crystal waterways and roadways, and the gates of glass. They all went back to their mother's house, and great was the welcome they got there.

And the boy that could not learn, he ate the Nuts of Knowledge. From that day, he knew all things, the talking of the wind and the whisper of the reeds and rushes, the call of birds, and the cry of beasts, and there was nothing in the whole wide world hidden from him after that day.

EDAIN THE QUEEN
Lady Wilde

Now it happened that the King of Munster one day saw a beautiful girl bathing, and he loved her and made her his queen. And in all the land was no woman so lovely to look upon as the fair Edain. And the fame of her beauty came to the ears of the great and powerful chief and king of the Tuatha-de-Danann, Midar by name. So he disguised himself and went to the court of the King of Munster as a wandering bard that he might look on the beauty of Edain. And he challenged the king to a game of chess.

'Who is this man that I should play chess with him?' said the king.

'Try me,' said the stranger. 'You will find me a worthy foe.'

Then the king said, 'But the chessboard is in the queen's apartment, and I cannot disturb her.'

However, when the queen heard that a stranger had challenged the king to chess, she sent her page in with the chessboard and then came herself to greet the stranger. And

Midar was so dazzled with her beauty that he could not speak, he could only gaze on her. And the queen also seemed troubled, and after a time she left them alone.

'Now, what shall we play for?' asked the king.

'Let the conquerer name the reward,' answered the stranger, 'and whatever he desires let it be granted to him.'

'Agreed,' replied the monarch.

Then they played the game and the stranger won.

'What is your demand now?' cried the king. 'I have given my word that whatever you name shall be yours.'

'I demand the Lady Edain, the queen, as my reward,' replied the stranger. 'But I shall not ask you to give her up to me till this day year.' And the stranger departed.

Now the king was utterly perplexed and confounded, but he took good note of the time and, on that night just a twelvemonth after, he made a great feast at Tara for all the princes, and he placed three lines of his chosen warriors all round the palace, and forbade any stranger to enter on pain of death. So all being secure, as he thought, he took his place at the feast with the beautiful Edain beside him, all glittering with jewels and a golden crown on her head, and the revelry went on till midnight. Just then, to his horror, the king looked up, and there stood the stranger in the middle of the hall, but no one seemed to perceive him save only the king. He fixed his eyes on the queen, and coming towards her, he struck the golden harp he had in his hand and sang in a low sweet voice:

'O Edain, will you come with me
To a wonderful palace that is mine?
White are the teeth there, and black the brows,
And crimson as the mead are the lips of the lovers.

O woman, if you come to my proud people,
'Tis a golden crown shall circle your head,
You shall dwell by the sweet streams of my land,
And drink of the mead and wine in the arms of your lover.'

Then he gently put his arms round the queen's waist, and drew her up from her royal throne, and went forth with her through the midst of all the guests, none hindering, and the king himself was like one in a dream, and could neither speak nor move. But when he recovered himself, then he knew that the stranger was one of the fairy chiefs of the Tuatha-de-Danann who had carried off the beautiful Edain to his fairy mansion. So he sent round messengers to all the kings of Erin that they should destroy all the forts of the hated Tuatha race, and slay and kill and let none live till the queen, his young bride, was brought back to him.

Still she came not. Then the king out of revenge ordered his men to block up all the stables where the royal horses of the Dananns were kept, that so they might die of hunger. But the horses were of noble blood, and no bars or bolts could hold them, and they broke through the bars and rushed out like the whirlwind, and spread all over the country. And the kings, when they saw the beauty of the horses, forgot all about the search for Queen Edain, and only strove how they could seize and hold as many as possible for themselves of the fiery steeds with the silver hoofs and golden bridles.

Then the king raged in his wrath, and sent for the chief of the Druids, and told him he should be put to death unless he discovered the place where the queen lay hid. So the Druid went over all Ireland, and searched, and made spells with oghams on four wands of a hazel-tree. It was revealed to him that deep down in a hill in the very centre of Ireland, Queen Edain was hidden away in the enchanted palace of Midar the fairy chief.

Then the king gathered a great army, and they circled the hill, and dug down and down till they came to the very centre. And just as they reached the gate of the fairy palace, Midar by his enchantments sent forth fifty beautiful women from the hillside, to distract the attention of the warriors, all so like the queen in form and features and dress, that the king himself could not make out truly, if his own wife were amongst them or not.

But Edain, when she saw her husband so near her, was touched by love of him in her heart, and the power of the enchantment fell from her soul, and she came to him, and he lifted her up on his horse and kissed her tenderly, and brought her back safely to his royal palace of Tara, where they lived happily ever after.

But soon after, the power of the Tuatha-de-Danann was broken forever, and the remnant that was left took refuge in the caves where they exist to this day, and practise their magic, and work spells, and are safe from death until the judgement day.

HOW CUCHULAIN GOT
HIS NAME
Eleanor Hull

In Ulster, near Cuchulain's country, lived a mighty craftsman and smith, whose name was Culain. Now the custom is, that every man of means and every owner of land in Ulster, should, once in a year or so, invite the King and his chiefs to spend a few days, it may be a week or a fortnight, at his house, that he may give them entertainment. But Culain the smith owned no lands, nor was he rich, for only the fruit of his hammer, of his anvil and his tongs, had he. Nevertheless he desired to entertain the King at a banquet, and he went to Emain to invite his chief. But he said, 'I have no lands or store of wealth; I pray you, therefore, to bring with you only a few of your prime warriors, because my house cannot contain a great company of guests.' So the King said he would go, bringing but a small retinue with him.

Culain returned home to prepare his banquet, and when the day was come, towards evening the King set forth to reach the fort of Culain. He assumed his light, convenient travelling garb, and before starting he went down to the green to bid the boy-corps of guards farewell.

There he saw a sight so curious that he could not tear himself away. At one end of the green stood a group of a hundred and fifty youths, guarding one goal, all striving to prevent the ball of a single little boy, who was playing against the whole of them, from getting in; but for all that they could do, he won the game, and drove his ball home to the goal single-handed.

Then they changed sides, and the little lad defended his own goal against the hundred and fifty balls of the other youths, all sent at once across the ground. But though the youths played well, following up their balls, not one of them went into the hole, for the little boy caught them one after another just outside, driving them hither and thither, so that they could not make the goal. But when his turn came round again to make the counter-stroke, he was as successful as before; nay, he would get the entire set of a hundred and fifty balls into their hole, for all that they could do.

Then they played a game of getting each other's cloaks off without tearing them, and he would have their mantles off, one after the other, before they could, on their part, even unfasten the brooch that held his cloak. When they wrestled with each other, it was the same thing: he would have them on the ground before all of them together could upset him, or make him budge a foot.

As the King stood and watched all this, he said: ''Tis well for the country into which this boy has come! A clever child indeed is he; if only his acts as a grown man were to come up to the promise of his youth, he might be of some solid use to us; but this is not to be assumed.'

The King learned that the boy's name was Setanta. Then the King said, 'Have the child called, that we may take him with us to the banquet.'

So when Setanta came, the King invited him; but the boy

said, 'Excuse me now awhile; I cannot go just now.' 'How so?' said the King, surprised. 'Because the boy-corps have not yet had enough of play.' 'I cannot wait until they have,' replied the King: 'the night is growing late.' 'Wait not at all,' replied the child; 'I will even finish this one game, and will run after you.' 'But, young one, do you know the way?' asked the King. 'I will follow the trail made by your company, the wheels of their chariots and hoofs of the horses on the road,' he replied.

Thereupon King Conor starts; and in time for the banquet he reaches Culain's house, where, with due honour, he is received. Fresh rushes had been strewn upon the floor, the tables all decked out, the fires burning in the middle of the room. A great vat full of ale stood in the hall, a lofty candlestick gave light, and round the fires stood servants cooking savoury viands, holding them on forks or spits of wood. Each man of the King's guests entered in order of his rank, and sat at the feast in his own allotted place, hanging his weapons up above his head. The King occupied the central seat, his poets, counsellors, and chiefs sitting on either hand according to their state and dignity. As they were sitting down, the smith Culain came to Conor and asked him, 'Good now, O King, before we sit at meat I would even know whether anyone at all will follow you this night to my dwelling, or is your whole company gathered now within?' 'All are now here,' said the King, quite forgetting the wee boy; 'but why do you ask?'

'It is only that I have an excellent watch-dog, fierce and strong; and when his chain is taken off, and he is set free to guard the house, no one dare come anywhere within the same district with him; he is furious with all but me, and he has the strength and savage force of a hundred ordinary watch-dogs. This dog was brought to me from Spain, and no dog in the country can equal him.' 'Let him be set loose, for all are here,' said Conor; 'well will he guard this place for us.'

So Culain loosed the dog, and with one spring it bounded forth out of the court of the house and over the wall of the rath, making a circuit of the entire district; and when it came back panting, with its tongue hanging from its jaws, it took up its usual position in front of the house, and there crouched with its head upon its paws, watching the high road to Emain. Surely an extraordinarily cruel and fierce and savage dog was he.

When the boy-corps broke up that night, each of the lads returning to the house of his parent or his fosterer or guardian, Setanta, trusting to the trail of the company that went with Conor, struck out for Culain's house. With his club and ball he ran forward, and the distance seemed short on account of his interest in the game. As soon as he arrived on the green of Culain's fort, the mastiff noticed him, and set up such a howling as echoed loud through all the countryside. Inside the house the King and his followers heard and suddenly the King remembered Setanta, but he was struck dumb with fear, nor dared to move, thinking surely to find the little lad dead at the door of the fort. As for the hound himself, he thought with one fierce gulp to swallow Setanta whole. Now the little lad was without any means of defence beyond his ball and hurley-stick. He never left his play till he came near. Then, as the hound charged open-jawed, with all his strength he threw the ball right into the creature's mouth; and as for a moment the hound stopped short, choking as the ball passed down its throat, the lad seized hold of the mastiff's open jaws, grasping its throat with one hand and the back of its head with the other, and so violently did he strike its head against the pillars of the door, that it was no long time until the creature lay dead upon the ground.

When Culain and the warriors within had heard the mastiff howl, they asked each other, as soon as they got back their voices, 'What makes the watch-dog cry?' 'Alas!' the King said, ''tis no good luck that brought us on our present trip.' 'Why so?' inquired all. 'I mean that it is the little boy, my foster-son and Fergus's, Setanta, son of Sual-tach, who promised to come after me; now, even now, he is doubtless fallen by the hound of Culain.' Then, when they heard that it was Conor's foster-son who was without, on the instant and as one man they rose; and though the doors of the fort were thrown wide open they could not stand around, but out they stormed over the walls and ramparts of the fort to find the boy.

At the rampart's outer door they found the child, and the great hound dead beside him. Without a pause they picked up the boy and hoisted him on their shoulders, and thus, with all the heroes following, they came to Conor, and placed Setanta safe between the monarch's knees.

That was just how it was. But poor Culain. The smith went out to find his dog, and when he saw him lying there, knocked almost to pieces and quite dead, his heart was vexed within him. He went back to the house, and said,

"Twas no good luck that urged me to make this feast for you, O King; would I had not prepared a banquet. My life is a life lost, and my substance is but substance wasted without my dog. He was a defence and protection to our property and our cattle, to every beast we had and to our house. Little boy,' said he, 'you are welcome for your people's sake, you are not welcome for your own; that was a good member of my family you took from me, a guardian of house, of flocks and herds.' 'Be not vexed,' replied the child, 'for I myself will fix on my own punishment. This shall it be. If in all Ireland a whelp of that dog's breed is to be found, 'tis I myself will rear him up for you till he be fit to take the watch-dog's place. In the meantime, O Culain, I myself will be your hound for defence of your cattle and for your own defence, until the dog be grown and capable of action; I will defend your territory, and no cattle or beast or store of yours shall be taken from you, without my knowing it.'

'A good and just punishment,' they all said, 'and henceforward shall your name be changed; you shall no longer be called Setanta; Cu-Chulain, or the "Hound of Culain", shall your name be.'

'I like my own name best,' the child objected. 'Ah, say not so,' replied the King's druid, 'for one day will the name of Cuchulain ring in all men's mouths; among the brave ones of the whole wide world Cuchulain's name shall find a place. Renowned and famous shall he be, beloved and feared by all.' 'If that is so, then am I well content,' replied the boy.

So from that day forth the name Cuchulain clung to him, until the time came when he was no longer remembered as the Hound of Culain's Fort, but as the guardian and watch-dog of defence to the Province against her foes; and then men loved best to call him 'The Hound of Ulster'.

THE STORY OF DEIRDRE

Joseph Jacobs

There was a man in Ireland once who was called Malcolm
Harper. He was a right good man, with a goodly share of
this world's goods. He had a wife, but no family. What did
Malcolm hear one day, but that a soothsayer was travelling
in the neighbourhood, and as Malcolm Harper was a right
good man, he wished that the soothsayer might visit him.
Whether it was that he was invited or that he came of
himself, the soothsayer came to the house of Malcolm.

'Are you doing any soothsaying?' says Malcolm.

'Yes, I am doing a little. Are you in need of soothsaying?'

'Well, I do not mind taking soothsaying from you, if you
had soothsaying for me, and you would be willing to do it.'

'Well, I will do soothsaying for you. What kind of soothsaying do you want?'

'Well, the soothsaying I wanted was that you would tell
me my lot or what will happen to me, if you can give me
knowledge of it.'

'Well, I am going out, and when I return, I will tell you.'

162

And the soothsayer went forth out of the house and he was not long outside when he returned.

'Well,' said the soothsayer, 'I saw in my second sight that it is on account of a daughter of yours that the greatest amount of blood shall be shed that has ever been shed in Erin since time and race began. And the three most famous heroes that ever were found will lose their heads on her account.'

After a time a daughter was born to Malcolm, and he did not allow a living being to come to his house, only himself and the nurse. He asked this woman, 'Will you yourself bring up the child to keep her in hiding far away where eye will not see a sight of her nor ear hear a word about her?'

The woman said she would, so Malcolm got three men, and he took them away to a large mountain, distant and far from reach, without the knowledge or notice of anyone. He caused there a hillock, round and green, to be dug out of the middle of the mountain, and the hole thus made to be covered carefully over so that a little company could dwell there together. This was done.

Deirdre and her foster-mother dwelt in the bothy on the mountainside without the knowledge or the suspicion of any living person about them and without anything occurring, until Deirdre was sixteen years of age. Deirdre grew like the white sapling, straight and trim as the rash on the moss. She was the creature of fairest form, of loveliest aspect, and of gentlest nature that existed between earth and heaven in all Ireland – whatever colour of hue she had before, there was nobody that looked into her face but she would blush fiery red over it.

The woman that had charge of her, gave Deirdre every information and skill of which she herself had knowledge and skill. There was not a blade of grass growing from root, nor a bird singing in the wood, nor a star shining from heaven but Deirdre had a name for it. But one thing, the woman did not wish Deirdre to have either part or parley with any single living man of the rest of the world. But on a

gloomy winter night, with black, scowling clouds, a hunter
of game was wearily travelling the hills, and what happened
but that he missed the trail of the hunt, and lost his course
and companions. A drowsiness came upon the man as he
wearily wandered over the hills, and he lay down by the side
of the beautiful green knoll in which Deirdre lived, and he
slept. The man was faint from hunger and wandering, and
benumbed with cold, and a deep sleep fell upon him. When
he lay down beside the green hill where Deirdre was, a
troubled dream came to the man, and he thought that he
enjoyed the warmth of a fairy broch, the fairies being inside
playing music. The hunter shouted out in his dream, if there
was anyone in the broch, to let him in for the Holy One's
sake. Deirdre heard the voice and said to her foster-mother:
'O foster-mother, what cry is that?' 'It is nothing at all,
Deirdre – merely the birds of the air astray and seeking each
other. But let them go past to the bosky glade. There is no
shelter or house for them here.' 'Oh, foster-mother, the bird
asked to get inside for the sake of the God of the Elements,
and you yourself tell me that anything that is asked in His
name we ought to do. If you will not allow the bird that is
benumbed with cold, and done to death with hunger, to be
let in, I do not think much of your language or your faith.
But since I respect your language and your faith, which you
taught me, I will myself let in the bird.' And Deirdre arose
and drew the bolt from the leaf of the door, and she let in
the hunter. She placed a seat in the place for sitting, food in
the place for eating, and drink in the place for drinking for
the man who came to the house. 'Oh, for dear life, you man
that came in, keep restraint on your tongue!' said the old
woman. 'It is not a great task for you to keep your mouth
shut and your tongue quiet in return for a home and the
shelter of a hearth on a gloomy winter's night.' 'Well,' said
the hunter, 'I may do that – keep my mouth shut and my
tongue quiet, since I came to the house and received hospitality from you; but by the hand of thy father and grandfather

and by your own two hands, if some other of the people of the world saw this beautiful creature you have here hid away, they would not long leave her with you, I swear.'

'What men are these you refer to?' said Deirdre.

'Well, I will tell you, young woman,' said the hunter. 'They are Naois, son of Uisnech, and Allen and Arden his two brothers.'

'What like are these men when seen, if we were to see them?' said Deirdre.

'Why, the aspect and form of the men when seen are these,' said the hunter: 'they have the colour of the raven on their hair, their skin like swan on the wave in whiteness, and their cheeks as the blood of the brindled red calf, and their speed and their leap are those of the salmon of the torrent and the deer of the grey mountainside. And Naois is head and shoulders over the rest of the people of Erin.'

'However they are,' said the nurse, 'be you off from here and continue your journey. And, King of Light and Sun! in good sooth and certainty, little are my thanks for yourself or for her that let you in!'

The hunter went away, and went straight to the palace of King Connachar. He sent word in to the king that he wished to speak to him if he pleased. The king answered the message and came out to speak to the man. 'What is the reason of your journey?' said the king to the hunter.

'I have only to tell you, O king,' said the hunter, 'that I saw the fairest creature that ever was born in Erin, and I came to tell you of it.'

'Who is this beauty and where is she to be seen, when she was not seen till you saw her, if you did see her?'

'Well, I did see her,' said the hunter. 'But, if I did, no man else can see her unless he get directions from me as to where she is dwelling.'

'And will you direct me to where she dwells? and the reward of your directing me will be as good as the reward of your message,' said the king.

'Well, I will direct you, O king, although it is likely that this will not be what they want,' said the hunter.

Connachar, King of Ulster, sent for his nearest kinsmen, and he told them of his intent. Though early rose the song of the birds mid the rocky caves and the music of the birds in the grove, earlier than that did Connachar, King of Ulster, arise, with his little troop of dear friends, in the delightful twilight of the fresh and gentle May; the dew was heavy on each bush and flower and stem, as they went to bring Deirdre forth from the green knoll where she stayed. Many a youth was there who had a lithe leaping and lissom step when they started, but whose step was faint, failing, and faltering when they reached the bothy on account of the length of the way and roughness of the road. 'Yonder, now, on the mountainside at the top of the glen is the bothy where the woman dwells, but I will not go nearer than this to the old woman,' said the hunter.

Connachar with his band of kinsfolk went up to the green knoll where Deirdre dwelt and he knocked at the door of the bothy. The nurse replied, 'No less than a king's command and a king's army could put me out of my bothy tonight. And I should be obliged to you, were you to tell who it is that wants me to open my bothy door.' 'It is I, Connachar King of Ulster.' When the poor woman heard who was at the door, she rose with haste and let in the king and all that could get in of his retinue.

When the king saw the woman that was before him that he had been in quest of, he thought he never saw in the course of the day nor in the dream of night a creature so fair as Deirdre and he gave his full heart's weight of love to her. Deirdre was raised on the topmost of the heroes' shoulder, and she and her foster-mother were brought to the Court of King Connachar of Ulster.

With the love that Connachar had for her, he wanted to marry Deirdre right off there and then, no matter what. But she said to him, 'I would be obliged to you if you will giv-

me the respite of a year and a day.' He said, 'I will grant you that, hard though it is, if you will give me your unfailing promise that you will marry me at the year's end.' And she gave the promise. Connachar got for her a woman-teacher and merry modest maidens fair that would lie down and rise with her, that would play and speak with her. Deirdre was clever in maidenly duties and wifely understanding, and Connachar thought he never saw with bodily eye a creature that pleased him more.

Deirdre and her women companions were one day out on the hillock behind the house enjoying the scene, and drinking in the sun's heat. What did they see coming but three men a-journeying. Deirdre was looking at the men that were coming, and wondering at them. When the men neared them, Deirdre remembered the words of the huntsman, and she said to herself that these were the three sons of Uisnech, and that this was Naois, he being head and shoulders taller than all the men of Erin. The three brothers went past

without taking any notice of them, without even glancing at
the young girls on the hillock. What happened but that love
for Naois struck the heart of Deirdre, so that she could not
but follow after him. She girded up her robe and went after
the men that went past the base of the knoll, leaving her
women attendants there. Allen and Arden had heard of the
woman that Connachar, King of Ulster, had with him, and
they thought that, if Naois, their brother, saw Deirdre, he
would have her himself, more especially as she was not yet
married to the King. They perceived the woman coming,
and called on one another to hasten their step as they had a
long distance to travel, and the dusk of night was coming
on. They did so. Deirdre cried: 'Naois, son of Uisnech, will
you leave me?' 'What piercing, shrill cry is that – the most
melodious my ear ever heard, and the shrillest that ever
struck my heart of all the cries I ever heard?' 'It is nothing
else but the wail of the wave-swans of Connachar,' said his
brothers. 'No! yonder is a woman's cry of distress,' said
Naois, and he swore he would not go further until he saw
from whom the cry came, and Naois turned back. Naois
and Deirdre met, and Deirdre kissed Naois three times, and
a kiss each to his brothers. With the confusion that she was
in, Deirdre went into a crimson blaze of fire, and her colour
came and went as rapidly as the movement of the aspen by
the streamside. Naois thought he never saw a fairer creature,
and Naois gave Deirdre the love that he never before gave to
thing, to vision, or to creature but to herself.

Then Naois placed Deirdre on the topmost height of his
shoulder, and told his brothers to keep up their pace, and
they kept up their pace. Naois thought that it would not be
wise for him to remain in Erin on account of the way in
which Connachar, King of Ulster, his uncle's son, would
turn against him because of the woman, though he had not
married her; and Naois crossed over to Scotland. He reached
the side of Loch Ness and made his habitation near there.
He could kill the salmon of the torrent from out his own

door, and the deer of the grey gorge from out his window. Naois and Deirdre and Allen and Arden dwelt in a tower, and they were happy so long a time as they were there.

By this time the end of the year came at which Deirdre had promised to marry Connachar, King of Ulster. Connachar made up his mind to take Deirdre away by the sword whether she was married to Naois or not. So he prepared a great and gleeful feast. He sent word far and wide through Erin to all his kinspeople to come to the feast. Connachar thought to himself that Naois would not come even if he should bid him; and the scheme that arose in his mind was to send for his father's brother, Ferchar Mac Ro, and to send him on an embassy to Naois. He did so; and Connachar said to Ferchar, 'Tell Naois, son of Uisnech, that I am setting forth a great and gleeful feast to my friends and kinspeople throughout the wide extent of Erin, and that I shall not have rest by day nor sleep by night if he and Allen and Arden will not partake of the feast.'

Ferchar Mac Ro and his three sons went on their journey, and reached the tower where Naois was dwelling by the side of Loch Etive. The sons of Uisnech gave a cordial kindly welcome to Ferchar Mac Ro and his three sons, and asked him the news from Erin. 'The best news that I have for you,' said the hardy hero, 'is that Connachar, King of Ulster, is setting forth a great sumptuous feast to his friends and kinspeople throughout the wide extent of Erin, and he has vowed by the earth beneath him, by the high heaven above him, and by the sun that wends to the west, that he will have no rest by day nor sleep by night if the sons of Uisnech, the sons of his own father's brother, will not come back to the land of their home and the soil of their nativity, and to the feast likewise, and he has sent us on an embassy to invite you.'

'We will go with you,' said Naois.

'We will,' said his brothers.

But Deirdre did not wish to go with Ferchar Mac Ro, and

she tried every prayer to turn Naois from going back with him, saying:

'I saw a vision, Naois, and you may interpret it to me,' said Deirdre – then she sang:

> O Naois, son of Uisnech, hear
> What was shown in a dream to me.
>
> There came three white doves out of the South
> Flying over the sea,
> And drops of honey were in their mouth
> From the hive of the honey-bee.
>
> O Naois, son of Uisnech, hear,
> What was shown in a dream to me.
>
> I saw three grey hawks out of the South
> Come flying over the sea,
> And the red red drops they bare in their mouth
> They were dearer than life to me.

Said Naois: –

> It is nought but the fear of woman's heart,
> And a dream of the night, Deirdre.

'The day that Connachar sent the invitation to his feast will be unlucky for us if we don't go, O Deirdre.'

'You will go there,' said Ferchar Mac Ro; 'and if Connachar show kindness to you, show ye kindness to him; and if he will display wrath towards you, display ye wrath towards him, and I and my three sons will be with you.'

'We will,' said Daring Drop. 'We will,' said Hardy Holly. 'We will,' said Fiallan the Fair.

'I have three sons, and they are three heroes, and in any harm or danger that may befall you, they will be with you, and I myself will be along with them.' And Ferchar Mac Ro gave his vow and his word in presence of his arms that, in any harm or danger that came in the way of the sons of Uisnech, he and his three sons would not leave head on live body in Erin, despite sword or helmet, spear or shield, blade or mail, be they ever so good.

Deirdre was still most unwilling to leave Scotland, but she went with Naois. Deirdre wept tears in showers and she sang:

> *Dear is the land, the land over there,*
> *Scotland full of woods and lakes;*
> *Bitter to my heart is leaving thee,*
> *But I go away with Naois.*

Ferchar Mac Ro did not stop till he got the sons of Uisnech away with him, despite the suspicion of Deirdre.

> *The coracle was put to sea,*
> *The sail was hoisted to it;*
> *And the second morrow they arrived*
> *On the white shores of Erin.*

As soon as the sons of Uisnech landed in Erin, Ferchar Mac Ro sent word to Connachar, King of Ulster, that the men whom he wanted were come, and let him now show kindness to them. 'Well,' said Connachar, 'I did not expect that the sons of Uisnech would come, though I sent for them, and I am not quite ready to receive them. But there is a house down yonder where I keep strangers, and let them go down to it today, and my house will be ready for them tomorrow.'

But Connachar then felt it long that he was not getting word as to how matters were going on for those down in the house of the strangers. 'Go you, Gelban Grednach, son of Lochlin's King, go you down and bring me information as to whether her former hue and complexion are on Deirdre. If they are, I will take her back with edge of blade and point of sword, and if not, let Naois, son of Uisnech, have her for himself,' said Connachar.

Gelban, the cheering and charming son of Lochlin's King, went down to the place of the strangers, where Deirdre and the sons of Uisnech were staying. He looked in through the

peep-hole on the door-leaf. Now she that he gazed upo
used to go into a crimson blaze of blushes when anyon
looked at her. Naois looked at Deirdre and knew tha
someone was looking at her from the back of the door-lea
He seized one of the dice on the table before him and fired
through the peep-hole, and knocked the eye out of Gelba
Grednach the Cheerful and Charming, right through th
back of his head. Gelban returned back to the palace o
King Connachar.

'You were cheerful, charming, going away, but you ar
cheerless, charmless, returning. What has happened to yo
Gelban? But have you seen her, and are Deirdre's hue an
complexion as before?' said Connachar.

'Well, I have seen Deirdre, and I saw her also truly, an
while I was looking at her through the peep-hole on th
door, Naois, son of Uisnech, knocked out my eye with on
of the dice in his hand. But of a truth and verity, althoug
he put out even my eye, I would have liked still to remai
looking at her with the other eye, were it not for the hurr
you told me to be in,' said Gelban.

'That is true,' said Connachar; 'let three hundred brav
heroes go down to the abode of the strangers, and let the
bring hither to me Deirdre, and kill the rest.'

Connachar ordered three hundred active heroes to g
down to the abode of the strangers and to take Deirdre u
with them and kill the rest. 'The pursuit is coming,' said Dei
dre.

'Yes, but I will myself go out and stop the pursuit,' sai
Naois.

'It is not you, but we that will go,' said Daring Drop, an
Hardy Holly, and Fiallan the Fair; 'it is to us that our fathe
entrusted your defence from harm and danger when h
himself left for home.' And the gallant youths, full nobl
full manly, full handsome, with beautiful brown locks, wer
forth girt with battle arms fit for fierce fight and clothe
with combat dress for fierce contest fit, which wa

burnished, bright, brilliant, bladed, blazing, on which were many pictures of beasts and birds and creeping things, lions and lithe-limbed tigers, brown eagle and harrying hawk and adder fierce; and the young heroes laid low three-thirds of the company.

Connachar came out in haste and cried with wrath: 'Who is there on the battlefield, slaughtering my men?'

'We, the three sons of Ferchar Mac Ro.'

'Well,' said the king, 'I will give free passage to your grandfather, free passage to your father, and free passage each to you three brothers, if you come over to my side to-night.'

'Well, Connachar, we will not accept that offer from you nor thank you for it. Greater by far do we prefer to go home to our father and tell the deeds of heroism we have done, than accept anything on these terms from you. Naois, son of Uisnech, and Allen and Arden are as nearly related to yourself as they are to us, though you are so keen to shed their blood, and you would shed our blood also, Connachar.' And the noble, manly, handsome youths with beautiful brown locks returned inside. 'We are now,' said they, 'going home to tell our father that you are now safe from the hands of the king.' And the youths all fresh and tall and lithe and beautiful, went home to their father to tell that the sons of Uisnech were safe. This happened at the parting of the day and night in the morning twilight time, and Naois said they must go away, leave that house, and return to Scotland.

Naois and Deirdre, Allan and Arden started to return to Scotland. Word then came to the king that the company he was in pursuit of were gone. The king now sent for Duanan Gacha Druid, the best magician he had, and he spoke to him as follows: – 'Much wealth have I spent on you, Duanan Gacha Druid, to give schooling and learning and magic mystery to you. Must these people get away from me today without care, without consideration or regard for me, without chance of overtaking them, and you without power to stop them?'

'Well, I will stop them,' said the magician, 'until the company you send in pursuit return.' And the magician placed a wood before them through which no man could go but the sons of Uisnech marched through the wood without halt or hesitation, and Deirdre held onto Naois's hand.

'What is the good of that? that will not stop them,' said Connachar. 'They are off without bending of their feet or stopping of their step, without heed or respect to me, and I am without power to keep up to them or opportunity to turn them back this night.'

'I will try another plan on them,' said the druid; and he placed before them a grey sea instead of a green plain. The three heroes stripped and tied their clothes behind their heads, and Naois placed Deirdre on the top of his shoulder.

> They stretched their sides to the stream,
>   And sea and land were to them the same,
> The rough grey ocean was the same
>   As meadow-land green and plain.

'Though that be good, O Duanan, it will not make the heroes return,' said Connachar; 'they are gone without regard for me, and without honour to me, and without power on my part to pursue them or to force them to return this night.'

'We shall try another method on them, since yon one did not stop them,' said the druid. And the druid froze the grey ridged sea into hard rocky knobs, the sharpness of sword being on the one edge and the poison power of adders on the other. Then Arden cried that he was getting tired, and nearly giving over. 'Come you, Arden, and sit on my right shoulder,' said Naois. Arden came and sat on Naois's shoulder. Arden was long in this posture when he died; but though he was dead, Naois would not let him go. Allen then cried out that he was getting faint and nigh-well giving up

When Naois heard his prayer, he gave forth the piercing sigh of death, and asked Allen to lay hold of him and he would bring him to land.

But Allen was not long thus when the weakness of death came on him and his hold failed. Naois looked around, and when he saw his two well-beloved brothers dead, he cared not whether he lived or died, and he gave forth the bitter sigh of death, and his own heart burst.

'They are gone,' said Duanan Gacha Druid to the king, 'and I have done what you desired me. The sons of Uisnech are dead and they will trouble you no more; and you have your wife hale and whole to yourself.'

'Blessings for that upon you and may the good results accrue to me, Duanan. I count it no loss what I spent in the schooling and teaching of you. Now dry up the flood, and let me see if I can behold Deirdre,' said Connachar. And Duanan Gacha Druid dried up the flood from the plain and the three sons of Uisnech were lying together dead, without breath of life, side by side on the green meadow plain and Deirdre bending above showering down her tears.

Then Deirdre said this lament: 'Fair one, loved one, flower of beauty; beloved upright and strong; beloved noble and modest warrior. Fair one, blue-eyed, beloved of thy wife; lovely to me at the trysting-place came thy clear voice through the woods of Ireland. I cannot eat or smile henceforth. Break not today, my heart: soon enough shall I lie within my grave. Strong are the waves of sorrow, but stronger is sorrow's self, Connachar.'

The people then gathered round the heroes' bodies and asked Connachar what was to be done with them. The order that he gave was that they should dig a pit and put the three brothers in it side by side.

Deirdre kept sitting on the brink of the grave, constantly asking the gravediggers to dig the pit wide and free. When the bodies of the brothers were put in the grave, Deirdre said: –

Come over hither, Naois, my love,
Let Arden close to Allen lie;
If the dead had any sense to feel,
Ye would have made a place for Deirdre.

The men did as she told them. She jumped into the grave
and lay down by Naois, and she was dead by his side.

The king ordered the body to be raised from out the
grave and to be buried on the other side of the loch. It was
done as the king bade, and the pit closed. Thereupon a fir
shoot grew out of the grave of Deirdre and a fir shoot from
the grave of Naois, and the two shoots united in a knot
above the loch. The king ordered the shoots to be cut down,
and this was done twice, until, at the third time, the wife
whom the king had married caused him to stop this work of
evil and to cease his vengeance on the remains of the dead.

THE COMING OF FINN
Standish O'Grady

It was the Eve of Samhain, which we Christians call All Hallows' Eve.

The King of Ireland, Conn, the Hundred-Fighter, sat at supper in his palace at Tara. All his chiefs and mighty men were with him. On his right hand was his only son, Art the Solitary, so called because he had no brothers. The sons of Morna, who kept the boy Finn out of his rights and were at the time trying to kill him if they could, were here too. Chief amongst them was Gaul mac Morna, a huge and strong warrior, and Captain of all the Fians ever since that battle in which Finn's father had been killed.

And Gaul's men were with him. The great long table was spread for supper. A thousand wax candles shed their light through the chamber, and caused the vessels of gold, silver and bronze to shine. Yet, though it was a great feast, none of these warriors seemed to care about eating or drinking; every face was sad, and there was little conversation, and no music. It seemed as if they were expecting some calamity. Conn's sceptre, which was a plain staff of silver, lay beside him on the table, and there was a canopy of bright bronze over his head. Gaul mac Morna, Captain of the Fians, sat at the other end of the long table. Every warrior wore a bright banqueting mantle of silk or satin, scarlet or crimson, blue, green, or purple, fastened on the breast either with a great brooch or with a pin of gold or silver. Yet, though their raiment was bright and gay, and though all the usual instruments of festivity were there, and a thousand tall candles shed their light over the scene, no one looked happy.

Then was heard a low sound like thunder, and the earth seemed to tremble, and after that they distinctly heard a footfall like the slow, deliberate tread of a giant. These footfalls sent a chill into every heart, and every face, gloomy before, was now pale.

The King leaned past his son Art the Solitary, and said to a certain Druid who sat beside Art, 'Is this the son of Midna come before his time?' 'It is not,' said the Druid, 'but it is the man who is to conquer Midna. One is coming to Tara this night before whose glory all other glory shall wax dim.'

Shortly after that they heard the voices of the doorkeepers raised in argument, as if they would repel from the hall someone who wished to enter, then a slight scuffle, and after that a strange figure entered the chamber. He was dressed in the skins of wild beasts, and wore over his shoulders a huge thick cloak of wild boars' skins, fastened on the breast with a white tusk of the same animal. He wore a shield and two spears. Though of huge stature his face was that of a boy, smooth on the cheeks and lips. It was white and ruddy, and very handsome. His hair was like refined gold. A light seemed to go out from him, before which the candles burned dim. It was Finn.

He stood in the doorway, and cried out in a strong and sonorous, but musical, voice:

'O Conn the Hundred-Fighter, son of Felimy, the righteous

178

son of Tuthal the legitimate, O King of the Kings of Erin, a wronged and disinherited youth, possessing nowhere one rood of his patrimony, a wanderer and an outlaw, a hunter of the wildernesses and mountains, claims hospitality of you, illustrious prince, on the eve of the great festival of Samhain.'

'You are welcome whoever you are,' answered the King, 'and doubly welcome because you are unfortunate. I think, such is your face and form, that you are the son of some mighty king on whom disaster has fallen undeserved. The high gods of Erin grant you speedy restoration and strong vengeance of your many wrongs. Sit here, O noble youth, between me and my only son, Art, heir to my kingdom.'

An attendant took his weapons from the youth and hung them on the wall with the rest, and Finn sat down between the King of Ireland and his only son. Choice food was set before him, which he ate, and old ale, which he drank. From the moment he entered, no one thought of anything but him. When Finn had made an end of eating and drinking, he said to the King:

'O illustrious prince, though it is not right for a guest to even seem to observe anything amiss, or not as it should be, in the hall of his entertainer, yet the sorrow of a kindly host is a sorrow, too, to his guest, and sometimes unawares the man of the house finds succour and help in the stranger. There is sorrow in this chamber of festivity. If anyone who is dear to you and your people happens to be dead, I can do nothing. But I say it, and it is not a vain boast, that even if a person is at the point of death, I can restore him to life and health, for there are marvellous powers of life-giving in my two hands.'

Conn the Hundred-Fighter answered, 'Our grief is not such as you suppose; and why should I not tell a cause of shame, which is known far and wide? This, then, is the reason of our being together, and the gloom which is over us. There is a mighty enchanter whose dwelling is in the haunted mountains of Slieve Gullion in the north. His name is Allen, son of Midna, and his enmity to me is as great as his power. Once every year, at this season, it is his pleasure to burn Tara. Descending out of his wizard haunts, he stands over against the city and shoots balls of fire out of his mouth against it, till it is consumed. Then he goes away, mocking and triumphant. This annual building of Tara, only to be annually consumed, is a shame to me, and till this enchanter declared war against me, I have lived without reproach.'

'But,' said Finn, 'how is it that your young warriors, valiant and swift, do not repel him, or kill him?'

'Alas!' said Conn, 'all our valour is in vain against this man. Our hosts encompass Tara on all sides, keeping watch and ward when the fatal night comes. Then the son of Midna plays on his Druidic instrument of music, on his magic pipe and his magic lyre, and as the fairy music falls on our ears, our eyelids grow heavy, and soon all subside upon the grass in deep slumber. So comes this man against the city and shoots his fire-balls against it, and utterly consumes it. Nine years he has burnt Tara in that manner and this is the tenth. At midnight tonight he will come and do the same. Last year (though it was a shame to me that I who am the high King over all Ireland, should not be able myself to defend Tara) I summoned Gaul mac Morna and all the Fians to my assistance. They came, but the pipe and lyre of the son of Midna prevailed over them too, so that Tara was burned as at other times. Nor have we any reason to believe that the son of Midna will not burn the city again tonight, as he did last year. All the women and children have been sent out of Tara this day. We are only men of war here, waiting for the time. That, O noble youth, is why we are sad. The 'Pillars of Tara' are broken, and the might of the Fians is as nothing before the power of this man.'

'What shall be my reward if I kill this man and save Tara?' asked Finn.

'Your just inheritance,' answered the King, 'be it great or small, and whether it lies in Ireland or beyond Ireland; and for securities I give you my son Art and Gaul mac Morna and the Chief of the Fians.'

Gaul and the captains of the Fianna consented to that arrangement, though reluctantly, for they had misgivings about who the great youth might be.

After that all arose and armed themselves and ringed Tara round with horse and foot, and thrice Conn the Hundred-Fighter raised his awful regal voice, urging great vigilance upon his people, and thrice Gaul mac Morna did the same, addressing the Fians, and after that they all filled their ears with wax and wool, and kept a stern and fierce watch, and many of them thrust the points of their swords into their flesh.

Now Finn was alone in the banqueting chamber after the rest had gone out, and he washed his face and his hands in pure water, and he took from the bag that was at his belt the instruments of divination and magic, which had been his father's, and what use he made of them is not known; but ere long a man stood before him, holding a spear in one hand and a blue mantle in the other. There were twenty nails of gold of Arabia in the spear. The nails glittered like stars, and twinkled with live light as stars do in a frosty night, and the blade of it quivered like a tongue of white fire. From haft to blade-point that spear was alive. There were voices in it too, and the war-tunes of the enchanted races of Erin, whom they called the Tuatha De Danann, sounded from it. The mantle, too, was a wonder, for innumerable stars twinkled in the blue, and the likeness of clouds passed through it. The man gave these things to Finn, and when he had instructed him in their use, he disappeared.

Then Finn arose and armed himself, and took the magic spear and mantle and went out. There was a ring of flame round Tara that night, for the Fians and the warriors of

Conn had torches in their hands, and all the royal buildings of Tara showed clear in the light, and also the dark serpentine course of the Boyne river, which flowed past Tara on the north; and there, standing silent and alert, were the innumerable warriors of all Erin, with spear and shield, keeping watch and ward against the son of Midna, also the Four Pillars of Tara in four dense divisions around the high King, even Conn the Hundred-Fighter.

Finn stood with his back to the palace, which was called the House-of-the-going-round-of-Mead, between the palace and Conn, and he grasped the magic spear strongly with one hand and the mantle with the other.

As midnight drew nigh, he heard far away in the north, out of the mountains of Slieve Gullion, a fairy tune played, soft, low, and slow, as if on a silver flute; and at the same time the roar of Conn the Hundred-Fighter, and the voice of Gaul like thunder, and the responsive shouts of the captains, and the clamour of the host, for the host shouted all together, and clashed their swords against their shields in fierce defiance, when in spite of all obstructions the fairy music of the enchanter began to steal into their souls. That shout was heard all over Ireland, echoing from sea to sea, and the hollow buildings of Tara reverberated to the uproar. Yet through it all could be heard the low, slow, delicious music that came from Slieve Gullion. Finn put the point of the spear to his forehead. It burned him like fire, yet his stout heart did not fail. Then the roar of the host slowly faded away as in a dream, though the captains were still shouting, and two-thirds of the torches fell to the ground. And now, succeeding the flute music, sounded the music of a stringed instrument exceedingly sweet. Finn pressed the cruel spearhead closer to his forehead, and saw every torch fall, save one which wavered as if held by a drunken man, and beneath it a giant figure that reeled and tottered and strove in vain to keep its feet. It was Conn the Hundred-Fighter. As he fell there was a roar as of many waters; it was the

182

ocean mourning for the high King's fall. Finn passed through the fallen men and stood alone on the dark hillside. He heard the feet of the enchanter splashing through the Boyne, and saw his huge form ascending the slopes of Tara. When the enchanter saw that all was silent and dark there he laughed and from his mouth blew a red fire-ball, to set the city in flames. Finn caught the fire-ball in the magic mantle. The enchanter blew a second and a third, and Finn caught them both. The man saw that his power over Tara was at an end, and that his magic arts had been defeated. On the third occasion he saw Finn's face, and recognized his conqueror. He turned to flee, and though slow was his coming, swifter than the wind was his going, that he might recover the protection of his enchanted palace before the 'fair-faced youth clad in skins' should overtake him. Finn let fall the mantle as he had been instructed, and pursued him, but in vain. Soon he perceived that he could not possibly overtake the swift enchanter. Then he was aware that the magic spear struggled in his hand like a hound on a leash. 'Go, then, if you will,' he said, and, poising, cast the spear from him. It shot through the dark night, hissing and screaming. There was a track of fire behind it. Finn followed, and on the threshold of the enchanted palace, he found the body of the son of Midna. He was quite dead, with the blood pouring through a wound in the middle of his back; but the spear was gone. Finn drew his sword and cut off the enchanter's head, and returned with it to Tara. When he came to the spot where he had dropped the mantle it was not seen, but smoke and flame issued there from a hole in the ground. That hole was twenty feet deep in the earth, and at the bottom of it there was a fire always from that night, and it was never extinguished. It was called the fire of the son of Midna. It was in a depression on the north side of the hill of Tara, called the Glen of the Mantle, Glen-a-Brat.

Finn, bearing the head, passed through the sleepers into the palace and spiked the head on his own spear, and drove the spear-end into the ground at Conn's end of the great hall. Then the sickness and faintness of death came upon Finn, also a great horror and despair overshadowed him, so that he was about to give himself up for utterly lost. Yet he recalled one of his marvellous attributes, and approaching a silver vessel, into which pure water ever flowed and which was always full, he made a cup with his two hands and, lifting it to his mouth, drank, and the blood began to circulate in his veins again, and strength returned to his limbs, and the cheerful hue of rosy health to his cheeks.

Having rested himself sufficiently he went forth and shouted to the sleeping host, and called the captains by their names, beginning with Conn. They awoke and rose up, though dazed and stupid, for it was difficult for any man, no matter how he had stopped his ears, to avoid hearing Finn when he sent forth his voice of power. They were astonished to find that Tara was still standing, for though the night was dark, the palaces and temples, all of hewn timber, were brilliantly coloured and of many hues, for in those days men delighted in splendid colours.

When the captains came together, Finn said, 'I have slain Midna.' 'Where is his head?' they asked, not because they disbelieved him, but because the heads of men slain in battle were always brought away for trophies. 'Come and see,' answered Finn. Conn and his only son and Gaul mac Morna followed the young hero into the palace, where the spear-long waxen candles were still burning, and when they saw the head of the son of Midna impaled there at the end of the hall, the head of the man whom they believed to be immortal and not to be wounded or conquered, they were filled with great joy, and praised their deliverer and paid him many compliments.

'Who are you, O brave youth?' said Conn. 'Surely you are the son of some great king or champion, for heroic feats like these are not performed by the sons of inconsiderable and unknown men.'

Then Finn flung back his cloak of wild boars' skins, and holding his father's treasure-bag in his hand before them all, cried in a loud voice:

'I am Finn, the son of Cool, the son of Trenmor, the son of Basna; I am he whom the sons of Morna have been seeking to destroy from the time that I was born; and here tonight, O King of the Kings of Erin, I claim the fulfilment of your promise, and the restoration of my inheritance, which is the Fian leadership of Fail. Thereupon Gaul mac Morna put his right hand into Finn's, and became his man. Then his brothers and his sons, and the sons of his brothers, did so in succession, and after that all the chief men of the Fians did the same, and that night Finn was solemnly and surely installed in the Fian leadership of Erin, and put in possession of all the woods and forests and waste places, and all the hills and mountains and promontories, and all the streams and rivers of Erin, and the harbours and estuaries and the harbour-dues of the merchants, and all ships and boats and galleys with their mariners, and all that pertained of old time to the Fian leadership of Fail.

HOW FINN FOUND BRAN
Elizabeth Grierson

In the latter part of his life Finn was always followed by an enormous hound, who answered to the name of Bran. It not only accompanied him when he went a-hunting, but it went with him to battle, and woe betide the man or beast who had to fight against it.

For not only were its teeth long and sharp, but it had one great claw which was sharper than all the rest, and besides being sharper, it was venomous also; which means that, if it raised its foot and struck anyone with this claw, the wound was poisoned, and would not heal, but festered away until it destroyed the person's life.

Bran did not use this claw very often, however, for Finn had no wish to kill more people than he could help, so he had a golden shoe made for it, and the great hound always wore this shoe unless Finn were in danger, when he would call the faithful creature to his side, and take it off. Then, with open mouth and uplifted claw, Bran would fly at his master's enemies, and speedily overcome them.

How Finn Found Bran

Folk said that Bran came out of Faerie-land, and when you have read this story you will be inclined to say that they spoke true.

It chanced one day that Finn went out walking with no one to attend him; and as he walked, he met a man whom he had never seen before.

This was an unusual thing, for the great Chief knew everyone who lived in his dominions, so he stopped and asked the stranger what he was seeking, and where he was going.

'I am a good servant in search of employment,' answered the man.

'In what way are you a good servant?' asked Finn, for the fellow spoke as if he knew that what he said was true.

'I never slept a wink in my life,' answered he, 'and the master who hires me may find it useful to have someone who is always awake.'

'That is true,' said Finn, and he hired him on the spot.

He had not gone much farther before he met another man, whose face was also strange to him.

'Who are you, and what do you seek?' he asked.

The man answered in the same words that the first had done: 'I am a good servant in search of employment.'

'And what can you do?' said Finn, wondering what this fellow's answer would be.

'I hear all things,' answered the stranger. 'I can even hear the grass coming through the ground.'

'In truth, a useful accomplishment,' said Finn, and he hired this lad also.

Soon a third stranger made his appearance, and the Chief, half amused, half amazed, asked him his business.

His answer was once more the same. 'I am a good servant seeking employment.'

'And what can you do?'

'I am good at keeping hold of what I have got. When once I get a grip of anything, I never let it go.'

'Just the man for me,' said Finn, and he hired him too.

No sooner had he done so than a fourth man appeared, and the same question was asked, and the same answer given.

This man said that he was such a good thief that he would undertake to steal an egg from a heron's nest, while the bird was standing by, without its knowing it.

'If things go on like this, I shall soon have men who are able to do everything,' said Finn, and he engaged this clever thief on the spot.

Soon a fifth man appeared, and he claimed to be able to climb a wall, even although it was covered with the skins of eels, which, as everyone knows, are the most slippery things in the world.

He also was added to the band.

Then a sixth stranger came, who boasted that every stone he threw became part of a stone and lime wall.

'A cheap and easy way of building,' said Finn. 'It seems to me this good fortune cannot continue,' and he hired this last man without delay.

But there was still a seventh stranger to come, and he was such a good marksman that he promised to shoot an arrow at any object, and not to miss it by even a hair's breadth.

So he too was engaged, and after him came no more.

Finn continued his walk with his seven new servants behind him, and presently they came in sight of a King's Palace.

Then Finn noticed for the first time that he had walked far farther than he had intended, and that night was beginning to fall, and he was far from his own home.

So he went up to the Palace, and knocked at the great door, and when the porter opened it, he desired him to tell his Royal Master that the Chief of the Fian, Finn, the son of Cool, was without, and that he begged of him a night's shelter for himself and his men.

Now the name of Finn was known throughout the length

and breadth of Erin, and the King was delighted that such a mighty hero should come to his Palace, and he came out himself to welcome him.

But when he had brought Finn into his great hall, and ordered bread and wine, and all manner of meats to be set before him, Finn noticed how sad and downcast he was, and asked him if anything was troubling him.

'Ay,' said the King, 'I am sorely troubled. For I have had two children, and both of them have been stolen away, as soon as they were born, by faeries, or demons, or some such uncanny creatures. And this night a third child has been born to the Queen and myself, and our hearts are heavy within us, for we feel sure that this babe will be carried away also; for when one has to do with witchcraft or faerie folk, no watch that mortal man can keep avails against them. And something tells me that this child too will surely be stolen, even if we never take our eyes off his cradle.'

'That shall he not,' said Finn, 'so long as my men and I are in the house.' And he went out and called to his seven new servants.

He told them the story which he had just heard, and then he looked at the man who had never slept a wink in his life.

'This night you must sit in the Queen's chamber,' he said, 'and if ever you watched in your life, watch now.'

Then he beckoned to the man who could hear the grass coming through the earth. 'And you must sit in the Queen's ante-chamber,' he said, 'and if ever you listened in your life, listen now.'

'And you,' he went on, turning to the third man, the one who kept a tight grip of what he laid hold of. 'You had better sit near the baby's cradle, and whatever comes, be it giant, or witch, or imp, or demon, grip it with all your might.'

The men did as they were bid, and the King's household settled down for the night, though not to sleep; everyone was too anxious for that, and everyone set themselves to keep awake and watch.

For some time all went well, but just as the clock struck twelve Finn's servant in the ante-room stirred uneasily.

'My eyes begin to feel wondrous heavy,' he said.

'And so do ours,' chimed in the crowd of courtiers and attendants who were watching along with him.

Finn's servant stooped down and listened intently. 'I can hear far off distant music,' he said. 'Do you know where it comes from?'

At these words everyone started and looked at one another with terror written on their faces.

''Tis the Musical Harper,' they cried, 'we are undone. We have often heard tell of his wonderful music, although we have never heard it with our own ears; for it lulls everyone to sleep long before he approaches. And how can we watch if we be asleep?'

'I will take care of that,' cried the servant who sat in the Queen's chamber, 'for this Musical Harper may harp all night if he likes close to my ear, 'twill make no difference to me;' and he rose up, and went round all the rooms in the Palace, shaking the people he found there, so that they could not go to sleep.

Meanwhile the third man, he who was noted for his wonderful grip, who was sitting at the side of the baby's cradle, saw an enormously long skinny arm come right through the wall, and reach over to where the infant lay.

'Ah, you'd steal the Prince, would you?' he cried. 'Then feel the strength of my muscles,' and he jumped up and took tight hold of the mysterious hand.

At this it was drawn back with such a jerk that Finn's servant was pulled half out of the window. He held bravely on, however, and pulled, and pulled, until, with a crash, the arm parted from its unseen body, and the servant fell back on the floor gasping, grasping it tightly to his breast.

Everyone pressed forward in delight to look at it, for they felt that, now that it had been torn off, there was little risk that its crippled owner would try again to steal the baby.

Alas! alas! In their excitement they forgot to be watchful, and in an instant another long skinny hand was thrust into the room, and, passing over their heads, lifted the baby from its cradle, and was instantly withdrawn, leaving them staring at the wall through which it had passed, in horror-stricken silence.

When they came to themselves they rushed outside and ran madly up and down, seeking in vain for the lost child, but it had vanished completely.

Of course, as you may imagine, the poor King and Queen were almost heartbroken, while Finn could hardly find words in which to express his sorrow and vexation.

'I promised to guard the babe,' said he, 'and now, after all my promises, it's been carried off before our eyes.'

He strode across the room to where the King stood, trying to stifle his grief beside the empty cradle. 'May the sky make a nest in my head, and the earth a hollow in my feet, if I do not find the child for you,' he said solemnly.

Then, without wasting more words, Finn called his seven servants together, and passed in silence through the open door, and turned his face in the direction of home.

Now, down by the sea-shore, near the King's castle, was a wonderfully strong boat, which had been seven years and seven days a-building, and it had just been finished and newly tarred.

''Tis well that everything is ready,' Finn said to the workmen, 'for tomorrow I intend to set out in this boat to sail the proud seas.'

And accordingly, next day, he called together the seven servants whom he had met so strangely, and ordered them to make ready to accompany him.

'I am going to a strange land,' he said, 'perhaps I will find you useful there.'

So the eight of them made ready, and that same evening they climbed into the boat, and pushed off from the shore.

They sailed and they sailed, until at last, after many days, they came in sight of a wild and rocky country.

'This is the land I spoke of,' said Finn; 'here will we disembark, and see what we can discover.'

So they jumped ashore, and pulled up the boat on to the green grass, and then, having made it fast, they set out to explore.

At first they saw nothing but bare and desolate country, but at last they caught sight of a house, and when they came near it, they found that the walls, instead of being covered with mortar, were all covered with eel-skins.

'Ha!' said Finn, his eyes kindling, 'it looks as if one of my men would be useful here. Come, fellow,' he added, turning to the man who was good at climbing, 'climb up to the top of that house, and peep down the chimney, and see what you can see.'

Without a moment's hesitation the servant did as he was bid, and it was plain that he had not boasted of his skill in vain, for he went up the slippery eel-skin as if it had been a ladder.

He put one eye to the top of the chimney; then he drew back quickly, and beckoned to Finn to come close up under the wall.

'Master, Master!' he whispered joyously, 'I think we have found what we came to seek. For there is a Giant seated within. He is great and terrible, with one huge eye which glows like a furnace in the middle of his forehead. And, moreover, he has only one arm, and he is sitting gazing at an infant which he is holding in the palm of his hand, while other two children are playing at his feet.'

Then Finn looked round quickly, 'Where is the man who can steal an egg from the nest while the heron is looking on?' he asked.

Another servant stepped forward.

'If ever you stole well, steal well now,' said Finn. 'Put in your hand, and take the babes before the Monster has time to mark what is happening.'

The man did as he was bid. He lifted the latch and slipped into the house, and stealing noiselessly up behind the Giant, he seized the two boys who were playing on the floor, and the baby who was lying on his enormous palm; and he did all this so quietly, and in such a wonderfully stealthy manner, that the Giant never noticed him, but simply sat and rubbed his eye, and wondered where the children had gone to.

As the man was stealing away out of the room, he happened to notice three fine puppies which were lying curled up on a piece of matting in the corner.

'I may as well take these puppies while I am about it,' he said to himself, 'they seem fine dogs, and perchance my master would like them.'

So as he passed, he lifted the puppies, and then he crept noiselessly out of the door, shutting it softly behind him.

As you may think, Finn was overjoyed to see that his servant had accomplished his errand so successfully, but he hardly took time to speak to him, for he knew that the

instant the Giant realized that the children were really gone, he would rush out to look for them. So, taking one child in his arms, and ordering his men to keep close together, he turned and set out at their head in the direction of the sea.

They had not gone very far, however, before they heard a low, deep noise behind them, as if a dog were baying, and looking back, they saw a great tawny hound coming after them, with eyes that glowed like lamps, and deep-hanging jaws. And the curious thing about this hound was, that as it ran, it lifted one of its forefeet high in the air, as if it would strike some object in front of it.

'Quick! You that can throw stones, and turn them into a stone and lime wall,' cried Finn sharply, for he knew that if the hound overtook them, it was likely to tear one or other of them in pieces.

The man he spoke to began picking up stones as fast as he could, and throwing them in the direction of the advancing animal.

And, to everyone's amazement, wherever a stone fell there sprang up, as if by magic, a great piece of solid wall.

But no matter how high walls are, they do not check the progress of furious dogs; and as quickly as one wall sprang up, the hound jumped over it, so that it soon became plain that they could not hope to stop her in that way.

'Give her one of her puppies,' shouted Finn, for he did not want to lose the children for the sake of a dog.

So one of the puppies was set down on the ground and left behind, while the whole company hurried on as fast as they could.

When the great hound came to the tiny creature she stopped, and sniffed it all over, wagging her tail with joy, but she only paused in her chase for a minute or two, then she left the puppy behind and bounded onwards.

Finn looked over his shoulder. It was clear that she was gaining on them.

'Give her another,' he cried. So another puppy was left behind. This time the mother seemed satisfied, for she stopped her pursuit and remained where she was, fondling her baby with little cries of contentment.

Meanwhile Finn and his company had reached the place where the boat was lying, and had dragged it down to the water's edge and launched it, and were rowing away towards Erin as fast as they could.

They rowed, and they rowed, until at last they laid by their oars for a time, thinking they were quite safe from pursuit.

But when they looked behind them they saw something weird and strange, following them far away in the distance.

It was as though the sea were all on fire, with flashing streaks of light darting about in all directions, and in the middle of the light they could see that the water was foaming and frothing as if someone were beating it into fury.

This strange thing came on and on, until at last it was so

near that one of the men called out, 'It is the Giant; I can see his great face, and his one eye fixed on us, as if he would dearly like to destroy us.'

'And destroy us he surely will,' said Finn, 'if he reaches us. One touch of his little finger will be enough to wreck the boat. But we will outdo him yet! Where is the man who can work such wonders with his bow and arrow?'

In an instant the man was beside him, his bowstring at his ear. Straight and swift flew the arrow, and entered the Giant's eye.

The Monster uttered a cry of rage and pain, but still he swam on, and still the awful lights played round about him, and still the water rose high in the air.

'Shoot again,' said Finn, and once more the man drew his bow. This time the Giant was vanquished, for he threw up his one remaining arm in the air, and with a hoarse cry sank down dead.

Then were the hearts of Finn and his men filled with joy, for they knew that their dangers were at last overcome, and that they would reach Erin in safety.

And in due time they did so, and carried the three children in triumph to the King's Palace.

When the King saw them coming, and realized that Finn had brought back, not only the baby that had been lost, but his two little brothers also, he scarcely knew how to thank him.

'What can I offer you in return for this great service which you have rendered me, O Finn?' he said. 'Nothing is too much for you to ask. Take what you wish, even to the half of my Kingdom.'

But Finn shook his head.

'I ask not for reward, O King,' he replied, 'for the best reward I can have, have I already attained, for I have been able to keep my word to you. I promised to save your child, and I have fulfilled my promise; and, moreover, I have brought to you your other children also, whom you had given up for lost.'

'But I will keep this pup as a remembrance,' he added, lifting up the tiny creature and pressing it to his breast, 'for it has come from an enchanted land, and I perceive that on its forefoot it has a claw, such as I have never seen on any dog before, so that perchance it has powers that we know not of, and may prove to us a help and protection in the days that are to come.'

Which words, as old tales tell us, came abundantly true.

HOW FINN OBTAINED THE TOOTH OF KNOWLEDGE

Elizabeth Grierson

All the world knows that the great Irish hero, Finn, the son of Cool, Captain of the Fians, had a wonderful Tooth, called the Tooth of Knowledge, by the aid of which he could practise the art of divination.

Which means that he had but to place his thumb in his mouth, and press it against this tooth, and instantly the whole of the future lay bare before him, and he could tell what would happen in the coming days.

Long before he was born, an old soothsayer had told the people of Ireland that there was a certain magic Salmon, the Salmon of Knowledge, swimming about in a deep pool, the Pool of Linn-fec, in the River Boyne, and that some day a man named Finn would catch this Salmon and eat it; and that, as soon as he tasted it, the magic gift would pass from the Salmon to him, and he would be able to foretell the future.

No one paid much attention to this ancient prophecy
however, until at last, long years after the soothsayer had
died, an old poet, whose name also chanced to be Finn,
heard of it, and he at once determined that he would try to
catch the Salmon, and become the possessor of this marvellous gift of knowledge.

So he left his poetry and his books, and took up his abode
in a tent by the side of the pool, and spent the whole of his
time in fishing.

But although he managed to catch a great many other
kinds of fish, he never managed to catch the wonderful
Salmon. He did not lose heart, however, but went on
patiently, for he always hoped that he would have better
luck next time.

One day a little boy, who looked pinched and pale for
want of food, came walking along the river's bank, clad in
rough, coarse garments.

When he saw the tent, and the poet sitting fishing on a

three-legged stool by the edge of the river, his eyes brightened, for he was looking for work, and it was possible that this old man might be able to give it to him.

'Good-day, master,' he said timidly, 'I am seeking for work; maybe you'd be glad of someone to clean your pots and pans for you.'

'That would I,' said the poet, for he had been so engrossed with his fishing, he had never taken time to wash up his dishes properly after his meals, and everything in the tent was getting into a terrible state of disorder. 'What's your name?' he went on, looking at the little fellow sharply out of his keen grey eyes.

'My name is Demna,' said the boy, for he dare not tell him that his true name was Finn, and that he was the orphan son of Cool, who had been killed in battle just before he was born, and that he was flying in disguise from his father's enemies, who were looking for him in order to kill him.

Now the old poet liked the look of the lad, for he had a noble face, and a soft and gentle tongue; so he took him into his service, and set him to mend the fire, and clean the pots and pans, while he went on with his fishing.

Demna began to work at his new task with a light heart. He felt safe now, for he knew that, even if his enemies did chance to ride that way, they would not expect to find the son of Cool acting as servant to an old fisherman, so they would probably ride past without paying any heed to him.

He had just finished tidying up the tent, and was thinking of beginning to wash his own hands and face, when he was startled by a loud shout.

Thinking that some evil had befallen his master, he threw down his brush and ran as fast as he could to the bank of the stream.

But instead of finding the poet in any trouble, he found him in a state of great delight, for the old man had at last hooked the Salmon of Knowledge, and having landed it safely, he had laid it down on the green bank, and was dancing and leaping round it, fairly beside himself with joy.

When he saw Demna he stopped, and, pretending that he had only been warming himself, he picked up the Salmon and gave it to him, saying hurriedly –

'Take that, boy, and cook it for me, and see to it that you don't taste it while you are handling it, or I will dismiss you without further ado.'

Astonished at the sharpness of his tone, Demna took the fish, promising to do as he was bid, and not taste it, and, being an honest lad, he stuck to his promise, although he was very hungry, and the fish smelt deliciously as it was being cooked.

But he was not a very experienced cook, and he did not put enough water into the pot, and when he lifted the lid to see if it were ready, he saw that its skin had risen in a great big blister on one side.

'This will never do,' he thought to himself; 'my master will think that I am no servant at all,' and he put down his thumb, and drew it along the Salmon's silvery scales, as he had seen other cooks do, to smooth out the blister.

But the Salmon's skin was wondrous hot, and he drew back his thumb with a cry of pain, and popped it into his mouth to stop the smarting.

As he did so, it struck against one of his teeth, and from that moment that tooth possessed the Gift of Knowledge, for his thumb carried with it some of the gravy of the fish, and thus, by mistake as it were, he tasted it.

'Ah, ha!' he cried, licking his lips, 'I am not such a bad cook after all, I'm sure my old master will be pleased with my efforts.'

But when he had put the Salmon carefully on a dish, and garnished it daintily with wild parsley, and carried it to the Poet, the old man looked at him gravely.

'Have you tasted of it, boy?' he asked.

'Nay,' said Demna proudly. 'I gave you my word that I

would not do that, and when I give my word I keep it. But I scalded my thumb while I was cooking it, and I popped my thumb into my mouth to cool the burning heat, and in this way I know how delicious the flavour is.'

For an instant the old man fought with his terrible disappointment. He had caught the fish, but, behold, all unwittingly, his little serving-lad had tasted it before him, and gained the Prize of Knowledge.

Then the battle was won, and he laid his hand gently on the boy's head.

'Why did you tell me a lie, my child?' he said, 'for I believe your name cannot be Demna, it must be Finn.'

'How do you know that?' asked Demna, shrinking back in fear; then, feeling the old man's arm round him, and looking up into the kind old face, he told him all his story.

'I knew it must be so as soon as you told me that you'd licked your thumb, and tasted from thence the flavour of the Salmon,' said the Poet. 'I thought to have fulfilled the prophecy in myself, and for this end have I sat here and fished all these weary weeks; but the gods have ordered it otherwise, and it is fulfilled in you. And perchance it is better so, for you are young and I am old; and you are noble, while I am but lowly born, so you will be better able to use this Gift which you have received, for the good of the people of Erin.'

So it was in this manner that Finn became a Diviner and a Soothsayer.

THE TALKING HEAD
OF DONN-BO
Eleanor Hull

There is an old tale told in Erin of a lovable and bright and handsome youth named Donn-bo, who was the best singer of 'Songs of Idleness' and the best teller of 'King Stories' in the world. He could tell a tale of each king who reigned in Erin, from the 'Tale of the Destruction of Dind Righ', when Cova Coelbre was killed, down to the kings who reigned in his own time.

On a night before a battle, the warriors said, 'Sing tonight for us, Donn-bo.' But Donn-bo answered, 'No word at all will come on my lips tonight; therefore, for this night let the King-buffoon of Ireland amuse you. But tomorrow, at this hour, in whatever place they and I shall be, I will sing for the fighting men.' For the warriors had said that unless Donn-bo would go with them to that battle, not one of them would go.

The battle was past, and on the evening of the morrow at

that same hour Donn-bo lay dead, his fair young body stretched across the body of the King of Ireland, for he had died in defending his chief. But his head had rolled away among a wisp of growing rushes by the waterside.

At the feasting of the army on that night a warrior said, 'Where is Donn-bo, that he may sing for us, as he promised us at this hour yesternight, and that he may tell us the "King Stories of Erin"?'

A valiant champion of the men of Munster answered, 'I will go over the battlefield and seek for him.' He inquired among the living for Donn-bo, but he found him not, and then he searched hither and thither among the dead.

At last he came where the body of the King of Erin lay, and a young, fair corpse beside it. In all the air about there was the sound of singing, low and very sweet; dead bards and poets reciting in faint whispers old tales and poems to dead chiefs.

The wild, clear note of the battle-march, the *dord fiansa* played by the drooping hands of slain warriors upon the points of broken spears, low like the echo of an echo sounded in the clump of rushes nearby; and, above them all a voice, faint and very still, that sang a song that was sweeter than the tunes of the whole world beside.

The voice that sang was the voice of the head of Donn bo. The warrior stooped to pick up the head.

'Do not touch me,' said the head, 'for we are commanded by the King of the Plains of Heaven to make music tonight for our lord, the King of Erin, the shining one who lies dead beside us; and though all of us are lying dead likewise, no faintness or feebleness shall prevent us from obeying that command. Disturb me not.'

'The hosts of Leinster are asking you to sing for them, as you did promise them last night,' said the messenger.

'When my singing here is done, I will go with you,' said the head; 'but only if Christ, the Son of God, in whose presence I now am, go with me, and if you take me to m body again.' 'That shall be done, indeed,' said the messenger, and when it had ceased chanting for the King of Erin he carried away the head.

When the messenger came again amongst the warriors they stopped their feasting and gathered round him. 'Have you brought anything from the battlefield?' they cried.

'I have brought the head of Donn-bo,' said the man.

'Set it upon a pillar that we may see and hear it,' cried they all; and they said, 'It is no luck for you to be like that, Donn-bo, and you the most beautiful minstrel and the best in Erin. Make music, for the love of Jesus Christ, the Son of God. Entertain the Leinster men tonight as you entertained your master a while ago.'

Then Donn-bo turned his face to the wall, that the darkness might be around him, and he raised his melody in the quiet night; and the sound of that song was so piteous and sad that the hosts sat weeping at the sound of it. Then was the head taken to his body, and the neck joined itself to the shoulders again, and Donn-bo was at rest.

This is the story of the 'Talking Head of Donn-bo'.

MURTOUGH AND THE
WITCH WOMAN
Eleanor Hull

In the days when Murtough Mac Erca was in the High
Kingship of Ireland, the country was divided between the
old beliefs of paganism and the new doctrines of the Christian teaching. Some held with the old creed and some with
the new, and the thought of the people was troubled between
them, for they knew not which way to follow and which to
forsake. The faith of their forefathers clung close around
them, holding them by many fine and tender threads of
memory and custom and tradition; yet still the new faith
was making its way, and every day it spread wider and
wider through the land.

The family of Murtough had joined itself to the Christian
faith, and his three brothers were bishops and abbots of the
Church, but Murtough himself remained a pagan, for he
was a wild and lawless prince, and the peaceful teachings of
the Christian doctrine, with its forgiveness of enemies

pleased him not at all. Fierce and cruel was his life, filled with dark deeds and bloody wars, and savage and tragic was his death, as we shall hear.

Now Murtough was in the sunny summer palace of Cletty, which Cormac, son of Art, had built for a pleasure house on the brink of the slow-flowing Boyne, near the Fairy Fortress of Angus the Ever Young, the God of Youth and Beauty. A day of summer was that day, and the King came forth to hunt on the borders of the Fortress, with all his boon companions around him. But when the high-noon came the sun grew hot, and the King sat down to rest upon the fairy mound, and the hunt passed on beyond him, and he was left alone.

There was a witch woman in that country whose name was 'Sigh, Sough, Storm, Rough Wind, Winter Night, Cry, Wail, and Groan'. Star-bright and beautiful was she in face and form, but inwardly she was as cruel as her names. And she hated Murtough because he had scattered and destroyed the Ancient Peoples of the Fairy Tribes of Erin, her country and her fatherland, and because in the battle which he fought at Cerb on the Boyne her father and her mother and her sister had been slain. For in those days women went to battle side by side with men.

She knew, too, that with the coming of the new faith trouble would come upon the fairy folk, and their power and their great majesty would depart from them, and men would call them demons, and would drive them out with psalm-singing and with the saying of prayers, and with the sound of little tinkling bells. So trouble and anger worked upon the witch woman, and she waited the day to be revenged on Murtough, for he being yet a pagan, was still within her power to harm.

So when Sheen (for Sheen or 'Storm' was the name men gave to her) saw the King seated on the fairy mound and all his comrades parted from him, she arose softly, and combed her hair with her comb of silver adorned with little ribs of

207

gold, and she washed her hands in a silver basin wherein
were four golden birds sitting on the rim of the bowl, and
little bright gems of carbuncle set round about the rim. And
she donned her fairy mantle of flowing green, and her cloak,
wide and hooded, with silvery fringes, and a brooch of
fairest gold. On her head were tresses yellow like to gold,
plaited in four locks, with a golden drop at the end of each
long tress. The hue of her hair was like the flower of the iris
in summer or like red gold after the burnishing thereof. And
she wore on her breasts and at her shoulders marvellous
clasps of gold, finely worked with the tracery of the skilled
craftsman, and a golden twisted torque around her throat.
And when she was all splendidly adorned she went softly
and sat down beside Murtough on the turfy hunting mound.
And after a space Murtough perceived her sitting there, and
the sun shining upon her, so that the glittering of the gold
and of her golden hair and the bright shimmer of the green
silk of her garments, was like the yellow iris-beds upon the
lake on a sunny summer's day. Wonder and terror seized on
Murtough at her beauty, and he knew not if he loved her or
if he hated her the most; for at one moment all his nature
was filled with longing and with love of her, so that it
seemed to him that he would give the whole of Ireland for
the loan of one hour's space of dalliance with her; but after
that he felt a dread of her, because he knew his fate was in
her hands, and that she had come to work him ill. But he
welcomed her as if she were known to him and he asked her
wherefore she was come. 'I am come,' she said, 'because I
am beloved of Murtough, son of Erc, King of Erin, and I
come to seek him here.' Then Murtough was glad, and he
said, 'Do you not know me, maiden?' 'I do,' she answered,
'for all secret and mysterious things are known to me and
you and all the men of Erin are well known.'

After he had conversed with her awhile, she appeared to
him so fair that the King was ready to promise her anything
in life she wished, so long as she would go with him to

Cletty of the Boyne. 'My wish,' she said, 'is that you take me to your house, and that you put out from it your wife and your children because they are of the new faith, and all the clerics that are in your house, and that neither your wife nor any cleric be permitted to enter the house while I am there.'

'I will give you,' said the King, 'a hundred head of every herd of cattle that is within my kingdom, and a hundred drinking horns, and a hundred cups, and a hundred rings of gold, and a feast every other night in the summer palace of Cletty. But I pledge you my word, oh, maiden, it would be easier for me to give you half of Ireland than to do this thing that you ask.' For Murtough feared that when those that were of the Christian faith were put out of his house, she would work her spells upon him, and no power would be left with him to resist those spells.

'I will not take your gifts,' said the damsel, 'but only those things that I have asked; moreover, it is thus, that my name must never be uttered by you, nor must any man or woman learn it.'

'What is your name,' said Murtough, 'that it may not come upon my lips to utter it?'

In the end, 'Sigh, Sough, Storm, Rough Wind, Winter Night, Cry, Wail, Groan, this is my name, but men call me Sheen, for "Storm" or Sheen is my chief name, and storms are with me where I come.'

Nevertheless, Murtough was so fascinated by her that he brought her to his home, and drove out the clerics that were there, with his wife and children along with them, and drove out also the nobles of his own clan, the children of Niall, two great and gallant battalions. And Duivsech, his wife, went crying along the road with her children around her to seek Bishop Cairnech, the half-brother of her husband, and her own soul-friend, that she might obtain help and shelter from him.

But Sheen went gladly and light-heartedly into the House of Cletty, and when she saw the lovely lightsome house and the goodly nobles of the clan of Niall, and the feasting and banqueting and the playing of the minstrels and all the joyous noise of that kingly dwelling, her heart was lifted within her, and 'Fair as a fairy palace is this house of Cletty,' said she.

'Fair, indeed, it is,' replied the King; 'for neither the Kings of Leinster nor the Kings of mighty Ulster, nor the lords of the clans of Owen or of Niall, have such a house as this, nay, in Tara of the Kings itself, no house to equal this house of mine is found.' And that night the King robed himself in all the splendour of his royal dignity, and on his right hand he seated Sheen, and a great banquet was made before them, and men said that never on earth was to be seen a woman more goodly of appearance than she. And the King was astonished at her, and he began to ask her questions, for it seemed to him that the power of a great goddess of the ancient time was in her; and he asked her whence she came, and what manner was the power that he saw in her. He asked her, too, did she believe in the God of the clerics, or was she herself some goddess of the older world? For he feared her, feeling that his fate was in her hands.

She laughed a careless and a cruel laugh, for she knew that the King was in her power, now that she was there alone with him, and the clerics and the Christian teachers gone. 'Fear me not, O Murtough,' she cried; 'I am, like you, a daughter of the race of men of the ancient family of Adam and of Eve; fit and meet my comradeship with you; therefore, fear not nor regret. And as to that true God of yours, worker of miracles and helper of His people, no miracle in all the world is there that I, by my own unaided power, cannot work the like. I can create a sun and moon; the heavens I can sprinkle with radiant stars of night. I can call back to life men fiercely killed in conflict, slaughtering one another. I could make wine of the cold water of the Boyne, and sheep of lifeless stones, and swine of ferns. In the presence of the hosts I can make gold and silver, plenty and to spare; and hosts of famous fighting men I can produce from nothing. Now, tell me, can your God work the like?'

'Work for us,' says the King, 'some of these great wonders.' Then Sheen went forth out of the house, and she set herself to work spells on Murtough, so that he knew not whether he was in his right mind or no. She took of the water of the Boyne and made a magic wine from it, and she took ferns and spiked thistles and light puff-balls of the woods, and out of them she fashioned magic swine and sheep and goats, and with these she fed Murtough and the hosts. And when they had eaten, all their strength went from them, and the magic wine sent them into an uneasy sleep and restless slumbers. And out of stones and sods of earth she fashioned three battalions, and one of the battalions she placed at one side of the house, and the other at the further side beyond it, and one encircling the rest southward along the hollow windings of the glen. And thus were these

battalions, one of them all made of men stark-naked and
their colour blue, and the second with heads of goats with
shaggy beards and horned; but the third, more terrible than
they, for these were headless men, fighting like human
beings, yet finished at the neck; and the sound of heavy
shouting as of hosts and multitudes came from the first and
the second battalion, but from the third no sound save only
that they waved their arms and struck their weapons together, and smote the ground with their feet impatiently.
And though terrible was the shout of the blue men and the
bleating of the goats with human limbs, more horrible yet
was the stamping and the rage of those headless men,
finished at the neck.

And Murtough, in his sleep and in his dreams, heard the
battle-shout, and he rose impetuously from off his bed, but
the wine overcame him, and his strength departed from him,
and he fell helplessly upon the floor. Then he heard the
challenge a second time, and the stamping of the feet outside,
and he rose again, and madly, fiercely, he set upon them,
charging the hosts and scattering them before him, as he
thought, back into their fairy fortress. But all his strength
was lost in fighting phantoms, for they were but stones and
sods and withered leaves of the forest that he took for
fighting men.

Now Duivsech, Murtough's wife, knew what was going
on. She called upon Cairnech to arise and to gather together
the clans of the children of his people, the men of Owen and
of Niall, and together they went to the fort; but Sheen
guarded it well, so that they could by no means find an
entrance. Then Cairnech was angry, and he cursed the
place, and he dug a grave before the door, and he stood up
upon the mound of the grave, and rang his bells and cursed
the King and his house, and prophesied his downfall. But he
blessed the clans of Owen and of Niall, and they returned to
their own country.

Then Cairnech sent messengers to seek Murtough and to

draw him away from the witch woman who sought his destruction, but because she was so lovely the King would believe no evil of her; and whenever he made any sign to go to Cairnech, she threw her spell upon the King, so that he could not break away. When he was so weak and faint that he had no power left, she cast a sleep upon him, and she went round the house, putting everything in readiness. She called upon her magic host of warriors, and set them round the fortress, with their spears and javelins pointed inwards towards the house, so that the King would not dare to go out amongst them. And that night was a night of Samhaintide, the eve of Wednesday after All Souls' Day.

Then she went everywhere throughout the house, and took lighted brands and burning torches, and scattered them in every part of the dwelling. And she returned into the room wherein Murtough slept, and lay down by his side. And she caused a great wind to spring up, and it came soughing through the house from the north-west; and the King said, 'This is the sigh of the winter night.' And Sheen smiled, because, unwittingly, the King had spoken her name, for she knew by that that the hour of her revenge had come. "Tis I myself that am Sigh and Winter Night,' she said, 'and I am Rough Wind and Storm, a daughter of fair nobles; and I am Cry and Wail, the maid of elfin birth, who brings ill-luck to men.'

After that she caused a great snowstorm to come round the house; and like the noise of troops and the rage of battle was the storm, beating and pouring in on every side, so that drifts of deep snow were piled against the walls, blocking the doors and chilling the folk that were feasting within the house. But the King was lying in a heavy, unresting sleep, and Sheen was at his side. Suddenly he screamed out of his sleep and stirred himself, for he heard the crash of falling timbers and the noise of the magic hosts, and he smelled the strong smell of fire in the palace.

He sprang up. 'It seems to me,' he cried, 'that hosts of

213

demons are around the house, and that they are slaughtering my people, and that the house of Cletty is on fire.' 'It was but a dream,' the witch maiden said. Then he slept again, and he saw a vision, to wit, that he was tossing in a ship at sea, and the ship floundered, and above his head a griffin, with sharp beak and talons, sailed, her wings outspread and covering all the sun, so that it was dark as middle-night; and lo! as she rose on high, her plumes quivered for a moment in the air; then down she swooped and picked him from the waves, carrying him to her eyrie on the dismal cliff outhanging above the ocean; and the griffin began to pierce him and to prod him with her talons, and to pick out pieces of his flesh with her beak; and this went on awhile, and then a flame, that came he knew not whence, rose from the nest, and he and the griffin were enveloped in the flame. Then in her beak the griffin picked him up, and together they fell downward over the cliff's edge into the seething ocean; so that, half by fire and half by water, he died a miserable death.

When the King saw that vision, he rose screaming from his sleep, and donned his arms; and he made one plunge forward seeking for the magic hosts, but he found no man to answer him. The damsel went forth from the house, and Murtough made to follow her, but as he turned the flames leaped out, and all between him and the door was one vast sheet of flame. He saw no way of escape, save the vat of Boyne wine that stood in the banqueting hall, and into that he got; but the burning timbers of the roof fell upon his head and the hails of fiery sparks rained on him, so that half of him was burned and half was drowned, as he had seen in his dream.

The next day, amid the embers, the clerics found his corpse, and they took it up and washed it in the Boyne, and carried it to Tuilen to bury it. And they said, 'Alas! that Mac Erca, High King of Erin, of the noble race of Conn and of the descendants of Ugaine the Great, should die fighting with sods and stones! Alas! that the Cross of Christ was not signed upon his face that he might have known the witcheries of the maiden for what they were.'

As they went thus, bewailing the death of Murtough and bearing him to his grave, Duivsech, wife of Murtough, met them, and when she found her husband dead, she struck her hands together and she made a great and mournful lamentation; and because weakness came upon her she leaned her back against the ancient tree that is in Aenech Reil; and a burst of blood broke from her heart, and there she died, grieving for her husband. And the grave of Murtough was made wide and deep, and there they laid the Queen beside him, two in the one grave, near the north side of the little church that is in Tuilen.

Now, when the burial was finished, and the clerics were reciting over his grave the deeds of the King, and were making prayers for Murtough's soul that it might be brought out of hell, for Cairnech showed great care for this, they saw coming towards them across the sward a lonely woman, star-bright and beautiful, and a kirtle of priceless silk upon her, and a shimmering green mantle with its fringes of silver thread flowing to the ground. She reached the place where the clerics were, and saluted them, and they saluted her. And they marvelled at her beauty, but they perceived on her an appearance of sadness and of heavy grief. They asked of her, 'Who are you, maiden, and why do you come to the house of mourning? For a king lies buried here.' 'A king lies buried here, indeed,' said she, 'and I it was who slew him, Murtough of the many deeds, of the race of Conn and Niall, High King of Ireland and of the West. And though it was I who worked his death, I myself will die for grief of him.'

And they said, 'Tell us, maiden, why you brought him to his death, if he was dear to you?' And she said, 'Murtough was dear to me, indeed, dearest of the men of the whole world; for I am Sheen, the daughter of Sige, the son of Dian, from whom Ath Sigi or the "Ford of Sige" is called today.

But Murtough slew my father, and my mother and sister were slain along with him, in the battle of Cerb upon the Boyne, and there was none of my house to avenge their death, save myself alone. Moreover, in his time the Ancient Peoples of the Fairy Tribes of Erin were scattered and destroyed, the folk of the underworld and of my fatherland; and to avenge the wrong and loss he caused them I slew the man I loved. I made poison for him; alas! I made for him magic drink and food which took his strength away, and out of the sods of earth and puff-balls that float down the wind, I made men and armies of headless, hideous folk, till all his senses were distraught. And, now, take me to thee, O Cairnech, in fervent and true repentance, and sign the Cross of Christ upon my brow, for the time of my death is come.'

Then she repented the sin that she had sinned, and she died there upon the grave of grief and of sorrow after the King. And they digged a grave lengthways across the foot of the wide grave of Murtough and his spouse, and there they laid the maiden who had done them wrong. And the clerics wondered at those things, and they wrote them and revised them in a book.

FAIR, BROWN, AND
TREMBLING

Jeremiah Curtin

King Hugh Curucha lived in Tir Conal, and he had three
daughters, whose names were Fair, Brown, and Trembling.

Fair and Brown had new dresses, and went to church
every Sunday. Trembling was kept at home to do the
cooking and work. They would not let her go out of the
house at all; for she was more beautiful than the other
two, and they were in dread she might marry before themselves.

They carried on in this way for seven years. At the end of
seven years the son of the king of Emania fell in love with
the eldest sister.

One Sunday morning, after the other two had gone to
church, the old henwife came into the kitchen to Trembling,
and said: 'It's at church you ought to be this day, instead of
working here at home.'

'How could I go?' said Trembling. 'I have no clothes good

217

enough to wear at church; and if my sisters were to see me there, they'd kill me for going out of the house.'

'I'll give you,' said the henwife, 'a finer dress than either of them has ever seen. And now tell me what dress will you have?'

'I'll have,' said Trembling, 'a dress as white as snow, and green shoes for my feet.'

Then the henwife put on the cloak of darkness, clipped a piece from the old clothes the young woman had on, and asked for the whitest robes in the world and the most beautiful that could be found, and a pair of green shoes.

That moment she had the robe and the shoes, and she brought them to Trembling, who put them on. When Trembling was dressed and ready, the henwife said: 'I have a honey-bird here to sit on your right shoulder, and a honey-suckle flower to put on your left. At the door stands a milk-white mare, with a golden saddle for you to sit on, and a golden bridle to hold in your hand.'

Trembling sat on the golden saddle; and when she was ready to start, the henwife said: 'You must not go inside the door of the church, and the minute the people rise up at the end of Mass, do you make off, and ride home as fast as the mare will carry you.'

When Trembling came to the door of the church there was no one inside who could get a glimpse of her but was striving to know who she was; and when they saw her hurrying away at the end of Mass, they ran out to overtake her. But no use in their running; she was away before any man could come near her. From the minute she left the church till she got home, she overtook the wind before her, and outstripped the wind behind.

She came down at the door, went in, and found the henwife had dinner ready. She put off the white robes, and had on her old dress in a twinkling.

When the two sisters came home the henwife asked: 'Have you any news today from the church?'

'We have great news,' said they. 'We saw a wonderful grand lady at the church-door. The like of the robes she had we have never seen on woman before. It's little that was thought of our dresses beside what she had on; and there wasn't a man at the church, from the king to the beggar, but was trying to get a look at her and know who she was.'

The sisters would give no peace till they had two dresses like the robes of the strange lady; but honey-birds and honeysuckles were not to be found.

Next Sunday the two sisters went to church again, and left the youngest at home to cook the dinner.

After they had gone, the henwife came in and asked: 'Will you go to church today?'

'I would go,' said Trembling, 'if I could get the going.'

'What robe will you wear?' asked the henwife.

'The finest black satin that can be found, and red shoes for my feet.'

'What colour do you want the mare to be?'

'I want her to be so black and so glossy that I can see myself in her body.'

The henwife put on the cloak of darkness, and asked for the robes and the mare. That moment she had them. When Trembling was dressed, the henwife put the honey-bird on her right shoulder and the honeysuckle on her left. The saddle on the mare was silver, and so was the bridle.

When Trembling sat in the saddle and was going away, the henwife ordered her strictly not to go inside the door of the church, but to rush away as soon as the people rose at the end of Mass, and hurry home on the mare before any man could stop her.

That Sunday the people were more astonished than ever, and gazed at her more than the first time; and all they were thinking of was to know who she was. But they had no chance; for the moment the people rose at the end of Mass she slipped from the church, was in the silver saddle, and home before a man could stop her or talk to her.

The henwife had the dinner ready. Trembling took off her satin robe, and had on her old clothes before her sisters got home.

'What news have you today?' asked the henwife of the sisters when they came from the church.

'Oh, we saw the grand strange lady again! And it's little that any man could think of our dresses after looking at the robes of satin that she had on! And all at church, from high to low, had their mouths open, gazing at her, and no man was looking at us.'

The two sisters gave neither rest nor peace till they got dresses as nearly like the strange lady's robes as they could find. Of course they were not so good; for the like of those robes could not be found in Erin.

When the third Sunday came, Fair and Brown went to church dressed in black satin. They left Trembling at home to work in the kitchen, and told her to be sure and have dinner ready when they came back.

After they had gone and were out of sight, the henwife came to the kitchen and said: 'Well, my dear, are you for church today?'

'I would go if I had a new dress to wear.'

'I'll get you any dress you ask for. What dress would you like?' asked the henwife.

'A dress red as a rose from the waist down, and white as snow from the waist up; a cape of green on my shoulders; and a hat on my head with a red, a white, and a green feather in it; and shoes for my feet with the toes red, the middle white, and the backs and heels green.'

The henwife put on the cloak of darkness, wished for all these things, and had them. When Trembling was dressed, the henwife put the honey-bird on her right shoulder and the honeysuckle on her left, and, placing the hat on her head, clipped a few hairs from one lock and a few from another with her scissors, and that moment the most beautiful golden hair was flowing down over the girl's shoulders.

Then the henwife asked what kind of a mare she would ride. She said white, with blue and gold-coloured diamond-shaped spots all over her body, on her back a saddle of gold, and on her head a golden bridle.

The mare stood there before the door, and a bird sitting between her ears, which began to sing as soon as Trembling was in the saddle, and never stopped till she came home from the church.

The fame of the beautiful strange lady had gone out through the world, and all the princes and great men that were in it came to church that Sunday, each one hoping that it was himself would have her home with him after Mass.

The son of the king of Emania forgot all about the eldest sister, and remained outside the church, so as to catch the strange lady before she could hurry away.

The church was more crowded than ever before, and there were three times as many outside. There was such a throng before the church that Trembling could only come inside the gate.

As soon as the people were rising at the end of Mass, the lady slipped out through the gate, was in the golden saddle in an instant, and sweeping away ahead of the wind. But if she was, the prince of Emania was at her side, and, seizing her by the foot, he ran with the mare for two hundred metres, and never let go of the beautiful lady till the shoe was pulled from her foot, and he was left behind with it in his hand. She came home as fast as the mare could carry her, and was thinking all the time that the henwife would kill her for losing the shoe.

Seeing her so vexed and so changed in the face, the old woman asked: 'What's the trouble that's on you now?'

'Oh! I've lost one of the shoes off my feet,' said Trembling.

'Don't mind that; don't be vexed,' said the henwife; 'maybe it's the best thing that ever happened to you.'

Then Trembling gave up all the things she had to the

221

henwife, put on her old clothes, and went to work in the kitchen. When the sisters came home, the henwife asked: 'Have you any news from the church?'

'We have indeed,' said they, 'for we saw the grandest sight today. The strange lady came again, in grander array than before. On herself and the horse she rode were the finest colours of the world, and between the ears of the horse was a bird which never stopped singing from the time she came till she went away. The lady herself is the most beautiful woman ever seen by man in Erin.'

After Trembling had disappeared from the church, the son of the king of Emania said to the other kings' sons: 'I will have that lady for my own.'

They all said: 'You didn't win her just by taking the shoe off her foot; you'll have to win her by the point of the sword; you'll have to fight for her with us before you can call her your own.'

'Well,' said the son of the king of Emania, 'when I find the lady that shoe will fit, I'll fight for her, never fear, before I leave her to any of you.'

Then all the kings' sons were uneasy, and anxious to know who was she that lost the shoe; and they began to travel all over Erin to find her. The prince of Emania and all the others went in a great company together, and made the round of Erin; they went everywhere – north, south, east and west. They visited every place where a woman was to be found, and left not a house in the kingdom unsearched, to find the woman the shoe would fit, not caring whether she was rich or poor, of high or low degree.

The prince of Emania always kept the shoe; and when the young women saw it, they had great hopes, for it was of proper size, neither large nor small, and it would beat any man to know of what material it was made. One thought it would fit her if she cut a little from her great toe; and another, with too short a foot, put something in the tip of her stocking. But no use; they only spoiled their feet, and were curing them for months afterwards.

The two sisters, Fair and Brown, heard that the princes of the world were looking all over Erin for the woman that could wear the shoe, and every day they were talking of trying it on; and one day Trembling spoke up and said: 'Maybe it's my foot that the shoe will fit.'

'Oh, such moonshine! Why say that when you were at home every Sunday?'

They were that way waiting, and scolding the younger sister, till the princes were near the place. The day they were to come, the sisters put Trembling in a closet, and locked the door on her. When the company came to the house, the prince of Emania gave the shoe to the sisters. But though they tried and tried, it would fit neither of them.

'Is there any other young woman in the house?' asked the prince.

'There is,' said Trembling, speaking up in the closet; 'I'm here.'

'Oh! ignore that one – we have her for nothing but to put out the ashes,' said the sisters.

But the prince and the others wouldn't leave the house till they had seen her; so the two sisters had to open the door. When Trembling came out, the shoe was given to her, and it fitted exactly.

The prince of Emania looked at her and said: 'You are the woman the shoe fits, and you are the woman I took the shoe from.'

Then Trembling spoke up, and said: 'Please stay here till I return.'

Then she went to the henwife's house. The old woman put on the cloak of darkness, got everything for her she had the first Sunday at church, and put her on the white mare in the same fashion. Then Trembling rode along the highway to the front of the house. All who had seen her the first time said: 'This is the lady we saw at church.'

Then she went away a second time, and a second time came back on the black mare in the second dress which the henwife gave her. All who had seen her the second Sunday said: 'That is the lady we saw at church.'

A third time she asked for a short absence, and soon came back on the third mare and in the third dress. All who had seen her the third time said: 'That is the lady we saw at church.' Every man was now satisfied, and knew that she was the woman.

Then all the princes and great men spoke up, and said to the son of the king of Emania: 'You'll have to fight now for her before we let her go with you.'

'I'm here before you, ready for combat,' answered the prince.

Then the son of the king of Lochlin stepped forth. The struggle began, and a terrible struggle it was. They fought for nine hours; and then the son of the king of Lochlin stopped, gave up his claim, and left the field. Next day the son of the king of Spain fought six hours, and yielded his claim. On the third day the son of the king of Nyerfói fought eight hours, and stopped. The fourth day the son of the king of Greece fought six hours, and stopped. On the fifth day no more foreign princes wanted to fight; and all the sons of kings in Erin said they would not fight with a man of their own land, that the strangers had had their chance, and, as no others came to claim the woman, she belonged of right to the son of the king of Emania.

The marriage-day was fixed, and the invitations were sent out. The wedding lasted for a year and a day. When the wedding was over, the king's son brought home the bride, and when the time came a son was born. The young woman sent for her eldest sister, Fair, to be with her and care for her. One day, when Trembling was well, and when her husband was away hunting, the two sisters went out to walk; and when they came to the seaside, the eldest pushed the youngest sister in. A great whale came and swallowed her.

The eldest sister came home alone, and the husband asked, 'Where is your sister?'

'She has gone home to her father in Ballyshannon; now that I am well, I don't need her.'

'Well,' said the husband, looking at her, 'I'm in dread it's my wife that has gone.'

'Oh! no,' said she; 'I'm well, it's my sister Fair that's gone.'

Since the sisters were very much alike, the prince was in doubt. That night he put his sword between their beds, and said: 'If you are my wife, this sword will get warm; if not, it will stay cold.'

In the morning when he rose up, the sword was as cold as when he put it there.

It happened, when the two sisters were walking by the seashore, that a little cowboy was down by the water minding cattle, and saw Fair push Trembling into the sea; and next day, when the tide came in, he saw the whale swim up and throw her out on the sand. When she was on the sand she said to the cowboy: 'When you go home in the evening with the cows, tell the master that my sister Fair pushed me into the sea yesterday; that a whale swallowed me, and then threw me out, but will come again and swallow me with the coming of the next tide; then he'll go out with the tide, and come again with tomorrow's tide, and throw me again on the strand. The whale will cast me out three times. I'm under the enchantment of this whale, and cannot leave the beach or escape myself. Unless my husband saves me before I'm swallowed the fourth time, I shall be lost. He must come and shoot the whale with a silver bullet when he turns on the broad of his back. Under the breast-fin of the whale is a reddish-brown spot. My husband must hit him in that spot, for it is the only place in which he can be killed.'

When the cowboy got home with this story, the eldest sister gave him a sleeping potion, and he did not tell the prince.

Next day the boy went again to the sea. The whale came

and cast Trembling on shore again. She asked the boy: 'Did you tell the master what I told you to tell him?'

'I did not,' said he; 'I forgot.'

'How did you forget?' asked she.

'The woman of the house gave me a drink that made me forget.'

'Well, don't forget telling the prince this night; and if she gives you a drink, don't take it from her.'

As soon as the cowboy came home, the eldest sister offered him a drink. He refused to take it till he had delivered his message and told all to the master. The third day the prince went down to the shore with his gun and a silver bullet in it. He was not long there when the whale came and threw Trembling upon the beach as he had done the two days before. She had no power to speak to her husband till he had killed the whale. Then the whale went out, turned over once on the broad of his back, and showed the spot for a moment only. That moment the prince fired. He had but the one chance, and a short one at that; but he took it, and hit the spot, and the whale, mad with pain, made the sea all around red with blood, and died.

That minute Trembling was able to speak, and went home with her husband, who sent word to her father what the eldest sister had done. The father came, and told him any death he chose to give her to give it. The prince told the father he would leave her life and death with himself. The father had her put out then on the sea in a barrel, with provisions in it for seven years.

In time Trembling had a second child, a daughter. The prince and she sent the cowboy to school, and trained him up as one of their own children, and said: 'If the little girl that is born to us now lives, no other man in the world will get her but him.'

The cowboy and the prince's daughter lived on till they were married. The mother said to her husband: 'You could not have saved me from the whale but for the little cowboy; on that account I don't grudge him my daughter.'

The prince of Emania and Trembling had fourteen children, and they lived happily till the two died of old age.

THE LAZY BEAUTY AND
HER AUNTS

Patrick Kennedy

There was once a poor widow woman, who had a daughter
that was as handsome as the day, and as lazy as a pig,
saving your presence. The poor mother was the most industrious person in the townland, and was a particularly good
hand at the spinning-wheel. It was the wish of her heart that
her daughter should be as handy as herself; but she'd get up
late, eat her breakfast before she'd finished her prayers, and
then go about dawdling, and anything she handled seemed
to be burning her fingers. She drawled her words as if it was
a great trouble to her to speak, or as if her tongue was as
lazy as her body. Many a heart-scald her poor mother got
with her, and still she was only improving like dead fowl in
August.

Well, one morning that things were as bad as they could
be, and the poor woman was giving tongue at the rate of a
mill-clapper, who should be riding by but the king's son.

'Oh dear, oh dear, good woman!' said he, 'you must have a very bad child to make you scold so terribly. Sure it can't be this handsome girl that vexed you!' 'Oh, please your Majesty, not at all,' says the old dissembler. 'I was only checking her for working herself too much. Would your Majesty believe it? She spins three pounds of flax in a day, weaves it into linen the next, and makes it all into shirts the day after.' 'My gracious,' says the prince, 'she's the very lady that will just fill my mother's eye, and herself's the greatest spinner in the kingdom. Will you put on your daughter's bonnet and cloak, if you please, ma'am, and set her behind me? Why, my mother will be so delighted with her, that perhaps she'll make her her daughter-in-law in a week, that is, if the young woman herself is agreeable.'

Well, between the confusion, and the joy, and the fear of being found out, the women didn't know what to do; and before they could make up their minds, young Anty (Anastasia) was set behind the prince, and away he and his attendants went, and a good heavy purse was left behind with the mother. She *pullillued* a long time after all was gone, in dread of something bad happening to the poor girl.

The prince couldn't judge of the girl's breeding or wit from the few answers he pulled out of her. The queen was struck in a heap when she saw a young country girl sitting behind her son, but when she saw her handsome face, and heard all she could do, she didn't think she could make too much of her. The prince took an opportunity of whispering to her that if she didn't object to be his wife she must strive to please his mother. Well, the evening went by, and the prince and Anty were getting fonder and fonder of one another, but the thought of the spinning used to send the cold to her heart every moment. When bed-time came, the old queen went along with her to a beautiful bedroom, and when she was bidding her good-night, she pointed to a heap of fine flax, and said, 'You may begin as soon as you like tomorrow morning, and I'll expect to see these three pounds

229

in nice thread the morning after.' Little did the poor girl sleep that night. She kept crying and lamenting that she didn't mind her mother's advice better. When she was left alone next morning, she began with a heavy heart; and though she had a nice mahogany wheel and the finest flax you ever saw, the thread was breaking every moment. One while it was as fine as a cobweb, and the next as coarse as a little boy's whipcord. At last she pushed her chair back, let her hands fall in her lap, and burst out a-crying.

A small, old woman with surprising big feet appeared before her at the same moment, and said, 'What ails you, you handsome colleen?' 'An' haven't I all that flax to spin before tomorrow morning, and I'll never be able to have even five yards of fine thread of it put together.' 'An' would you think bad to ask poor Colliach Cushmōr (Old woman Big-foot) to your wedding with the young prince? If you promise me that, all your three pounds will be made into the finest of thread while you're taking your sleep tonight.'

'Indeed, you must be there and welcome, and I'll honour you all the days of your life.' 'Very well; stay in your room till tea-time, and tell the queen she may come in for her thread as early as she likes tomorrow morning.' It was all as she said; and the thread was finer and evener than the gut you see with fly-fishers. 'My brave girl you were!' says the queen. 'I'll get my own mahogany loom brought in to you, but you needn't do anything more today. Work and rest, work and rest, is my motto. Tomorrow you'll weave all this thread, and who knows what may happen?'

The poor girl was more frightened this time than the last, and she was so afraid to lose the prince. She didn't even know how to put the warp in the gears, nor how to use the shuttle, and she was sitting in the greatest grief, when a little woman, who was mighty well-shouldered about the hips, all at once appeared to her, told her her name was Colliach Cromanmōr, and made the same bargain with her as Colliach Cushmōr. Great was the queen's pleasure when she found early in the morning a web as fine and white as the finest paper you ever saw. 'The darling you were!' says she. 'Take your ease with the ladies and gentlemen today and if you have all this made into nice shirts tomorrow you may present one of them to my son, and be married to him out of hand.'

Oh, wouldn't you pity poor Anty the next day, she was now so near the prince, and, maybe, would be soon so far from him. But she waited as patiently as she could with scissors, needle, and thread in hand, till a minute after noon. Then she was rejoiced to see the third woman appear. She had a big red nose, and informed Anty that people called her Shron Mor Rua on that account. She was as good to her as the others, for a dozen fine shirts were lying on the table when the queen paid her an early visit.

Now there was nothing talked of but the wedding, and I needn't tell you it was grand. The poor mother was there along with the rest, and at the dinner the old queen could talk of nothing but the lovely shirts, and how happy herself and the bride would be after the honeymoon, spinning, and weaving, and sewing shirts and shifts without end. The bridegroom didn't like the discourse, and the bride liked it less, and he was going to say something, when the footman came up to the head of the table and said to the bride, 'Your ladyship's aunt, Colliach Cushmōr, bade me ask might she come in.' The bride blushed and wished she was seven miles under the floor, but well became the prince. 'Tell Mrs Cushmōr,' said he, 'that any relation of my bride's will be always heartily welcome wherever she and I are.' In came the woman with the big foot, and got a seat near the prince. The old queen didn't like it much, and after a few words she asked rather spitefully, 'Dear ma'am, what's the reason your foot is so big?' '*Musha*, faith, your majesty, I was standing almost all my life at the spinning-wheel, and that's the reason.' 'I declare to you, my darling,' said the prince, 'I'll never allow you to spend one hour at the same spinning-wheel.' The same footman said again, 'Your ladyship's aunt, Colliach Cromanmōr, wishes to come in, if the genteels and yourself have no objection.' Very *sharoose* (displeased) was Princess Anty, but the prince sent her welcome, and she took her seat, and drank healths apiece to the company. 'May I ask, ma'am?' says the old queen, 'why you're so wide half-way between the head and the feet?' 'That, your majesty, is owing to sitting all my life at the loom.' 'By my sceptre,' says the prince, 'my wife shall never sit there an hour.' The footman again came up. 'Your ladyship's aunt, Colliach Shron Mor Rua, is asking leave to come into the banquet.' More blushing on the bride's face, but the bridegroom spoke out cordially, 'Tell Mrs Shron Mor Rua she's doing us an honour.' In came the old woman, and great respect she got near the top of the table, but the people down low put up their tumblers and glasses to their noses to hide the grins. 'Ma'am,' says the old queen, 'will you tell us, if you please, why your nose is so big and red?' 'Throth, your majesty, my head was bent down over the stitching all my life, and all the blood in my body ran into my nose.' 'My darling,' said the prince to Anty, 'if ever I see a needle in your hand, I'll run a hundred miles from you.'

'And in troth, girls and boys, though it's a diverting story, I don't think the moral is good; and if any of you *thuckeens* go about imitating Anty in her laziness, you'll find it won't thrive with you as it did with her. She was beautiful beyond compare, which none of you are, and she had three powerful fairies to help her besides. There's no fairies now, and no prince or lord to ride by, and catch you idling or working; and maybe, after all, the prince and herself were not so very happy when the cares of the world or old age came on them.'

Thus was the tale ended by poor old Shebale (Sybilla), Father Murphy's housekeeper, in Coolbawn, Barony of Bantry, about half a century since.

KING O'TOOLE AND
HIS GOOSE
Joseph Jacobs [after Samuel Lover]

Och, I thought all the world, far and near, had heerd o'
King O'Toole – well, well, but the darkness of mankind is
untellible! Well, sir, you must know, as you didn't hear it
afore, that there was a king, called King O'Toole, who was
a fine old king in the old ancient times, long ago; and it was
he that owned the churches in the early days. The king, you
see, was the right sort; he was a great lad, and loved sport
as he loved his life, and hunting in particular; and from the
rising o' the sun, up he got, and away he went over the
mountains after the deer; and fine times they were.

Well, it was all mighty good, as long as the king had his
health; but, you see, in course of time the king grew old,
stiff in his limbs, and when he got stricken in years, his
heart failed him, and he was lost entirely for want o'
diversion, because he couldn't go a-hunting no longer; and,
by dad, the poor king was obliged at last to get a goose to

divert him. Oh, you may laugh, if you like, but it's truth I'm telling you; and the way the goose diverted him was this-a-way: You see, the goose used to swim across the lake, and go diving for trout, and catch fish on a Friday for the king, and flew every other day round about the lake, diverting the poor king. All went on mighty well until, by dad, the goose got stricken in years like her master, and couldn't divert him no longer, and then it was that the poor king was lost entirely. The king was walkin' one mornin' by the edge of the lake, lamentin' his cruel fate, and thinking of drowning himself, that could get no diversion in life, when all of a sudden, turning round the corner, who should he meet but a mighty decent young man coming up to him.

'God save you,' says the king to the young man.

'God save you kindly, King O'Toole,' says the young man.

'True for you,' says the king. 'I am King O'Toole,' says he, 'prince and plennypennytinchery of these parts,' says he; 'but how came ye to know that?' says he.

'Oh, never mind,' says Saint Kavin.

You see it was Saint Kavin, sure enough – the saint himself in disguise, and nobody else. 'Oh, never mind,' says he, 'I know more than that. May I make bold to ask how is your goose, King O'Toole?' says he.

'Blur-an-agers, how came ye to know about my goose?' says the king.

'Oh, no matter; I was given to understand it,' says Saint Kavin.

After some more talk the king says, 'What are you?'

'I'm an honest man,' says Saint Kavin.

'Well, honest man,' says the king, 'and how is it you make your money so aisy?'

'By makin' old things as good as new,' says Saint Kavin.

'Is it a tinker you are?' says the king.

'No,' says the saint; 'I'm no tinker by trade, King O'Toole; I've a better trade than a tinker,' says he – 'what would you say,' says he, 'if I made your old goose as good as new?'

My dear, at the word of making his goose as good as new, you'd think the poor old king's eyes were ready to jump out of his head. With that the king whistled, and down came the poor goose, just like a hound, waddling up to the poor cripple, her master, and as like him as two peas. The minute the saint clapped his eyes on the goose, 'I'll do the job for you,' says he, 'King O'Toole.'

'By Jaminee!' says King O'Toole, 'if you do, I'll say you're the cleverest fellow in the seven parishes.'

'Oh, by dad,' says Saint Kavin, 'you must say more nor that – I'm not as soft-headed,' says he, 'as to repair your old goose for nothing; what'll you gi' me if I do the job for you? – that's the chat,' says Saint Kavin.

'I'll give you whatever you ask,' says the king; 'isn't that fair?'

'Divil a fairer,' says the saint; 'that's the way to do business. Now,' says he, 'this is the bargain I'll make with you, King O'Toole: will you gi' me all the ground the goose flies over, the first offer, after I make her as good as new?'

'I will,' says the king.

'You won't go back o' your word?' says Saint Kavin.

'Honour bright!' says King O'Toole, holding out his fist.

'Honour bright!' says Saint Kavin, back again, 'it's a bargain. Come here!' says he to the poor old goose – 'come here, you unfortunate ould cripple, and it's I that'll make you the sporting bird.' With that, my dear, he took up the goose by the two wings – 'Criss o' my cross an you,' says he, markin' her to grace with the blessed sign at the same minute – and throwing her up in the air, 'whew,' says he, just givin' her a blast to help her; and with that, my jewel, she took to her heels, flyin' like one o' the eagles themselves, and cutting as many capers as a swallow before a shower o' rain.

Well, my dear, it was a beautiful sight to see the king standing with his mouth open, looking at his poor old goose flying as light as a lark, and better than ever she was: and

236

when she lit at his feet, patted her on the head, and, '*Ma vourneen*,' says he, 'but you are the *darlint* o' the world.'

'And what do you say to me,' says Saint Kavin, 'for making her the like?'

'By Jabers,' says the king, 'I say nothing beats the art o' man, barring the bees.'

'And do you say no more nor that?' says Saint Kavin.

'And that I'm beholden to you,' says the king.

'But will you gi'e me all the ground the goose flew over?' says Saint Kavin.

'I will,' says King O'Toole, 'and you're welcome to it,' says he, 'though it's the last acre I have to give.'

'But you'll keep your word true?' says the saint.

'As true as the sun,' says the king.

'It's well for you, King O'Toole, that you said that word,' says he; 'for if you didn't say that word, the devil the bit o' your goose would ever fly agin.'

When the king was as good as his word, Saint Kavin was pleased with him, and then it was that he made himself known to the king. 'And,' says he, 'King O'Toole, you're a decent man, for I only came here to try you. You don't know me,' says he, 'because I'm disguised.'

'*Musha!* then,' says the king, 'who are you?'

'I'm Saint Kavin,' said the saint, blessing himself.

'Oh, queen of heaven!' says the king, making the sign of the cross between his eyes, and falling down on his knees before the saint; 'is it the great Saint Kavin,' says he, 'that I've been discoursing all this time without knowing it,' says he, 'all as one as if he was a lump of a *gossoon*? – and so you're a saint?' says the king.

'I am,' says Saint Kavin.

'By Jabers, I thought I was only talking to a dacent boy,' says the king.

'Well, you know the difference now,' says the saint. 'I'm Saint Kavin,' says he, 'the greatest of all the saints.'

And so the king had his goose as good as new, to divert

him until the day of his death – and that was soon after; for the poor goose thought he was catching a trout one Friday; but, my jewel, it was a mistake he made – and instead of a trout, it was a thieving horse-eel; and instead of the goose killing a trout for the king's supper – by dad, the eel killed the king's goose – and small blame to him; but he didn't ate her, because he darn't ate what Saint Kavin had laid his blessed hands on.

THE STORY OF THE
LITTLE BIRD

Thomas Crofton Croker

Many years ago there was a very religious and holy man,
one of the monks of a convent, and he was one day kneeling
at his prayers in the garden of his monastery, when he heard
a little bird singing in one of the rose-trees of the garden,
and there never was anything that he had heard in the world
so sweet as the song of that little bird.

And the holy man rose up from his knees where he was
kneeling at his prayers to listen to its song; for he thought he
never in all his life heard anything so heavenly.

And the little bird, after singing for some time longer on
the rose-tree, flew away to a grove at some distance from
the monastery, and the holy man followed it to listen to its
singing, for he felt as if he would never be tired of listening
to the sweet song it was singing out of its throat.

And the little bird after that went away to another distant
tree, and sung there for a while, and then to another tree,

and so on in the same manner, but ever farther and farther away from the monastery, and the holy man still following it farther, and farther, and farther still listening delighted to its enchanting song.

But at last he was obliged to give up, as it was growing late in the day, and he returned to the convent; and as he approached it in the evening, the sun was setting in the west with all the most heavenly colours that were ever seen in the world, and when he came into the convent, it was nightfall.

And he was quite surprised at everything he saw, for they were all strange faces about him in the monastery that he had never seen before, and the very place itself, and everything about it, seemed to be strangely altered; and, altogether, it seemed entirely different from what it was when he had left in the morning; and the garden was not like the garden where he had been kneeling at his devotion when he first heard the singing of the little bird.

And while he was wondering at all he saw, one of the monks of the convent came up to him, and the holy man questioned him, 'Brother, what is the cause of all these strange changes that have taken place here since the morning?'

And the monk that he spoke to seemed to wonder greatly at his question, and asked him what he meant by the change since morning? for, sure, there was no change; that all was just as before. And then he said, 'Brother, why do you ask these strange questions, and what is your name? for you wear the habit of our order, though we have never seen you before.'

So upon this the holy man told his name, and said that he had been at Mass in the chapel in the morning before he had wandered away from the garden listening to the song of a little bird that was singing among the rose-trees, near where he was kneeling at his prayers.

And the brother, while he was speaking, gazed at him very earnestly, and then told him that there was in the convent a tradition of a brother of his name, who had left it two hundred years before, but that what was become of him was never known.

And while he was speaking, the holy man said, 'My hour of death is come; blessed be the name of the Lord for all his mercies to me, through the merits of his only-begotten Son.'

And he kneeled down that very moment, and said, 'Brother, take my confession, for my soul is departing.'

And he made his confession, and received his absolution, and was anointed, and before midnight he died.

The little bird, you see, was an angel, one of the cherubims or seraphims; and that was the way the Almighty was pleased in His mercy to take to Himself the soul of that holy man.

ST BRIGID'S CLOAK
Patrick Kennedy

The King of Leinster at that time was not particularly generous, and St Brigid found it not easy to make him contribute in a respectable fashion to her many charities. One day when he proved more than usually niggardly, she at last said, as it were in jest: 'Well, at least grant me as much land as I can cover with my cloak.' And, to get rid of her importunity, he consented.

They were at the time standing on the highest point of ground of the Curragh, and she directed four of her sisters to spread out the cloak preparatory to her taking possession. They accordingly took up the garment, but instead of laying it flat on the turf, each virgin, with face turned to a different point of the compass, began to run swiftly, the cloth expanding at their wish in all directions. Other pious ladies, as the border enlarged, seized portions of it to preserve something of a circular shape, and the elastic extension continued till the breadth was a mile at least.

'Oh, St Brigid,' said the frighted King, 'what are you about?'

'I am – or rather my cloak is – about to cover your whole province to punish you for your stinginess to the poor.'

'Oh! Come! Come! This won't do. Call your maidens back. I will give you a decent plot of ground, and be more liberal for the future.'

The saint was easily persuaded. She obtained some acres, and if the King held his purse-strings tight on any future occasion, she had only to allude to her cloak's miraculous qualities to bring him to reason.

A LEGEND OF ST BRIGID

after Maud Joynt

St Brigid of Kildare once founded a convent and she wished
the Rule of Peter and Paul to be observed in it. But because
it was not the will of God that she should go to Rome
herself to learn the Rule, she sent seven of her people thither
to learn it on her behalf. But when they came back to her
from Rome, not one of the seven could remember a word of
it.

'The Son of God knows it, people make little profit if
they can only manage to make a small effort,' said Brigid to
them with a sigh.

So she sent another seven of her people on the long and
difficult pilgrimage to Rome to learn the Rule; and months
later, they too came back having forgotten it. A third time
she sent seven of her people, and this time she sent with
them a blind boy whom she trusted completely, for he never
forgot anything he had once heard. When this party were
sailing from Ireland to France, a gale battered their ship and
they had to anchor just off the Isle of Wight and ride out the

244

storm. And when the storm had passed, they tried to raise
their anchor and sail on, but they could not. The ship's
anchor was caught fast in the roof of a flooded church
beneath the sea, and it would not budge. So they cast lots to
see which of their number should dive down to try and free
the anchor; the lot fell on the blind boy, and he climbed
down the rope into the sea and freed the anchor, but he did
not come up again; so the boat sailed on its way to France
without him, and St Brigid's six remaining pilgrims com-
pleted their journey to Rome. When they were returning
home to Ireland a year later, a storm overtook their ship on
the very same spot, and again they had to anchor and ride
out the gale. And lo! after the storm had gone down, the
blind boy came clambering up the anchor-rope out of the
cold sea, carrying in his arm a bell; and he had with him
also the Rule of Peter and Paul, for he had learnt it by heart
in the church below the waves.

When they reached Ireland, none but the blind boy was
able to give Brigid the Rule, which was henceforth observed
in her convent. And the bell which the blind boy had
brought back was ever after the bell of her community.
Then it was that Brigid made these verses:

> *'Tis effort great and profit small*
> *To merely go to Rome;*
> *You cannot find Our Lord at all*
> *Unless you find him first at home.*
>
> *Since Death for all mankind is sure*
> *And swift the moments onward run,*
> *Is it not folly clear and pure*
> *To risk the wrath of God's own Son?*

HOW THE SHANNON
ACQUIRED ITS NAME
Patrick Kennedy

A long time ago there was a well in Ossory, shaded by a rowan tree. When the berries became ripe they would drop into the water, and be eaten by the salmon that had their residence in the well. Red spots would then appear on the fish, and they received the name of 'Salmon of Knowledge'. It was not so easy to take these salmon, for there were shelving banks, and they could also retreat into the cavern from which the waters issued that supplied the well.

However, one was occasionally caught, and the captor, as soon as he had made his repast on it, found himself gifted with extraordinary knowledge, even as Finn, son of Cool, when he had tasted of the broiled salmon of the Boyne.

It was understood that no woman could taste of this delicacy and live. Yet Sionan, a lady cursed with an extraordinary desire of knowledge, braved the danger, suspecting the report to be spread abroad and maintained by the male sex from merely selfish motives. So, in order to lose no time, she had a fire ready by the side of the well, and the unfortunate fish was scarcely flung out on the grass when he was frying on the coals.

Who can describe the rapture she felt from the burst of light that filled her mind on swallowing the first morsel! Alas – the next moment she was enveloped by the furious waters, which, bursting forth, swept westwards, and carried the unfortunate lady with them till they were lost in the great river which ever after bore her name.

FIOR USGA

Thomas Crofton Croker

A little way beyond the Gallows Green of Cork, and just outside the town, there is a great lough of water, where people in the winter go and skate for the sake of diversion. But the sport above the water is nothing to what is under it, because at the very bottom of this lough there are buildings and gardens far more beautiful than any now to be seen. And how they came there was in this manner.

Long before Saxon foot pressed Irish ground there was a great King, called Corc, whose palace stood where the lough is now, in a round green valley that was just a mile about. In the middle of the courtyard was a spring of fair water, so pure and so clear that it was the wonder of all the world. Much did the King rejoice at having so great a curiosity within his palace, but as people came in crowds from far and near to draw the precious water of this spring, he was sorely afraid that in time it might become dry.

So he caused a high wall to be built up around it, and would allow nobody to have the water, which was a very

248

great loss to the poor people living about the palace. Whenever he wanted any for himself he would send his daughter to get it, not liking to trust his servants with the key of the well-door, fearing they might give some of the water away.

One night the King gave a grand entertainment, and there were many great princes present, and lords and nobles without end. There were wonderful doings throughout the palace: there were bonfires, whose blaze reached up to the very sky; and dancing was there, to such sweet music that it ought to have waked up the dead out of their graves; and feasting was there in the greatest of plenty for all who came; nor was anyone turned away from the palace gates, but 'you're welcome – you're welcome heartily,' was the porter's salute for all.

Now it happened at this grand entertainment there was one young prince above all the rest mighty comely to behold, and as tall and as straight as ever eye would wish to look on. Right merrily did he dance that night with the old King's daughter, wheeling there, as light as a feather, and footing it away to the admiration of everyone. The musicians played the better for seeing their dancing; and they danced as if their lives depended upon it.

After all this dancing came the supper, and the young prince was seated at table by the side of his beautiful partner, who smiled upon him as often as he wished, for he had constantly to turn to the company and thank them for the many compliments passed upon his fair partner and himself.

In the midst of this banquet one of the great lords said to King Corc, 'May it please your Majesty, here is everything in abundance that heart can wish for, both to eat and drink, except water.'

'Water!' said the King, mightily pleased at someone calling for that of which purposely there was a want. 'Water shall you have, my lord, speedily, and that of such a delicious kind that I challenge all the world to equal it. Daughter,' said he, 'go and fetch some in the golden vessel which I caused to be made for the purpose.'

The King's daughter, who was called Fior Usga (which signifies 'Spring Water' in English), did not much like to be told to perform so menial a service before so many people; and though she did not venture to refuse the commands of her father, yet she hesitated to obey him, and looked down upon the ground.

The King, who loved his daughter very much, seeing this was sorry for what he had desired her to do, but having said the word he was never known to recall it. He therefore thought of a way to make his daughter go speedily to fetch the water, and this was by proposing that the young prince, her partner, should go along with her.

Accordingly, in a loud voice, he said, 'Daughter, I wonder not at your fearing to go alone so late at night; but I doubt not the young prince at your side will go with you.'

The prince was not displeased at hearing this and, taking the golden vessel in one hand, with the other he led the King's daughter out of the hall so gracefully that all present gazed after them with delight.

When they came to the spring of water, in the courtyard of the palace, the fair Usga unlocked the door with the greatest care. But stooping down with the golden vessel to take some of the water out of the well, she found the vessel so heavy that she lost her balance and fell in. The young prince tried to save her, but in vain, because the water rose and rose so fast that the entire courtyard was speedily covered with it, and he hastened back almost in a state of distraction to the King.

The door of the well being left open the water, so long confined, rejoiced at obtaining its liberty and rushed forth incessantly, every moment rising higher; it reached the hall of the entertainment sooner than the young prince himself, so that when he attempted to speak to the King he was up to his neck in water. At length the water rose to such a height that it filled the entire green valley in which the King's palace stood, and so the present Lough of Cork was formed.

Yet the King and his guests were not drowned, as would now happen if such an inundation were to take place. Neither was his daughter, the fair Usga, who returned to the banquet hall the very next night after this dreadful event. And every night since then the same entertainment and dancing goes on in the palace in the bottom of the lough, and it will last until someone has the luck to bring up out of it the golden vessel which was the cause of all the mischief.

Nobody can doubt this was a judgement upon the King for his shutting up the well in the courtyard from the poor people. And if there are any who do not credit my story, they might go and see the Lough of Cork, for there it is to be seen to this day. The road to Kinsale passes at one side of it and when its waters are low and clear the tops of towers and stately buildings may be plainly viewed in the bottom by those who have good eyesight, without the help of spectacles.

GLOSSARY

acushla: darling
avick (Ir. *a mhic*): my lad, my dear

baste: beast, rogue
bawn-wall: fortification
Bel/Beltaine: May Day festival (from Baal)
bodach: old man, goblin
brancheen: little branch

deeshy: smart
Diamond: the main square in an Irish market town

Emain: seat of the Kings of Ulster

Fians, or Fenians: a band of warriors

gossip: godparent
gossoon: lad, boy (from French *garçon*)

Lady Day: 25 March, Feast of the Annunciation

leprahaun (Ir. *leith bhrogan*): shoemaker, or 'artisan of the brogue', one of the fairy race

lusmore: foxglove

malivogue: wish evil upon

maneen: little man

mavourneen (Ir. *mo mhurnin*): my dear one

merrow (Ir. *moruadh*): sea fairy, or sea maiden. They wear a red cap (a *cohuleen driuth*), and if this is stolen, they cannot then go under the water.

Moy-Mell: the promised land of milk and honey

musha (Ir. *maiseadh*): expression of surprise

ochone (Ir. *ochoin*): alas! a lamentation

ogham: old Irish writing system

omadawn (Ir. *amadan*): fool

pishogue: a fairy spell. The four-leafed shamrock was a talisman or safeguard against a fairy pishogue.

phouka (Ir. *puca*): a puck, or kind of fairy which usually appears in the form of a horse, goat or bull.

poteen: a kind of whiskey, made from potatoes

rath: ruined hillfort or mound (hence placenames like Rathfarnham, Rathmullan, Rathmelton, Rathfriland)

Samhain: autumn festival, Hallowe'en

sheehogue (Ir. *sidheog*): land fairy, a diminutive of *sidhe*

sidhe: fairies, the people of the raths or mounds. Irish for the fairy people is *daoine sidhe*. The banshee (the fairy who prophesies a death) is *beansidhe* in Irish.

soorawn: dizziness

Tara: seat of the High Kings of Ireland

throng: busy

Tir nan Og: land of the young

Glossary

Tuatha De Danann: 'people of the goddess Dana', the fourth race of invaders of prehistoric Ireland. After their defeat by the Milesians, they were said to have withdrawn into the hills and caves and waters of Ireland. They were believed to possess magical powers, and the fairy race was said to be descended from them. They were thought to have shrunk to fairy size over the centuries, as people ceased to believe in them and offer them gifts.

OTHER TITLES

from

BLACKSTAFF PRESS

MICHAEL McLAVERTY

Collected Short Stories

'His tact and pacing, in the individual sentence
and the overall story, are beautiful: in his best work,
the elegiac is bodied forth in perfectly pondered
images and rhythms ... McLaverty's place in
our literature is secure.'

SEAMUS HEANEY

MICHAEL McLAVERTY, one of Ireland's most distin-
guished short story writers, painted with acute
precision and intensity the northern landscapes of his home-
land – lonely hill farms, rough island terrain and the tight
backstreets of Belfast. Focusing on moments of passion,
wonder or bitter disenchantment in lives that are a contin-
uous struggle towards the light, these stories, in the
compassion of the tone and the spare purity of the language,
are nothing short of masterly.

Illustrated with specially commissioned woodcuts by
Barbara Childs, and including an introduction by Seamus
Heaney and a foreword by Sophia Hillan, this handsome
hardback edition is a fitting celebration of a writer who has
been compared to both Joyce and Chekhov.

ISBN 0 85640 727 5

£14.99

undertow

JOHN F DEANE

Sheer survival is difficult enough for the people of a
small island off the west of Ireland – what chance
do they have of love or even of dignity?

In the 1950s the islanders' battle is with the savage forces of
poverty, disease and religious constraint. Terrible things
happen – rape, incest, bestiality – and yet somehow compassion, love and generosity of spirit manage to continue.
Brooding over it all is the elemental figure of Big Bucko,
symbolic of all that is brutal and disruptive.

Four decades later, the island is facing other dangers: the
Spanish fishing boats which threaten the livelihood of the
trawlermen, the encroachment of tourism and the gradual
disintegration of community. But still the people strive to
transcend their common legacy of suffering, to reach for love
and a new connectedness.

Soon past and present converge, as the secrets of the generations are disentangled and a complex, disturbing pattern is at
last revealed.

Mythic, lyrical and moving, this extraordinary novel sounds
the depths of our relationship with nature and with each
other, and bears witness to love's endurance in spite of all.

ISBN 0 85640 728 3

£8.99

LEO CULLEN

Clocking 90 on the road to Cloughjordan

Hilarious short stories from
Leo Cullen, author of the best-selling novel
Let's Twist Again

'The setting is rural Ireland in the 1950s, and the
subject is the adventures of the Connaughton family,
headed by Lally senior . . . a marvellous creation.
The final effect is atmospheric and poignant.'

ANTHONY GARDNER, *Daily Telegraph*

'Both subtle and funny . . . Leo Cullen memorably paints
the picture of Connaughton's worlds . . . and the realities
that drive him, in the emotional sense, at 90 miles per hour
along the back roads of Tipperary.'

OWEN KELLY, *Irish News*

'a heady mixture . . . demands shelf space
alongside O'Connor and O'Faolain'

SEAN McMAHON, *Irish Independent*

'I tried to remember when I had read a book
as funny. I couldn't find one . . . With this effort alone
the author has assured himself of a lasting place in
comic Irish literature.'

JOHN B. KEANE, *Sunday Independent*

ISBN 0 85640 722 4

£5.99

LEO CULLEN

Let's Twist Again

Moving, hilarious and totally
irresistible – the acclaimed new novel from
Leo Cullen, one of Ireland's most original –
and funniest – writers

'Young Lally Connaughton is trying to work out
where his life went off the rails. His father has married
Mam, and what's more, has moved himself and his five
children to live with Mam and her four children. The story
concentrates on the next decade in Lally's life – by turns
side-splittingly funny and heart-breakingly sad . . .
a delightful novel.'

GRANIA McFADDEN, *Belfast Telegraph*

'A gem of a novel . . . The ease and rich texture
of Cullen's prose sing from the page.'

CHRIS POWER, *The Times*

'Leo Cullen has created the most memorable fictional
child since at least Paddy Clarke . . . If Lally has to have any
literary siblings it's Frank O'Connor's child narrators he's
related to . . . In fact, Lally is out on his own . . . in this
funny, sad, multilayered and exceptionally readable novel.'

GEORGE O'BRIEN, *Irish Times*

ISBN 0 85640 721 6

£6.99